Becoming the

WHISKEY
PRINCESS

Becoming the

WHISKEY PRINCESS

A Taking Risks novel

NEW YORK TIMES BESTSELLING AUTHOR

TONI ALEO

Interior designed and formatted by

www.emtippettsbookdesigns.com

You think the dead we loved ever truly leave us? You think that we don't recall them more clearly than ever, in times of great trouble?

-Sirius Black

one
Amberlyn

I can't breathe.

The pain is unbearable.

It is all consuming.

My head is pounding, my body feels tingly, but most of all, my chest just burns with the pain of a thousand fires. I can feel my blood leaving my body. The heat of it running along my breast and armpit, gushing down the white gown I wear and staining it. I spent so much on that dress and now it is ruined.

Because he shot me.

I should have known better. The first time I saw him, I should have known he was nothing but a mistake. Since I'm not one to make mistakes, I really should have rethought that, but I didn't. I allowed him to play a little role in my life, and now I'm paying for it. My mom always said that you learn from your mistakes, but will I die from mine?

I knew from the beginning when we found Casey and Lena outside that it was going to be bad, but I never really thought it would end like this. That Casey really wanted to kill the love of my life. I couldn't let that happen. Not with all that Declan had to live for. So I did what any other woman would do. I stepped into the line of fire. There was no other choice. I couldn't let him die.

My ears still ring from the sound of the gun. It vibrates my soul and makes my skin break out in gooseflesh. Even with all this going on, I'm not scared. Even though the pain exploded throughout my chest, taking my breath away, I know I did the right thing. I'm not scared to die. I'm not saying it's ideal since I want to have a life with Declan, but I know I am dying for a good reason. Crumbling against him, I look into ice-blue eyes and I don't regret my choice.

I love him.

I would do anything for him.

Even die for him.

And that's exactly what I am about to do.

I can hear my favorite song falling off his sweet lips, and I want to stay. I want to be in his arms for the rest of my life, but I can't. I always thought that when you die, it would be like the scene in *Harry Potter* when Harry finds himself with Dumbledore in the train station. Get on the train to die or go back; that's always how I interpreted that part. It isn't like that though. There is no train; there is nothing but light, and thankfully, the pain is gone. Nothing. I feel nothing. It's almost as if I am floating. I look around for some sign of life, some sign of what I am to do next, and to my surprise, she stands there in all her ethereal glory.

My mother.

Dressed in only white, her gown sparkles much like mine as she stands with her arms extended out to me. Her dark red hair falls in a mass of curls down her shoulders. Her eyes, the same aquamarine as mine, are bright and happy, unlike how they had been when she was dying. She is smiling, her eyes welling up with tears, and I find myself fighting for breath again. Looking at her, I feel as if I am consumed with all the love in the world, and I honestly can't believe it.

My mommy is here.

Running to her, I wrap my arms around her middle as her nose and lips press against the top of my head. My tears stain her dress as her arms hold me in close. She feels like I remember. Like home. And she smells like roses. Sweet, beautiful roses.

"Ah, my sweetheart, my Amberlyn. Love, look at me," she whispers against my temple, and I sob as she tips my head up, her fingers light against my cheeks as I meet her gaze. "So beautiful," she says, kissing the side of my mouth.

"Mommy," I cry as my heart jumps into my throat. Searching her eyes, I want to believe this is real, but it can't be. Or is it? I can feel her; I can smell her. I am holding my mother. It has to be real. "I miss you so much."

"Oh sunshine, I miss you more," she says, holding me to her, her fingers running slowly through my hair like she used to do when I was a child. There wasn't a day that passed where I wouldn't lay my head in her lap and she would thread her fingers or braid my hair. It was perfect, but as I blink back the tears, she studies me with a look I've seen before. It was the same one she had when she told me she was dying.

Clearing her throat, she says, "But this isn't how you are going to die."

"Huh? I'm not dead?"

"No, and you're not going to die. Not today. You are going to go back."

My heart sinks. "But I don't want to leave you. Or Daddy! Where is Daddy?"

Her eyes soften as her lips curve up in a grin. "He's here and he loves you so much. He's so proud of you, but sweetheart, you have to go back."

My chest burns again, but this time with sobs as I cling to my mother, not wanting to let her go. "But I don't want to lose you again."

"But Declan is waiting," she whispers in my ear. "He loves you so, my sweetheart. He is good for ya. You are going to have a beautiful life together."

I know this is true, and I want to go back to Declan, I do, but I don't want to lose my mother again. I already did that. Not again.

"No, Mom, come with me," I beg. "Please don't leave me."

I don't know why, but space is being put between us. She is letting me go, while I try wildly to get ahold of her. "No, Mommy! Please! Don't leave me! Don't let go!"

"Go back to Declan, live the life you deserve, a long and beautiful one. Go, baby."

"No! Mommy! Please!" I cry, still trying to reach for her.

"I love you, Amberlyn love. So much."

She is slowly disappearing, and I don't know how to keep her with me. I keep trying to reach for her, but she is out of my reach though still smiling. How can she be smiling when she is leaving me?

"Mom! No! Don't leave me!"

"I'll never leave you, my sunshine. I am always with you."

"But I miss you," I whisper as my lip wobbles. "I don't want to live without you."

"Amberlyn, the sun is shining and so shall you. Live a beautiful life. We are watching and cheering you on."

And then she is gone.

"Amberlyn, Amberlyn, wake up, you're scaring me."

My eyes flutter open as the tears slowly roll down the sides of my face. The pain is back in my chest and I feel stiff. My heart is racing, I feel sweat rolling down my temple, and everything just hurts. When my cousin Fiona comes into my line of vision, her eyes are full of worry and her hair in a crazy heap on the top of her head. I blink back the tears and allow a sob to leave my lips.

I should be glad I am alive, but I just let my mother go again.

I can see the panic in Fiona's eyes as she reaches for my shoulders, shaking me slightly, causing pain to shoot through my chest. I flinch, crying out, and thankfully she lets go right away.

"Oh fuck! My bad! So sorry, ya were screaming weird though. Are ya okay?"

Blinking away the tears, I can only look at her as the pain of watching my mother disappear and the gunshot wound in my chest throbs. I didn't want to let her go.

"Are you okay? Please, I'm sorry. Did I hurt you more?"

I clear my throat and with a croak ask, "Declan?"

I feel all discombobulated. Almost as if I don't belong here. No, I feel empty. Alone. Where is Declan?

"Amberlyn, honey, are you okay? He went to the bathroom," my Aunt Shelia says.

"What happened?" I hear, and I quickly look at the door, meeting Declan's gaze. My lip starts to wobble as the tears run down my face. He looks dashing in a pair of khaki shorts and a blue button-down shirt. His hair is a mess of curls on top of his head, and I want to smile at the hair on his jaw, but then I want to cry at the look of pure distress on his beautiful, chiseled face.

He closes the distance between us, and I reach up for him as he gathers me in his arms, careful of my wound as he holds me close to his strong chest. Kissing my temple, he whispers that everything is fine, that it was only a dream, as he slowly rocks me back and forth.

Closing my eyes, I slowly remember that I am still in the hospital in Ireland and have been here for almost two weeks. Squeezing my eyes shut, I realize that it's the fourth time I've had that same dream since being shot by Casey Burke and woken up completely out of it. I don't understand the dream and hate the empty feeling it leaves me with, but, thankfully, Declan comes along and he fills the empty. He makes it better.

Nuzzling into his chest, I cling to him like a life preserver as my heart slows in my chest. As I look up at him, his mouth slowly pulls up at the side as he runs his fingers through my hair and behind my ear. I always feel so beautiful in his gaze. I know I probably don't look it, but in his eyes, I could almost think I am.

"Same dream?" I nod slowly and he kisses my nose. "It's all better now; I'm here."

"I miss her," I whisper, and he tightens his arms around me.

"I know, *mo stór*, I know," he says softly, kissing my cheek and the side of my mouth. "Everything is okay now. We are leaving soon, and then you can sleep in your bed. Maybe the dreams will stop."

While I would love to stop waking up in complete distress, I don't want to stop seeing my mother. But I know the dreams need to end, and hopefully being home will help that. Snuggling closer to him, I squeeze my eyes shut and know he is right. I hate that these dreams have started. I know that I went through something tragic, losing my mother, and then to step in front of Declan, leading to the gunshot wound in my chest that could have killed me, but why are the dreams starting now?

Is it her way of reaching out to me to tell me that my decision to marry Declan is a good one? It's crazy and insane, I know that. I mean, I've only known him three months, been dating for two, and we haven't even had sex yet, but I know this is real. I know that I've found my missing piece. I felt lost before, and like a guiding light, I found my way to him. That has to mean something. He is special, but am I having second thoughts? Is this my mother's way of reassuring me?

Looking up at Declan, I move my nose along his jaw and he smiles as he cups my face.

"I love you," he whispers, kissing the side of my mouth again, his hand running slowly down my arm as his gaze holds mine.

I need no reassurance. I made the right decision.

Am I scared? Out of my mind.

Will I be a good wife? Will I fit in to his world? And most of all, what if he doesn't like me after he sleeps with me? There are so many things that could go wrong, but our love has been so steady and strong since the beginning. I will never forget when I fell in love with him. It was when he held me in his arms as I cried for my mother in his large library. I remember feeling so safe and whole again, something I hadn't felt since I'd watched my mother die. It was only a couple weeks ago, but with the shooting, I feel like it's been years.

I feel as though we've been through so much, that together we can do anything. We are made for each other. He is so sweet and romantic, and from the start, I knew he was different. I knew he was someone I could be with my whole life. I know we are young, but when you know, you know. As he holds me, I can't help but think of what my mother said. How he is good for me. While, yes, it was a dream, I believe that she's right, and I believe in us. I made the right choice.

I know I did.

Reaching up, I hold his jaw and smile. "I love you too."

two
Declan

I hate seeing her in pain.

It breaks my heart something tragic.

As I stand here, watching as they slowly clean her wound and bandage it up, I hate the way her face cringes and how the tears are welling up in her eyes. I would give anything to have five minutes with that gobshite Casey Burke. I'd tear him limb from limb, that's for fucking sure. I have never hated someone as much as I hate him. Nor will I ever.

He not only hurt my sister, raped her and left her in the cold; he shot the love of my life. I want him to burn for what he's done. I want him to feel the pain I've felt—watching my sister try to be the person she was before the rape, waking up each day and trying to be happy. I want him to feel what my family has gone through, the pain, the embarrassment, and the guilt. It was our job to protect her and we failed.

The same with Amberlyn. I had one job, which was to love and protect her. I know that's what her father would say to me if he were here, God rest his soul, and her mother too. They aren't here to do it; someone needs to be, and I want that job, but I couldn't even keep her from being shot. So not only do I have the guilt and pain from Casey hurting my sister, but now I have the same feelings from his almost killing Amberlyn.

How can a person cause this much pain in someone's life and get away with it?

When Amberlyn cries out, I have to look away, my hand squeezing hers as the tears burn in my eyes. It's my fault. All my fucking fault. If I would have seen the severity of the situation, taken the wanker seriously, maybe this wouldn't have happened. I should have pushed Lena and Amberlyn to the side, out of harm's way. Taken him with my bare hands. But instead, I stood there. And laughed in his face. Like a fucking eejit.

I stood there while the gun went off, and still, I didn't believe it was happening. I thought it was all a joke, but then she slammed into me. The blood spilled from her beautiful body, staining everything red, and all I could do was hold her close to me and pray that she'd make it. I have never loved anyone the way I love her. I felt completely and utterly lost as I watched her blood leave her body. I didn't know how to fix it. My hand wasn't stopping the bleeding, and I couldn't save her. I was crying like a wee baby. I remember singing her song, but it was more for me than her. I needed something to keep me calm, and imagining the words coming from her sweet lips did it.

It was horrible. Something I never want to experience again.

I honestly don't know how she made it. The doctors were worried, which made me worry more. What would I do if I lost her? Would I shut down again? Would I lose everything? Surely my da would have made an exception, but what if he wouldn't? I couldn't blame him because I wouldn't find anyone else. Amberlyn is it. She is my future.

Honestly though, I still can't believe she wants to marry me. I think I knew from the start that I would make her my wife, but I never expected her to be so willing with only knowin' me a couple months. She is making a huge commitment to me, and I thought maybe I'd see fear or something, but nothing but love is in her sweet aquamarine eyes. She loves me, and Lord knows I love her even more. We are young, and this may be a little mental, but I believe in us. I know we will be grand.

Together. As long as I can protect her.

"Stop looking like that. I'm fine," I hear her sweet voice say.

I turn to look at her and she is smiling. She is wearing a tank and some sweat pants that Fiona had brought her. Her hair is high on her head, her eyes bright, but her skin is still pale. I can see the pain in her eyes but also the undying love. I don't know how she can be smiling. I don't want to smile; I feel like shite, and I honestly don't know how to feel anything but. All I keep doing is seeing her bleeding everywhere, dying in my arms.

But she isn't dead. She is here, and maybe that should make me smile.

Reaching over, I take her cheek in my hand and try to smile, but I just can't. I feel so horrible that this has happened.

"I just worry about ya, love."

"I know," she says, covering my hand with her own. "But I'm here. I'm alive and we are fine."

I nod slowly, looking deep into the eyes that hold my forever. "I love you, Amberlyn."

"I love you," she says softly, stepping in closer to me. "I love saying that."

"Me too," I admit, holding her close and kissing her nose. "Are you ready to go home?"

"I am," she agrees.

I want to take her to my home, but I know that is out of the question. I hope that Mr. and Mrs. Maclaster don't mind my hanging out because I have to make sure she is okay.

Or I'll drive myself mad.

ONCE WE are back to the Maclaster home, Mrs. Maclaster fusses over Amberlyn, leaving me to stand off to the side, awkwardly unsure what to do. Mr. Maclaster stands beside me, and he hasn't talked to me since the shooting. He doesn't even look me in the eye, and I know it's because he feels the same I do.

That this is my fault.

Even Mrs. Maclaster isn't looking at me like she used to. She used to admire my family, obsess a bit, but now I think she thinks I'm as good as shite. It upsets me since they are the closest thing to parents that Amberlyn has. I want them to like me, but then again, do I even deserve their blessing?

When I see Amberlyn cringe from how tight Mrs. Maclaster is tucking her in, I ask, "Are you all right like that?"

I receive a look from Mrs. Maclaster as she says, "Now, Declan, I've been tucking babies into bed for years. I'm sure I've got it."

"Mom, she looks in pain," Fiona points out, thank God. She is the only one who doesn't look at me like I was the one who fired the gun.

She gives me a small smile as Amberlyn says, "I'm fine. Honestly, no reason to fuss over me."

"It's our jobs. I promised your ma and da, so hush, let me fuss if I please," she says, and I can see her choking back her tears. "I already failed them a bit."

Amberlyn gives her a loving smile as she slowly shakes her head. "No, you didn't, and don't think that. I made my own decision. I couldn't let anything happen to him."

"Yeah, sure, but in the process of protecting him, we failed to protect you," she says sternly, shaking her head. "It's over. Let me wallow in my guilt and pray you get better."

Amberlyn reaches out, squeezing her aunt's hand, setting her with a look.

"I am going to be fine. I already feel so much better just being home. Don't worry. You've done everything you're supposed to. If I weren't so loved by you guys, then I wouldn't have had the instinct to jump in front of Declan to protect him. You've helped mold me into a woman my mom and dad would be proud of. Remember that."

Looking at the floor, I close my eyes as the room falls silent.

"No one is at fault here."

"That wanker is," Fiona says with a vengeance, and I couldn't agree more.

"Yes, he is, but we have to forgive him because he is lost and isn't loved like we are."

"I'll never forgive him," Fiona promises, and again, I agree.

"No, you have to because we should pity him, not hate him. It takes so much out of a person to hate someone; don't let him have that power over you. I've forgiven him, I'm moving on, I am going to make this life the best one yet. I only have one."

Tears sting my eyes as I think that she almost lost that life for me. She is so uplifting, so positive, and I wish I could be an ounce like her. I can't forgive him, I want to kill him, and it worries me. Does that mean I'm not the man she deserves? Because I want to be the man she wanted to die for. But what if I'm not?

"You are a beautiful soul, Amberlyn. I love you so," Mrs. Maclaster says, kissing her cheek softly before cupping her face.

"I love you too, all of you. Everything is going to be fine. From here we can only go up," she says with a bright grin.

"I'll let you rest," Mrs. Maclaster says before lightly touching her shoulder and heading toward the door, only giving me a sideways look.

"Call if you need us," Mr. Maclaster says, sending her a grin. He then looks at me and says, "Are you staying in here with her?"

"If that's okay."

I can see in his eyes that he wants nothing more than to tell me to fuck off, but he nods. "That's fine. Let her rest."

"Of course," I agree as I turn to see Fiona kiss Amberlyn's cheek.

"I'm right next door."

"I know, I'm fine."

She nods before squeezing her hand and then heading for the door. Clasping my shoulder, she smiles and says, "Hang in there, big guy."

I scoff. "Trying."

When the door shuts, I look over at my love and smile. Pulling the blanket back, she beckons me to her. "Come lie with me."

I don't hesitate. Kicking my shoes off, I head to the bed, crawling in slowly, making sure not to shake her too much as I settle in beside her. Wrapping my arms around her as softly as I can manage, I kiss her temple and close my eyes.

"Get some rest."

She smiles against my jaw. "I've been resting for two weeks."

"Being shot is a big deal, sweetheart. Ya need your rest."

"I feel fine."

"Please just rest," I practically beg.

"But I miss just being us."

"We never stop being us, my love," I reassure her. "I never stop loving you."

"As do I, but I mean, we haven't just laughed in forever."

"Amberlyn, there really isn't anything to laugh about right now. It's all still so fresh and new. I could have lost you."

Bringing her head up, she looks at me and cups my face, her eyes searching mine. "But you didn't. I'm fine and you are fine. Our lives are about to change forever, and I don't want to wallow in the past. I want to move forward."

"And we will, slowly. I don't want to rush you."

"Um, you only have three months before you lose your distillery. We don't have time *not* to rush."

I shake my head before she finishes talking. "Don't worry your head about that right now. I'll worry about it. Now, I want you to recover."

Setting me with a look that says she means business, she says, "I will worry because it deals with me. I want you to be happy, and that means us getting married. Me becoming the Whiskey Princess. So we need to get started on that."

I look away, biting my lip as my hand comes up to run through my curls. Ugh, she's gonna stress me the hell out.

"What is it? Do you not want to marry me anymore?"

I look back at her quickly and shake my head. "No, Amberlyn, I've dreamed of making you my wife since I met you."

Smiling, she asks, "Really?"

A true smile pulls at my lips as I nod. "Yes, I always knew you were it."

Still grinning at me, she asks, "Then what is the problem?"

Clearing my throat, I look up at the ceiling and take in a deep breath before saying, "I just don't think I'm the man you deserve."

When she doesn't say anything, I meet her gaze to find her brows pulled in. "And why is that?"

"I should be the one with the gunshot wound, not you. I failed ya."

She rolls her eyes, obviously completely annoyed with me. "Declan, you've done no such thing. And if you weren't the man for me, then why did I step in front of that bullet? I did it because I know you are, because I love you and I want you to have everything you ever wanted."

"But I couldn't have it without you."

She smiles, cupping my face, her thumb slowly moving along my lip. "You're completely right. I'm here, so let's figure everything out."

She is too damn headstrong, and I know that if she had her way, she'd plan everything now. She is such a planner and always ahead of the game. I know she just wants to ignore what happened and move on, but we all need to heal from this. We need time.

I'm a little worried we don't have it though.

She's right; it does need to be planned, but she needs to let me worry about it. One look in her eyes though, tells me that isn't gonna happen.

"One week. Rest for one more week, and then we'll figure everything out." She eyes me. "But we are getting married?"

I smile, covering her hands with mine. "If you'll have me, yes."

"I've already said yes."

"I was a bit worried it was the drugs," I tease and she smiles.

"Nope, I know what I want, and I want you. So damn much," she says before pressing her lips to mine. Instantly my eyes fall shut as our mouths move together and a euphoric feeling washes over me. Her tongue moves with mine, her body molding against mine, catching me completely on fire. This is the first time since the shooting that we've actually kissed like this. Probably because we've never been alone. It's always been soft, sweet kisses, not toe-curling ones like the one she is giving me now. My heart is pounding in my chest, my cock is growing, and I want more. But this can't be good for her. No, it can't, but my God, I want her. I want her so badly, I can't see straight.

But not yet.

Pulling away, I meet her heated gaze and shake my head. "You are supposed to be resting."

Her sparkling eyes lock with mine, her breathing is erratic, her breasts pressing into my chest with each breath she sucks in. As I search her eyes, waiting for her answer, I can see that her eyes are slowly starting to fill with tears. Shite! Did I hurt her?

"Amberlyn, my love, what's wrong?"

Tears run down her face as she shakes her head. "I want to forget, Declan. I want to forget that any of it happened. I want to start our life together, I want to be happy, I don't want to rest and feel sad that my chest hurts, I want to feel whole again. I don't want him to own anything on me, and the more time we allow me to rest and lie around, the more he is winning. I want to get on with everything. I want to start our life. I want to feel alive."

Clearing my throat free of the sob that is threatening to come out, I say, "Amberlyn, I want all that too, but I also don't want to rush you into this."

"You're not. I want this. I want you."

As I cuddle her in my arms, her face presses into my neck and I close my eyes. "I want you too, *mo stór*, but please, give me one week. I just want to make sure you are okay. Please give me that."

Pulling away a bit, she looks deep into my eyes and says, "Only if you stop blaming yourself."

Looking away, I suck in a deep breath. She sees right through me, doesn't she? "It isn't your fault. I've told you this so many times, and I can see in your eyes that you are blaming yourself. That has to stop or we can't move forward. I made the choice; I had to protect you—"

"But it isn't your job to protect me, yeah?" I point out.

"You protect the ones you love, and I did that. I know you'd do the same for me."

"But I didn't."

"Declan, he was shooting at you."

"I should have known he wasn't playing around."

"Maybe so, but whatever. It's over. It's time to move forward. In no way, shape, or form do I think this is your fault. I hold no one responsible but him. I love you."

I move my fingers along her jaw as I focus on her lips. I don't know how to let go of my guilt, but I know I need to try. I have to, or this beautiful woman who has taken me as hers will plan a wedding within a week with not a care in the world for the wound on her chest. Since that wouldn't be protecting her, I have to push all the guilt aside and focus on her. Meeting her gaze, I say, "Fine, I won't blame myself anymore. It's all that gobshite's fault."

Still holding my gaze, she says, "You have to forgive him."

"Over my dead body," I spit back. "I can forgive myself, but I hope he rots."

She shakes her head as she slowly shrugs her shoulders. "Fine, but please try."

"Sure," I say, but we both know I won't.

"We have better things to do."

I smile. "Oh?"

"Yup, wedding to plan 'cause I want a huge one. I'm becoming a princess for goodness' sakes," she says with a wink, and I smile.

"I'll give you the biggest damn wedding ever as long as you keep smiling like that."

Her smile doesn't move as she wraps her arms around my neck. "Good, but we do have one other thing to worry about."

"Yeah?"

"Yup, the small matter of my virginity."

I close my eyes as I shake my head. "Ah, Amberlyn, later on that. I couldn't imagine that right now. My need for ya is so fuckin' wild, I'd probably tear ya to pieces."

She giggles beside me. "Isn't that the point?"

I shake my head against hers, my cock throbbing in my shorts as I gaze into my future wife's eyes. "A week. Give me a week and we'll talk everything out."

"So if I got naked right now, you wouldn't take me?"

I groan loudly as her laughter fills the room. I smile widely and look over at her. "You wanted a laugh."

"I did."

"At my expense?"

She nods, cuddling into me. "I just want us to feel normal."

Taking her tightly in my arms, I kiss her fully on her lips and then smile against them. "It feels great for sure, my love. Thank you."

She grins, running her fingers through my hair. "I love you."

"I love you more, sweetheart," I say against her lips. "And if you were naked right now..."

"Yeah?" she asks with a teasing grin.

"I think I might die from the pure beauty of ya."

She giggles and shakes her head as I continue, "But if I don't, then I'm hightailing it out of here. Your uncle is sure to have me killed if he caught us."

That has her dissolving in giggles. Which is what I want. I want her happy.

Because she is everything to me.

three
Declan

*L*ike I wanted, Amberlyn falls asleep with her nose against my neck. It's cold, but I don't mind; hopefully, she'll warm up a bit. Closing my eyes, I want to fall asleep too. I'm so damn tired. It's been a long two weeks. Worrying constantly if she is okay and praying that she would heal. By the grace of God, she is, but still I'm finding it hard to sleep. My mind is going a hundred kilometers per hour.

She is so set on marrying me, but I can't help but think I did this all wrong. I was wrong for holding that part of me from her. I should have told her about the deadline, but I didn't. I was wrong to ask her when she was drugged out of her mind, even if she wanted it. I just feel wrong. I didn't even ask Mr. Maclaster if I could marry her. I went about this completely wrong, and I just have this dire need to fix it.

I honestly wish I could go back and change everything. I wish I had made Lena and Amberlyn go inside. I wish I would have taken care of Casey myself, been done with him and then gone inside to confront the issue at hand. She had every right to be mad at me. I was wrong to hold that from her, and I needed to make it right. But it all went to shit. And now I am going to marry a girl that when we get older, our babies running around us, she'll go, "Your da and I got married after I was shot. And he asked me in the hospital because he was gonna lose his distillery, and I couldn't let that happen." I don't want that to be the memory of my asking her. I want it to be beautiful and to blow her away.

Detangling myself from her, I kiss the side of her mouth before slowly getting out of the bed. When I look down, she is still sleeping blissfully. I pray she doesn't have those dreams she's been having. They scare me, but at the same time, comfort me. I believe in spirits and all that, and to know her ma came back to say she approves of me is straight wicked. But still, they upset Amberlyn and have her on edge. I just want her to sleep soundly, with no cares in the world. I need her to heal. I want to make a life with her.

Making sure she is covered well, I head out the door, and when I shut it, Fiona opens hers. She looks at me and then behind me, her brow raised. "Whaddya doin'?"

"I'm gonna go talk to your da."

Her brows don't move as she asks, "For what? Do you want me to sit with her?"

"You can, but she is dead to the world."

"Okay, what you want with my da?"

"Wanna ask him if it's okay to marry her," I say slowly, my eyes trained on hers. "She already said yes, but I feel wrong about it. I want to mend my wrongs with rights."

She nods, crossing her arms across her chest. "He's mad that you didn't ask."

"I figured."

"And the fact that she blocked a shot for you."

"Again, I know, and while I wish I could take it ba—"

"Ya can't, and she wouldn't want you to. She loves ya, Declan, and she did it because of that."

I look down, running my fingers through my hair with a nod. "I love her."

"Good. Go on then, ask my da. I'll keep my door open in case she wakes up."

"Thank you," I say, sharing a long look with her. She is so good for my best mate, Kane, it's insane. I always believe that people were born for other people, and Fiona is that for Kane. As my Amberlyn is for me.

Turning to go downstairs, I pause and look back at her. "Do you think we're mad?"

She smiled. "Yeah, I think it'd be mad to get married now, but she told me about the distillery and she isn't budging. I tried," she says sheepishly. "She's so young, but like I said, she loves you, and I believe in yous two. She doesn't make careless choices. She believes that she is making a sound decision, and I believe in her."

I know she is right and it does derail me a bit, but then I know we are going to have a good life together. We are young, yes, but it will work. I pray, at least, it will. "You know I'll love her until I die."

"Oh, I know. If I didn't, I wouldn't be so agreeable."

She sends me a grin and I can't help but to throw one back at her. Having

Fiona's approval is almost enough. She doesn't hold anything back. She lets the world know what she is thinking. She means a lot to Amberlyn, and to know she supports us is good. Real good. Turning to head down the stairs, my heart starts to knock against my chest. I know that the Maclasters don't think too highly of me right now, but I feel doing this will better their view of me.

I find them downstairs, Mrs. Maclaster in her chair reading and Mr. Maclaster on the computer.

When she sees me, she flies out of her chair, her eyes wild as she asks, "She okay?"

"Yes, of course. I'm sorry, didn't mean to alarm ya."

She places her hand on her chest, and I notice that Mr. Maclaster stands too, the same look of distress on his face. "You look worried."

"Oh, sorry, that's because I've come to ask for your blessing to marry Amberlyn," I say, and I really wish I would have thought that out a bit. They are both taken aback as they look at me in disbelief.

"What?" Mrs. Maclaster asks. "Didn't you already ask her?"

Mr. Maclaster crosses his arms across his wide chest, his dark eyes set on me as I nod slowly. "Yes, I did. But I don't feel right the way it happened. I know I am supposed to ask you two first, but with everything that happened, I kind of got lost in the process. I apologize for that."

They both eye me for a moment as sweat breaks out across my forehead. "She's so young. Only twenty."

"Yes, I know—"

"Just because you can lose your distillery doesn't mean she should have to marry you. You've only dated a short time," Mr. Maclaster says, his voice sharp.

Yeah, this is not going well. Not at all.

"I know. While the distillery issue is the reason that I asked so early, I've always known I was gonna marry her. She's beautiful, smart, and so damn perfect in my eyes."

"We know all that," Mrs. Maclaster says. "But she hasn't lived. She went from caring for her mother and not having any interaction with anyone to coming here, and bam! You are in her face. She hasn't experienced heartbreak, or university, nothing. She's still so young and naïve to it all. You come in, a prince of Mayo, and what girl wouldn't jump at the chance to marry ya? I think yer a sweet man, Declan, I do, but I feel this is rushing it a bit. How do you know that this is going to work? I know you don't believe in divorce, so what happens when she isn't happy?"

"I'll do everything to make her happy," I say, a little more sharply than I intended, but I feel under attack. Something I don't care for one bit. "I understand you perfectly, truly, but I love her. So much, and she loves me. I know we are young, I know this is rushed, but I promise you, she won't ever be unhappy. And if the moment comes when she is, I'll fix it. I'll make her happy;

I'll give her the world. If, after all, she decides she doesn't want to be with me, then I'll let her go. I'll lose it all for her. As long as she is happy."

Silence falls in the room, the only sound the breeze from the window, the curtains smacking against the wall. The TV is on mute, and my heart is pounding in my ears. I swallow hard as Mr. Maclaster clears his throat, looking deep into my eyes.

"That's the thing, she won't let you go. She's a fixer, a caring, sweet soul. She'll be unhappy before she allows anyone to hurt. And that's what worries me. Is she marrying you to save your distillery, or because she actually loves you?"

I nod. "I couldn't agree more, Mr. Maclaster, but if she didn't love me, then why did she almost die for me?"

His eyes darken as he nods slowly, looking away and falling into his seat. Mrs. Maclaster doesn't move, her eyes still trained on mine as she asks, "Can you not see if you can get more time? A year maybe?"

"I can," I agreed. "I planned to anyway, but I'd still like your blessing."

Mrs. Maclaster looks over at her husband, and they share a long look. I feel like it's a private moment, so I look away as I fight for breath. If they say no, what will I do? Can I marry Amberlyn without their consent?

Yeah. I can.

I know that is horrible, but I can't live without her. I just can't.

"Declan, you are a good man. We know you'll take good care of her. We'd like for ya to wait a little bit, but if that can't happen, then yes, you have our blessing," she says as she comes toward me. Placing her hands on my arms, she smiles. "Thank you for giving us this chance to talk to you."

"I should have done it before."

"Yes, but I am thankful you did now."

I nod and she cups my cheek as she searches my eyes. Clearing her throat, she says, "I think my brother would have liked you. I know that my sister-in-law would have. You remind me a lot of my Tomas, God rest his soul. He was a driven man, to himself, until Ciara came along. She bewitched him from the start, and I know that Amberlyn has done the same for ya."

"She has," I agree, holding her gaze. "And to honor her parents, I'll love Amberlyn enough for them and myself."

Mrs. Maclaster smiles, her eyes filling with tears as she nods. "Yes, well, on with ya then. You have our blessing."

I DON'T even remember driving to the offices of the distillery.

When I get there, I park the car beside my da's and lock it as I head inside. It's been two weeks since I've set foot near these offices or even the distillery I am fighting to keep, but thankfully, nothing looks out of sorts. Things have been running without a glitch from what Kane has said.

I greet my da's assistant before pushing his door open without her consent. If he doesn't want to see me, that's just too damn bad. We have things to discuss. Thankfully, he is alone and looks up from his desk, obviously surprised to see me.

"Everything all right?"

I nod as I drop down into the chair in front of his desk. "Yes, Amberlyn is home sleeping."

"Grand, I'm glad she is recovering."

"Me too," I agree. "Have I missed much?"

My fingers tap nervously on the arms of the chair as I wait for his answer.

"Not really. Although, Mindy has notes for ya from the last two meetings. Everyone understood your absence. Your ma has done well, keeping it pretty cut-and-dried for the media. The extra security around the hospital helped too. I am just glad that she is okay."

"Me too. Thank you for everything you've done."

"She saved my son; I owe her more than what I've done."

This is a different side to my da and I'm still not used to it, but thankful, nonetheless. Things haven't been as strained between us. We have actually been getting along all right.

Clearing my throat, I sit at the edge of the chair and meet his gaze. "Since we are on the topic of Amberlyn, I want to talk to you about something."

"Sure, what is it?" he asks, his eyebrows coming up before he shuts his laptop.

"I asked her to marry me," I say, and a small smile graces my da's usually stern face.

"I may have thought differently before, but after the way she has conducted herself, I can't help but respect the girl. You were right, she is something, and I look forward to getting to know her."

"She is amazing," I boast, my heart soaring for her. "But she is young, Da, only twenty. I know I have a deadline that will be up in three months, but surely you can give me some more time. Let us have a long engagement."

The smile drops so quickly, I almost don't believe it was ever on his face. Shaking his head, he says, "No, Declan, I can't do that. You have till October seventeenth to marry the girl or you'll lose the distillery, and that's final, son."

"But Da, I'm her first boyfriend. What if it doesn't work out?"

"Then you end it now," he says with an annoyed look. "You have three months. Either marry her or let her go."

"I won't let her go," I say with a vengeance. "I love her."

"I guess we have a wedding to plan, then?" he says simply, looking down at his calendar. "October seventeenth a good day? It's a Saturday. Be a nice enough time for a wedding, I guess."

Tears burn my eyes as I look at my legs. "Da, please, a year. Give me a year. Just to make sure she wants to marry me."

"If you aren't sure yet, Declan, let her go. You are wasting your time. You need a wife."

"We've only dated two months, Da!" I protest, but he isn't budging.

"Do ya love her?"

"I do, you know that! That's why I want to give her more time to make sure she loves me and wants to be with me for the rest of her life."

"No, you either know or you don't. Your ma and I met young, Declan, and look at us. I love her more now than I did then."

"But Da—"

"No. Should we start planning a wedding or not?"

Shaking my head, I know that if I tell him no then Amberlyn will have my arse. She wants this, but it worries me that she won't ten years down the road. But what am I to do? I won't let her go, and I know she won't allow me to give up the distillery, nor do I want to. As much as I don't want to rush her, I feel we have no other choice in the matter.

Looking up at my father, I nod. "Yes, we will need to plan one."

four
Amberlyn

I'm cold.

Why am I cold?

Blinking awake, I look to the right to see that Declan isn't there like he is supposed to be. Like he was when I fell into blissful sleep. That was by far the best nap I've ever had. Not sure if it was the drugs or if it was falling asleep with Declan close to me, but it was damn well needed. But where is he now?

"He went to talk to Ma and Da and then left. Hasn't been back yet."

I look across the room to find Fiona sitting with her computer in her lap. She smiles at me as she closes the laptop and says, "Good morning, by the way."

I glance at the window and see that the sun is shining bright.

"Jeez, what time is it?"

"Nine. You were knocked out. Do you need anything?"

I shake my head. "Damn. No, I'm fine." I get up slowly, my chest sore as I push back the covers. Cringing a bit, I sit up and meet Fiona's gaze. "I wonder why he left. Wait, what did he have to talk to your dad and mom for?"

"Ask for your hand in marriage," she says simply, leaning on her knees.

"What for? I already said yes."

"Yeah, but he said it was done all wrong. Trying to right his wrongs."

I roll my eyes. "I don't understand that, but okay," I say, reaching for my phone to text him. I see that there is a text from him, saying to call him once I wake up. Rubbing my eyes, I look up at Fiona. "What did they say?"

"They say you're too young," she says, and I look up from my phone. "Oh?"

"Yeah, and I tend to agree," she admits. "Are you sure, Amberlyn? You can say no. You don't have to do this because of everything he is gonna lose."

"You're right, I don't, but I want to."

"You aren't doing this because of everything with the distillery?"

I shake my head. "No, not at all. It may rush us a bit, but I want to marry him because I love him. I believe with my whole heart that my mom sent him to me for a reason. He completes me, Fiona. I love him."

"It's just mad is all. So quick and everything."

"Maybe, but I don't see myself with anyone but him."

"'Cause he's all you had. Hell, you ain't even had him!"

I smile. "True, but I will, and it will be perfect."

"Or it could go to hell and then you'll be stuck in a sucky sex life."

I laugh as I roll my eyes. "I doubt that will happen, but I can guarantee you, we will have sex before we marry."

"Thank God." Fiona decides with a shake of her head.

"Yeah, just to make sure, but I know it will be great. We just get each other. On so many levels."

"I guess, I mean yous are cute and all sugary sweet for each other, but it just worries me is all."

"Why?"

"I feel like you'll regret it later."

"No, I won't," I say with all the conviction in my heart. "I know he is who I am supposed to marry, I just do. In my gut."

"I don't know about that gut of yours. You not only dated Casey Burke, but then you blocked a shot for Declan. That gut gets you in trouble," she says with a grin, but I set her with a look.

"First, didn't you date Casey?"

"Oh, fuck off," is her response and I laugh.

"And if someone were about to shoot Kane, wouldn't you try to save him?"

She stops laughing for a moment and sends me a look. Slowly, she nods. "I would."

"Okay, and if Kane asked you to marry him, wouldn't you?"

"You're making this a losing battle for me," she says and I smile.

"Because it is. I may be young, but I know what I'm doing."

"Okay," she agrees. "I'll be right beside you all the way through, then."

"Thanks, couldn't do it without my maid of honor."

"Damn right, ya couldn't!"

Smiling, Fiona gets up and closes the distance between us. Wrapping an arm around my waist, she hugs me tightly to her and I lean my head to hers. In the short time since I met her, I feel as if I've known her my whole life. She is the sister I never had, and I couldn't replace her if I tried. While I respect what she just did here, I'm pretty sure I would have been a little broken if she hadn't agreed to stand beside me.

"I love you, Fiona," I whisper, and her arms tighten around me.

"I love you, too," she says softly. "I worry for ya, you know that."

"I do."

"That's why I said something. It isn't that I don't believe in yous two, I do. I think yous two are made for each other, but it just makes me nervous. Getting married isn't something to toy with, ya know?"

"I do, but I also know that this kind of love doesn't come around. Back in America, I never would have met someone like Declan. Someone who would love me without sex."

"Shit, ya usually wouldn't get that here. Declan is one of a kind."

"And all mine," I say with a grin.

We don't say anything for a moment as we hold on to each other. Within the next couple months, so much is gonna change. I'm going to move out, I'll be a married woman, and I won't have this time to just hug my cousin. It scares me, but then I think I'll be so unbelievably loved by the most amazing man on this earth.

My Declan.

"You're going to be the Whiskey Princess."

I smile. "Weird, huh?"

"Yeah, especially since you have to be dressed to the nines eighty percent of the time."

I hadn't thought about that. Ew. "Eh, I'm sure that won't apply to me."

She laughs. "If you say so. They'll have you walking in heels and your hair and makeup done every morning. No more buns or jeans, I can tell you that."

Pulling away, I look over at her. "No. Ugh."

"Bet ya! Those O'Callaghans are pristine all the time."

"Well, I'll be pristine in a pair of shorts and a tee, working the bar."

She laughed again. "You have no clue what you are getting into. You won't be working at the bar anymore. You'll be going to have tea with old people and shite."

"No way," I say with a shake of my head. "I'm not going to change who I am."

She eyes me for a second and slowly nods her head. "I sure as hell hope not."

I can see in her eyes that she is doubtful, but I don't believe a word she says. They may be basically royalty and perfect, but being an O'Callaghan isn't going to change me.

I'll still be me.

And that's how Declan will want me.

"Hey, girls."

I look up to see my aunt standing in the doorway, a smile on her face.

"Howya, Ma," Fiona says. "What's up?"

"Come on to the pub with me for a minute."

We comply, and I hate the way they treat me like a fragile piece of glass. Holding my hand and making sure I don't die on the way. It's annoying, but I know they do it because they love me. When we reach the pub after a short walk, we go through the side door, and as I come through, the room erupts in cheers. I smile as I take in all my regular patrons and then the big "Welcome Home, Amberlyn" sign. Tears sting my eyes as I am passed around, hugged softly, and kissed by almost everyone. I have missed my pub family; some of these people I see every day. I know that Mr. Little loves his corned beef hash. That Mrs. Kettle needs lavender in her tea. That Timmy loves his whiskey straight. That Brian would marry me or Fiona, or hell, even my aunt. I know these people. Their life stories. They are my family.

When I'm seated at the bar with Richard in front of me, I smile. He comes in every single Sunday with his guitar to sing. His wife, Laney, sits at the table to the left as he sings songs with his soft, crooning voice. It reminds me so much of my father's, and that's why he is probably my favorite person.

Cupping my face, he says, "You gave us all a scare."

I smile. "I'm sorry. It's so good to be home though."

"Sure, sure. Now, let me play for ya."

Pulling my knees up to my chest, I lean on them softly as I nod my head. With a grin on his face, he starts to sing a song I've heard many times before. One he knows is one of my favorites, "Wild Mountain Thyme." My dad used to sing it a lot, and it made my heart just sing in my chest. When the whole pub starts to sing along with him, I join in and it feels so right. Closing my eyes, I sing like I was singing with my dad while my mom sat to the side, tapping her foot on the floor as she read. I can see it so vividly. I can smell my father's cologne and the roast in the Crock-Pot, and I can recall the feeling of being so surrounded by the love he gave me. His dark eyes would be on me while his fingers ran along the strings of his guitar.

"Sing for me, love," he would say and I would.

Soon my mom would join in, and we would all start to laugh because she couldn't sing for shit, but it was her. And we loved her.

When the song ends, I open my eyes and smile. "Beautiful."

"Your voice, it is. I didn't know you could sing, Amberlyn," he says, his eyes playful. "I'll have to do duets with ya from now on!"

Everyone cheers for that, causing my face to burn with embarrassment. "No way! I was just singing along."

"Ah, hush, you have the voice of an angel. Sing for me!"

"No!" I say, giggling as I wave him off. Soon everyone is urging me on, and

I shake my head, still laughing. "You guys are crazy!"

"Come on then, Amberlyn! Do it!" Fiona calls and I shoot her a dirty look, but I know they aren't gonna give in until I do what they ask.

"Fine. Pick a song I know," I say to Richard.

"'Parting Glass,' yeah? I've heard you hum it before," he asks and I smile.

"Yeah," I nod, and I pray I can get through the song without tearing up. Clearing my throat, I am surprised by how much I want to do this. I always said I would never sing it without my dad, but now, after facing death, I feel like singing it will bring him even closer to me. Keep his memory alive and burning in my heart.

Not waiting for Richard to start playing, I start to sing, causing the pub to go quiet. When Richard joins in, our voices harmonize together almost like my dad's and mine used to. My eyes are locked on his as we sing the verses I learned from my dad. He lets me take the lead, harmonizing with me, and it's such a lovely sound. I wait for everyone to join in, but they don't. It's just me and Richard.

As I sing the last line, Richard does a flair with the guitar, causing everyone to cheer out loudly as my throat goes tight. I miss my dad so much. Every dream I have, he is never there, only my mom, and I would do anything to see his face again. Even in a dream. Standing up, Richard wraps his arm around me, hugging me softly as a lone tear rolls down my face.

In my ear, he whispers, "I've sung that with your da many times, my dear. Let me just say, he raised one hell of a singer, and what a beauty she is." Pulling away, he meets my gaze and wipes away my tear. "He'd be very proud of ya."

"Thank you," I say softly.

"Simply stunning."

I whip my head to the side to see Declan standing there, a grin on his face. "Hey!"

I hop off the stool and into his arms. Pain explodes across my chest, and I scold myself for that dumb move, but I've missed him. He's been a constant presence since I got shot, and I don't think I like being apart. As I kiss his lips softly, he smiles against mine, and I know it's because we are in front of the whole pub, but I don't give two shits. He's my man!

Parting, I smile up at him, running my finger along his jaw. "They threw me a little welcome home party."

"It was Declan's idea," I hear Fiona say, and my grin grows as his cheeks warm with color.

"Oh, really?"

He shrugs. "Sure. Everyone's missed ya."

I grin and he sends me a grin back before he unlocks my arms from around his neck. My brows come together as he says, "Sit down, sweetheart."

I do as he asks, and then he takes my hand in his. "I heard this song a couple years ago. I saw the artist perform it here, right, Fiona?"

Fiona grins as she nods. "Yeah."

He meets my gaze again and kisses my knuckles before saying, "And yeah, he was amazing, but I never thought about this song until about an hour ago." He pauses, lacing our fingers together, and I can feel the nerves coming off him in waves. He hates crowds, and I am surprised he is saying this much, but I appreciate it. "I was in my library and the thought of you was heavy on my mind. Like always," he says, sending me a grin that I return. "And all of a sudden, this song comes to mind. This is how I feel for ya, and it describes ya perfectly. So, yeah, let's have at it."

Richard starts to play and I fully expect him to start singing, but to my surprise, it is Declan who starts to sing. It is a lovely sound too! Deep but with a little bit of a softness to it. I recognize the song almost immediately as Ed Sheeran's "Fall." It is one of my favorites, and hearing Declan sing it has my heart coming out of my chest. While he doesn't have the voice Ed Sheeran has, his voice is beautiful just the same, and I am in complete awe of him. The song lyrics talk about how much he loves falling for the girl he loves, and it rattles my soul seeing my boyfriend, I mean fiancé, sing so beautifully. Just for me.

The whole pub has fallen silent again, and everyone is in total shock. As am I. Out of the corner of my eye, I see someone hold up their phone but Fiona takes it away, shaking her head. She really is so amazing. I meet Declan's gaze again and can see that he is nervous, but my God, he has no reason to be. He is beyond amazing. Squeezing his hand as his voice fills the pub, I am flabbergasted.

As the song ends, I stand up, wrapping my arms around his neck as I kiss his lips while everyone claps and hollers out for him. Love explodes in my heart for him, sending tingles through my body as we share a long kiss. His fingers are tight at my waist, and I can feel his heart beating against my chest, almost in time with mine. Parting, we share a smile, but when I go to say something, he shakes his head before falling down to one knee.

Holding my hand in his, he looks up at me and my heart kicks into hyperspeed. I know what he is doing, but seeing him down there just makes it extremely real.

"I would have never done that before," he says softly. "Sing for ya like that."

"Sure the hell wouldn't," I hear Kane call out, and I hadn't realized he was here, but he is, wrapped around Fiona like a glove.

Smiling, I look back down at Declan and cup his jaw. "It was beautiful. Thank you."

"Anything for ya, Amberlyn. Really. Anything and everything you want, you'll have because I honestly can't live this life without you. I can't believe I found ya, across a lake, looking so gorgeous. You stunned me. First glance, I was a goner. When I first talked to you and you poked me in the middle of my forehead, I knew I was going to love you my whole damn life. You've taken over my thoughts, my heart, and brought me out of the shell I've lived in for so long. I became alive when I met you."

Tears burn my eyes as I hold his gaze. "Oh, Declan," I say softly, and he smiles.

"Nothing feels like you. Nothing can add up to what you give me. I want to say I chose ya first, but I didn't. My heart did, and by the time my brain and the rest of my body caught up, I was gone with ya. I never want to let ya go. So," he says, pausing. I glance over to where he is looking as Fiona hands him a book. Meeting my gaze again, he says, "I want you to have this."

When he places it in my lap, I look up at him in shock. It's his *Pride and Prejudice* first edition.

"No, this is your great-times-ten-grandma's," I say, running my fingers down the front of it. I love this book and would love to say it was mine, but it isn't, and I can't allow him to give it to me. No matter how much I want it.

"Yeah, it was and so is what is inside."

Intrigued, I open the book but don't see anything. "Huh?"

He pulls on the little string bookmark, and at the bottom of the fabric is a ring tied to it. Blinking in complete shock, I pick it up and gawk at the gorgeousness of this ring. A huge oval diamond sits on a gold band that is encrusted with smaller diamonds. It is stunning and beautiful, very vintage. So completely me. I meet Declan's gaze, and he smiles as he takes the ring from my fingers and unties it. Holding it out, he looks deep into my eyes, and I can see the tears welling up in his own eyes. He is so beautiful, his ice-blue eyes burning with love for me. I can see every single one of his emotions, and I can't believe that, so quickly, I can read him like this. He is nervous but completely in love with me, just the way I want him.

"My grandma who wore this ring and bought this book was married for forty-six years to my grandda. They were mad for each other, and she loved this ring and this book, but I want you to have them."

A tear escapes my eye, and I try to hold in the others, but it doesn't work well. He smiles as his fingers thread with mine while his other hand holds the ring out to me. "These things are part of my history, and I want you to have them because you are my future."

"Declan," I gasp, my lip wobbling as I hold his gaze.

"I love ya, Amberlyn, and I would like nothing more than for you to be my wife. To make this life worth living because without ya, I'm nothing. So will ya have me?"

I don't even answer him. I let my lips do the talking and ignore the sting in my chest or the exclamation of the audience. I mark the pain off as my heart exploding in my chest, and I couldn't care less about the people in the room. The only thing that matters is the fact I'll never love anyone the way I love Declan O'Callaghan.

five
Amberlyn

I am finally feeling like myself.

It's been almost four weeks since I was shot, and I feel fantastic. Yeah, it still hurts a bit here and there when I do things, but I know that I am healed. My wound is scabbed over and isn't swollen anymore. The doctor gave me a clean bill of health, which is such a blessing since they thought I would die when it all first happened. But like my mom said, it wasn't my time. Which is fine with me. While I miss her and my dad so much, I am about to spend the rest of my life with Declan.

Swoon...

It's been a week since he proposed "the right way," as he says. I still can't believe how extraordinarily romantic it all was. I never expected that from him. I was fine with the way he did it in the hospital and thought that was how he operated, but then he blew my flipping mind with his *real* proposal. I swear I'll never forget the way his eyes sparkled as he looked deep into mine. The way he sang to me, only for me. Or the way he held the ring up to me as his eyes pleaded for my forever.

Which he already had.

He's changing right before my eyes, and I love it. I remember the first time I met him, when he was looking at me, his brow furrowed with the worst case of resting bitchface! He was so closed-off, almost scared of me, although it didn't take much to pull him from his shell. Now when he looks at me, I feel nothing but indescribable love.

I know that Fiona and even my aunt and uncle think I'm crazy. That this is all insane, but I know it's not crazy. It's real. If my mom were here, she would believe in this. She always told me to fight for what I believe in. To never give up. That she'd rather I stand for what I believe in alone than stand for something I don't. I know that it's fast, and that it wouldn't hurt to be engaged for a long time, but why wait when we are so in love? I know they think it's because of the distillery, but that has nothing to do with it. I know he would give it up for me; though, I would never allow him to do that.

We are getting married because we love each other.

The distillery issue just rushed us along.

Coming down the stairs, I smile at my aunt as I reach for my shoes.

"Where ya off to?" she asks with a grin on her face.

"Declan is picking me up for dinner with his family."

"Oh, that's nice," she says before looking down at the newspaper she is reading. Rolling my eyes, I hate that she is being so standoffish about it all. I know she doesn't agree, but can't she support me? Heading for her, I pause when I see the headline on her paper.

Will Amberlyn Reilly, the future Whiskey Princess, testify against her shooter?

"Why do you read that crap?" I find myself asking as I sit on the arm of her chair. Meeting my gaze with the same dark brown eyes of my father, she smiles.

"'Cause I'm nosy as shite. Have to know what they are saying about you."

"And?" I ask, even though I don't care.

"They think you won't."

I shake my head. "I want him to be punished for what he did to me. Of course I will."

"Oh, I know that, but Noreen is making sure that no one knows anything about you. It's kinda spooky how much she is hidin'," she says with a nod. "Good, though. She is protecting you."

"Yeah," I agree, wrapping my arm around her, ignoring the sting in my chest. As I lean my head against hers, she kisses my temple and smiles against it.

"Make sure to tell her thank you," she reminds me.

"I will," I say softly. I can feel the tension in her body, and it worries me that I put it there. "Are you mad at me?"

She shakes her head. "No, I'm worried a bit, that's all. I just want to make sure I am doing right by my brother's and your ma's memory, is all."

"I think you are," I say, leaning back to look at her. "I know you are."

"It's scary. You're so young, my love. I don't want you to waste this life you have on the first boy you fall for."

"I don't see it as a waste. I wish you could feel what I feel. The overpowering burst of love that rattles me to the core. I love him. And I want to marry him.

My mom married her first love."

"Yes, but she had some duds before that," she says, cupping my face. "You've had none."

"Good, so I'll never know the feeling of heartbreak. I take that as a good thing in my book."

She shakes her head and then sucks in a deep breath before letting it out. She looks over at me with all the love in the world and I smile. Since I came to Ireland, she has done nothing but treat me like her own. It's amazing how much she means to me. I always knew about her, spoke to her a few times on the phone, but now, I know I couldn't go a day without speaking to her.

"You're an adult, my love. You do as you please. I'll be here to guide you, and, above all, love ya like yer ma and da would."

I smile as I lean my forehead to hers. "That's all I could ever ask for."

She kisses my nose, and I giggle as I pull back. "We need to go dress shopping."

She nods. "Sure, when?"

"Soon, the wedding is October seventeenth."

"My goodness, so soon, yes?"

"Yeah, that's his deadline," I say with a shrug.

I kind of wanted to be a June bride, like my mom had been. She had even gotten married out beside the B&B when she was my age, but I won't be a June bride. Declan's father isn't budging, and while Declan has told me repeatedly he'd throw it all away to make me happy, I won't be happy if he does. So October bride I am! It's really no big deal, I guess. Orange will look great on Fiona, so that's a plus.

With an unpleasant sound, my aunt's thought on the matter is, "Ah, gobshite of a deadline, it is."

I laugh as I nod. "It is, but that's how those O'Callaghans work."

She squeezes my hand, tears gathering in her eyes. "You'll be one of them soon."

"Yeah, but I'll always be a Reilly deep down," I say with a wink as the doorbell rings.

Kissing her cheek loudly, I get up and head to the door. Pulling it open, I smile when my gaze meets Declan's. His lips curve up at the sides before he reaches for me, bringing me up to my tippy toes as his lips move with mine. Desire swims in my belly as my hands run up his chest and around his neck. I just love kissing him. Parting, he grins down at me before tucking a stray piece of my hair behind my ear.

"Howya," he says softly, running his thumb along my bottom lip. "You're beautiful."

I smile shyly as I lace my fingers with his. He's wearing a suit, not a tuxedo, but a dark blue suit with a light blue shirt underneath the jacket. The first few buttons are open, giving me a delectable view of his sexy neck. He isn't wearing the beanie either. I've noticed he hasn't been wearing it at all lately. "So are you," I say. "I feel a little underdressed."

He shakes his head, taking a step back before drinking in the sight of me. I hope he sees that I've taken time straightening my hair and doing my makeup since Fiona had to work. The dress I'm wearing is sweet enough, I guess; it's a pale green color, the skirt long with a cute little bird design all over it while the bodice is sparkling and tied around my neck. Smiling down at me, he gathers me in his arms before running his lips along mine.

"You're stunning,"

I kiss his jaw and close my eyes, leaning against him. I've missed him. He had to work all day yesterday and most of the days since I was shot, and it's sucked being so far away from him all day. Thankfully, I start back at work tomorrow, so I won't be so lonely.

"I missed you," I whisper against this jaw, the blond hair tickling my lips.

"I've missed ya too, my love. I got something for ya."

I lean back and meet his gaze. "Yeah?"

He lets me go to reach into his pocket and pulls out my engagement ring. His great-grandmother's ring. It didn't fit, it was too big, so he took it to be resized. I thought it would take longer to get here, but knowing Declan, he probably had it rushed. I am still in such awe of the beauty of the ring. The diamond is so big, almost a little gaudy, but the diamonds on the sides accent it beautifully, and it really is stunning.

Taking my hand, he slides it on my finger and smiles at me. Kissing the ring on my finger, he massages my hand with his thumb. "Perfect fit, yeah?"

I nod, my heart pounding against my ribs. "It is."

"You ready?"

"Yeah, let's go," I say, looking back at my aunt. "We are off."

"Howya, Mrs. Maclaster."

"Howya, Declan, good to see ya," she says and I actually believe her.

"You too, we'll be back later."

"Sure, give your parents my best."

"Will do," he says with a nod.

He then pulls me out the door and to his car.

We don't say much as we head to the O'Callaghan estate. My fingers are laced with his, resting on his leg as we drive. I feel so complete. It's such a euphoric feeling he brings me. Glancing over at him, I take in the beauty that is my fiancé. His eyes are trained on the road he is following, and I notice that his hair is getting longer. It's curling around his ears in a cute little way. The hair on his jaw is longer than normal too. He looks all unkempt, and I have to admit, it's rather sexy.

But then I notice the tension in his jaw. My brows come together as I ask,

"What's wrong?"

He smiles as he shakes his head. "Know me too well, ya think?"

"I don't think, I know."

Clearing his throat, he says, "Yeah, I guess ya do." Squeezing my hand, he glances at me for a moment before looking back at the road. "I don't know how I feel about this. I don't trust my da and ma."

I scoff. "What do you mean? We are going to dinner."

"Yeah, but I feel like it's gonna be a pain."

"Anything you don't want to do is a pain," I supply and he laughs.

"True, but promise me something," he says softly, meeting my gaze. "You feel uncomfortable, at any time, you tell me, yeah?"

I nod. "Of course."

"Good," he says with a nod, bringing my hand up to his mouth to kiss softly. "I love you."

"I love you," I say automatically as my stomach does a little flip-flop. There is something about the way he tells me he loves me that hits me in the gut every time. It's all sexy and rough and Irish. And I know it's all for me. As I watch him work his lip as he drives, I hate that he is nervous about going to dinner with his family. It reminds me of when we were going to the ball. Hm. That reminds me. "It's been a week."

His brows come in. "Sure, yeah? So?"

"You said we would talk about everything when a week was up. It's actually been a week and a half."

He chuckles. "Sweetheart, let's get through dinner."

I smile. "So you don't want to talk about having sex."

I'm surprised we don't crash the way he jerks the car to the side before righting the steering wheel and then looking at me. "Jaysus, Amberlyn! Run me off the road, will ya?"

I giggle. "Just asking."

"That's not something you ask, though; you let it happen," he says, kissing the back of my hand. "Give it time."

"We were gonna have sex the night I got shot," I point out and he closes his eyes.

"You're killin' me, Amberlyn. Shh, don't talk about it. I won't make it through dinner with my family if ya keep it up," he practically begs and I giggle.

"So saying that I want you very, very badly is frowned upon until a moment where we aren't going to dinner with your family?"

His eyes drift shut as he nods his head, his fingers squeezing mine. "You like torturing me, yeah?"

I smile. "Yeah, I do."

It's just so easy.

Amberlyn
six

"You look well, Amberlyn. That's very good."

I look up and smile across the table at Mr. O'Callaghan. Declan's mother and Lena smile fondly at me while her fiancé, Micah, just looks at me. He is very proper. Doesn't really talk much, but he is gorgeous. He'd have to be to be with someone like Lena. She is stunning. Tall as a model and a body like one too. The dress she wears puts mine to shame. It sparkles like a mirror ball and is short, showing off her beautiful long legs. Micah doesn't take his eyes off her much, and I don't blame him. I feel a little self-conscious around her. If Declan didn't look at me like I was the best looking piece of pie in the world, I'd probably leave.

Thankfully, he does though.

"Thank you," I say, tearing my gaze away from Micah and on to Mr. O'Callaghan. "I feel great."

"That's grand, Amberlyn, we've all been so worried," Mrs. O'Callaghan says.

"Sorry for that," I say because I have no clue what else to say.

"No, not at all. We owe you everything for protecting Declan the way you did," she says softly, squeezing Declan's arm. He sends her a smile before glancing at me with a grin. Good God, he is sexy. Heat burns throughout me. While it is fun to torture him with my need, it's just that; I crave him. I want to feel his naked body against mine. I want touch my lips to his body, taste him, and have the most unbelievable connection with him. I need it. I need him.

"You're flushed. Are you okay?"

I glance over at him as my skin burns with more color. "Yes, fine. It's hot in here."

He chuckles as Lena says, "I love your accent. It's so different from ours. It's so funny that we are both marrying non-Irish folks, Dec! Poor kids of ours won't know who to sound like."

Declan laughs as he nods. "I hope they all sound like Amberlyn. That would be a blessing, yeah."

I smile as I lean into him and Lena giggles. "Such a softy he is. Wish ya talked to me like that, Micah."

Micah scoffs to that as he shakes his head. "Like I don't. You know I do."

His voice is very English. He's from London from my understanding. They met when she went there on a holiday with her grandmother. Lena's laughter fills the room as she nods her head.

"I do," she says with a wink, and you can just see their love coming off them in waves. I wonder if it looks that way for Declan and me.

"When are you two getting married?" I ask and Lena smiles.

"May, next year. We want to wait till his mother gets back from Africa. She is doing missionary work," Lena informs me and I smile.

"That's amazing."

"Yeah, she's a doctor. I'm to go over this November to help build some house. Trying to talk Lena into going with me."

Lena laughs as Declan scoffs. "She wouldn't last an hour and you know it."

Micah smiles as he looks over at her. "Yeah, she wouldn't, but it's gonna be hard being away from her."

"I might try," Lena announces, but that has everyone at the table laughing. "Ah! Whatever."

"You know you need your hair and makeup done, and I doubt that your designer will come to Africa to design yer dresses," Declan says, pointing his fork at her. "And I'm pretty sure they don't have air conditioning."

"Oh, off with ya." She sneers back at him with a wave of her hand. "I don't need that stuff."

"Sure," Declan laughs and I smile at the family banter. Fiona and I can be the same way.

"Speaking of Marc, Amberlyn, we will need to get you in with him. Have him design you some clothes. He won't have time to do your wedding gown, but he'll have your wardrobe done for after the wedding," Mrs. O'Callaghan says.

I look over at her, confused. "My wardrobe?"

"Of course, you can't run around in jeans and T-shirts, my dear. You'll need nice clothes."

"You'll love him! We can go together! A girls' trip!" Lena exclaims.

"I like my clothes," I say, which silences the table. Looking around at all the faces staring at me, my heart jackhammers against my chest. "I like being comfortable."

"Oh, he'll make sure you are comfortable! Promise," Lena assures me, but I have seen what she wears, and if they think I'm strolling through the pub in heels, they have another thing coming.

Before I can make that known though, Mrs. O'Callaghan says, "When do you want to go pick out a dress? I'd love to come and so would Lena."

Not that I have anything against Declan's mom or sister, but I really wanted to do that with my aunt and my cousin. Since I don't want to offend them, I say, "I think we are planning that next week."

"Oh, it will be a blast! Ma, you'll have to call to make sure they have tea and everything set up."

When I glance back at Mrs. O'Callaghan, she's on her phone, nodding her head. "Already penciled it in. I'll call in the morning. I am so excited."

I smile, but I know it doesn't reach my eyes as Mr. O'Callaghan says, "You'll get married here, right, Declan?"

Declan nods. "Sure, Da."

"Um," I say, and all eyes shift to me. "My mom and dad got married on the B&B land, by the lake under the tree. I'd love to get married there."

"Oh, of course," Declan says quickly. "We'll have to make sure Mr. and Mrs. Maclaster are okay with that, but yeah, I want that too."

He smiles widely at me before returning to his plate, but when I look up, I can see that his parents don't like that idea.

"Will it hold everyone?"

"Everyone?" I ask, looking at Declan.

"Yeah, it will be fine. I have a huge family, friends, and stuff. It will be grand."

"Oh," Mrs. O'Callaghan says, her shoulders falling. "We've all gotten married on this land."

"Well, things change, Ma. I have to respect Amberlyn's wishes too," he says without looking at her, and I bite the inside of my cheek. I won't give on this. No matter how disappointed his mother looks. I want her to like me, but I won't budge on this.

"That's settled then," Mr. O'Callaghan says.

"Yes, I guess it is," Mrs. O'Callaghan sighs as Declan looks over at me.

He sends me a grin before leaning over to kiss my lips softly. It's way too quick in my opinion, and as he pulls back, he whispers, "I can't wait to be married to you."

"Me neither," I say back, running my thumb along his lip to wipe away some of my lip gloss.

He gives me a wink before returning back to his plate. Leaning back in my seat, stuffed from the duck that was prepared, I look across the table as Mr.

O'Callaghan asks, "Will you be moving in before or after the wedding?"

Moving in?

"We haven't talked about that yet, Da," Declan says without looking up. "We haven't discussed a lot of things. Been waiting for her to heal and all."

"That's well and all," Mr. O'Callaghan says, "but it's coming up quick. The wedding, that is, and we want to make sure she is comfortable."

"Sure, Da, let us talk privately about that."

"Of course," he says with a nod.

"Micah, you live here?" I find myself asking.

And to my surprise, he nods. "I do when I'm in here, and Lena stays with me in London."

"Oh."

"Are you one of those people who wait to move in until marriage?" Lena asks, a playful grin on her face.

"Lena, shut it," Declan says before glancing at me. "Don't pay her any mind. She obviously is off her meds today."

She sticks her tongue out at him as everyone starts to laugh, but I just poke at my carrots. I don't want to live here with his family.

Is that weird?

"Amberlyn, I'll need you to come to tea with us with the Fadmish ladies in two weeks, please," Mrs. O'Callaghan says once she's stopped laughing. "I just remembered, and they are so excited to meet you. Maybe you could wear something of Lena's."

My brows come up as I shake my head. "While I'm flattered by the fact you think I could wear Lena's clothes, I'm pretty sure my butt and boobs wouldn't fit."

"Sure wouldn't," is Declan's response, which causes my cheeks to redden as I playfully lean into him. "But gorgeous, just the same," he says, kissing my cheek and hugging me tightly to him.

Meeting Mrs. O'Callaghan's gaze once more, I notice her eyes are a little sharper. "I guess you're right. You should go shopping with Lena before then."

I tilt my head to the side. "I'm sure I have something."

She waves me off with a smile on her face. I'm not sure if she is joking or being serious. "You'll need to be dressed accordingly."

"Isn't it just tea? I'm sure I have something."

"A pantsuit?"

"A pantsuit?" I ask incredulously. "For tea?"

Lena laughs, and I notice that now Mr. O'Callaghan is watching me intently. Almost expectantly. I remember Declan telling me that his da thinks I'm not ready for this life. Well, he's got another thing coming.

"Or a tea dress. I'll take ya out," Lena says, but I don't want to go get new clothes. However, I swallow that and smile.

"Sure, it will be fun," I say with a nod, but I'm pretty sure it will be anything but.

"Grand!" Mrs. O'Callaghan says with a big grin before squeezing Declan's hand. He smiles up at her and then me before taking a sip of his whiskey. "We need to plan the engagement party quickly since the wedding is going to be here before we know it."

"Wouldn't be that way if Da would give me more time," Declan says, leaning back in his chair and crossing his arms. "Give us a year to plan."

"Well—" Mrs. O'Callaghan starts, but Mr. O'Callaghan interrupts her.

"No, you'll be married soon, or good ol' Micah will be taking over operations at the distillery. I want to travel, son. I am done here; it's time for me and your ma to leave, enjoy our retirement," he says, joining his fingers with hers.

I can see the tick in Declan's jaw and I hate that. This is the stupidest thing I've ever heard, and I'm more than a little annoyed with his father. While we really don't need time, I understand Declan wanting it for me. He's nervous and I understand that, but I'm not going anywhere.

"So when should we do the engagement party?" I say, lacing my fingers with his, and then I cover our hands with my other one. He glances at me and I smile. He leans to me, his lips close to my ear as he whispers, "You don't have to do this. You don't have to entertain them."

When he pulls back, his eyes locked with mine, I can read everything on his face. He is nervous and annoyed, but, above all, he loves me. I never thought I could look into the eyes of someone other than my parents and just know they love me. Getting lost in the blue of his eyes, I know that he is right, but at the same time, why shouldn't we experience it all? If they are going to give us a lavish engagement party, hell, let's do it. If she wants to show me off to every tea party, let's go. I'll do anything to ensure that Declan knows I am here for him. We have things to discuss, but in the end, I'm his. Completely and fully his. So cupping his face, I say the only thing I am thinking. The only thing I am always thinking.

"I love you."

Declan seven

I want to tell her no.

I want to tell her she doesn't have to do any of it. That all she has to do is be with me. Love me. But even I know that all this goes with being an O'Callaghan woman. They go to tea with stuck-up old ladies, they shop for expensive clothes that half the time don't even look good on them, and they plan parties. I know that this isn't what Amberlyn's scene is, and that makes me a bit nervous. How much is she gonna take before it's too much? I'm going to have to have a talk with my family.

And her.

I really don't want to upset her though. She is happy for the most part but still in some pain, something I still blame myself for. Not that I would admit it to her. I just don't know anymore. I am tiptoeing on the line between knowing what is right and not knowing at all. I know I want to marry her, be with her forever, but can I do that and still keep her happy? I want to think I can, trust I can. But I can't help but realize she isn't from my world, and I am plucking her from hers and putting her in mine, expecting it to all go well.

Glancing over at her, I see that she is watching me, a little smile on her beautiful lips as she holds my hand with both of hers. She looks gorgeous tonight; the skirt she's wearing is long, and it almost seems as if she is floating through the halls of my home. I love walking with her like this, but more so, I love seeing her in my home. I can't wait until the moment that she never leaves.

That when I come home, she's here, waiting for me. We will bring our children here, raise them. I can see it. I can.

"You're quiet."

I smile, squeezing her hand as I nod. "Just thinking."

"About?"

"Us."

Leaning her head on my shoulder, she says, "Good thing to think about."

"I think so too," I say. "I'm sorry if my family offended ya."

"They didn't." She looks up at me and shrugs. "It's just weird."

"It's going to take some getting used to," I say, but then I pause. Something flickers in her eyes, something almost like resistance. Like she wanted to say something but is holding back. "What?"

She shakes her head, but I push on. "Tell me."

Meeting my gaze again, she goes, "Fiona says that you guys are going to change me. That I can't be me and be an O'Callaghan."

I nod before stopping and turning to her. "I mean, there are expectations of us."

She watches me for a moment and asks, "What kind of expectations?"

I bite my lip and let out a long breath. "You have to dress the part, go to tea with people you don't know or like. You have to, shite, I don't know, Amberlyn. I don't care about that stuff. All I care about is you. I want you."

"I want that too," she says quietly as she looks down, lacing her fingers together. "I'll admit they make me nervous. I don't want to change me. I love me, but I also don't want to live a moment without you."

"I love you too, and I would never ask you to be something you're not. My parents might try though; I'm not going to lie. I'll talk to them, and hopefully, it won't be that bad."

She still looks unsure, so I say, "But Amberlyn, things are going to change. You won't be Amberlyn Reilly anymore. You'll be Amberlyn O'Callaghan, my wife, and with that, we have to do parties and stupid shite, when really, I'd rather lie in bed with you and never leave. So, this is your out, my love. I tried to get a year so that you could see more of my life and how it works, but I couldn't. If you're not ready for it, please, tell me, and I'll let you go. I want you to be happy. I want you to live the life you deserve."

With a grin, she steps to me, wrapping her arms around my neck. "I'm not going anywhere. The life I deserve is with you."

"Ya sure?" I ask 'cause I'm sure that I see differently in her sweet eyes.

"Very. I know you won't make me do something I don't want to do."

"I won't," I promise.

"So we're good. I'll go with it, but the moment I feel something isn't right, I'll say something."

"Good, I wouldn't want it any other way."

"So, while we are discussing that, I don't want to move in here."

My brows come together as I eye her. "What do you mean?"

"I don't want to move in with your parents. That's weird. We are adults. We have to have our own place."

What?

I see Lena and Micah coming toward us over her shoulder, and I don't want them to hear us. Taking her hand in mine, I lead her down the hall and up the stairs.

"Where are we going?"

I look back at her. "My room."

"Oh," is her answer as we go down another hall.

"My family lives in the North Wing, which is eight rooms, twelve bathrooms, two dining rooms, a huge kitchen, and three studies. It is also broken up into the three stories. My room is at the top with no one else. Lena is on the second, and my parents are on the main. I'll have to take you on a tour of the whole house," I say as I reach for my door and push it open.

I move to the side and watch her face as she enters. "Holy crap, it's a like a penthouse."

I smile. "Yeah. Have my own bathroom, balcony, and sitting area. Through that door is the bedroom," I say, walking past her to open the door to my bedroom. The room is large with big stained glass windows and another door that leads to the bathroom. In the middle is a huge four-poster bed that is fit for a king, as my ma always says. I've slept in that bed since I was a baby. Amberlyn walks in, an expression of awe on her face as she looks around.

"I like the blue."

"It's my favorite color."

She smiles back at me before pointing the door to the right. "What's in there?"

"I wish I could say it was something cool like a room of sex toys, but no, it's a closet," I joke as I push the door open. She peeks in, her eyes going wide.

"This is a whole other room! Why do you need all this space?"

I laugh as she goes in, hitting the light. One side is full of all my suits, hung in order by color. Below them are all my shoes. On the other rack are all my shirts and shorts and a few pair of jeans and slacks. More shoes and some of my winter equipment. The other side, though, is completely bare.

"For my wife," I say, answering her question. "This closet was redone when I turned sixteen since that's when I started looking for a wife. Or so my parents thought. I think my mom's goal was to lure a woman with a huge closet if she married me. I was a little dorky back then."

She laughs, "I highly doubt that."

"Ah, let's say the curls weren't tamed then. Pretty sure I have a Brillo pad head."

She turns to me, wrapping her arms around my midsection. "I would still find you crazy hot and want you. Brillo pad head and all."

I chuckle as I wrap my arms around her, holding her close. My body catches fire immediately, as always. There is something about this gorgeous girl's body against mine that drives me mad. Insanely mad. Capturing her mouth with mine, I hold her to me as my mouth works with hers. I gasp against her lips as her fingers move up my neck, as my hands drift down her arse. Squeezing the two globes, I lift her up without really thinking. Am I sure about this?

When her legs wrap around my waist, her tongue moving into my mouth, I know I am.

Carrying her to my bed, I lay her down, kissing down her jaw and neck as I press myself into her. She is so soft, while I am beyond hard. I can feel the heat coming off her in waves, and I don't know if I can handle this. Kissing down her neck to her chest, I pause at the gunshot wound and close my eyes. This spot will always remind me of what Casey's arse did to her, but it will also always remind me of the unconditional love she has for me.

Kissing the spot below it, I move up so I can look down into her flushed face. Pressing my hard cock into her, I am rewarded with a gasp as her face reddens more.

"I need ya, Amberlyn," I say, my voice raspy and full of desire.

"I'm yours," she answers, moving her hand up to my face, running her thumb along my jaw.

"Are ya sure?" I ask, my control slipping as I wait for the answer I need. Maybe she wants to wait until we are married or something. Shite, I don't know, I just fucking want her.

"Yeah."

Fuck. Thank God.

Dropping my mouth to hers, I kiss her long and hard as my other hand moves her skirt up her thighs so I can cup her bare arse. Grunting against her lips, I squeeze her as I press into her, wanting her so bad, I am shaking. Pulling back, I go up on my knees and then pull her up to me. Her lips meet mine as I gather her dress in my hands before pulling away so I can slowly lift the dress up her body. Throwing it to the side, I take in the beauty of my fiancée. Her skin is as white as December but with splotches of red from her desire for me. This is the first time I've seen her almost completely naked for me, so perfect and all wanton just for me.

It's a sight that I'll hold in my mind for the rest of my life.

"You are stunning, my love," I whisper against her lips as I pull the cups of her bra down, taking her nipple into my mouth. Swirling my tongue along it, my hand creeps down her ribs to her hips when the lace of her panties lies. I push them down as I kiss from her breast down her stomach to the spot above her pussy. She is wet, her desire all over the hair along her lips.

Looking up at her, I say, "I'm going to take you in my mouth, *mo stór.*"

She nods, her breathing labored and her eyes blazing with need. Watching her, I drop my head and take her into my mouth. Her eyes roll back as I move my tongue along her, opening her farther so I can get to all of her. Her fingers bite into my shoulders when I start to flick my tongue against her clit, her cries getting louder with each flick. She is squirming, crying out, and I know I'm about to lose it. She is so hot, so responsive, and I want her so damn bad.

Coming undone, she tries to squeezes her thighs shut, but I hold them open, pressing my tongue to her clit to lengthen the orgasm. Her legs are shaking against my elbows as I slowly run my tongue along her, licking up her desire. She tastes like heaven, and the thought that I get to do this for the rest of my life is a little mind-blowing. How does one get this lucky? To find someone who completes them?

I'm not sure, but I know I have to be in her. Though I know if I do, I'm going to come the second I am inside. Going up on my knees again, I release my cock from my pants and take it in my hand as I stare down at her. Reaching down for her, I bring her to me, moving my mouth with hers. I need to come real quick, and then I'll get in her. I should have done this before I took her to bed, but I wasn't thinking clearly then. Now, I have to take care of this before I embarrass myself.

"What are you doing?" she asks, moving her hands along my chest under my shirt. "Aren't I supposed to do that?"

I smile shyly before pausing my stroke to take my jacket off and then my shirt. Shaking my head, I say, "Just kiss me. It'll be quick, and then I'll take care of you again."

"But aren't you supposed to be inside me now?" she asks as I start to stroke myself again.

"No, if I get in you, I'll be done. Gotta get this first one out," I pant as my body goes taut. I want to come so badly, but she is looking at me like I have three heads!

"Well, let me do it, then."

"No, not yet. Soon," I say, picking up speed. "Kiss me."

I don't know why I thought she'd do as I said. With a sneaky grin on her face, she stops my strokes and takes my cock into her hand. Everything goes still—my body, my mind, everything as I watch her discover me. She runs her hand along me, cupping my balls, but then she goes to lower her mouth to me, and I don't know why, but I stop her.

"*Mo stór,* what are you doing?"

"I'm going to suck you off."

"What? Have you done it before?"

She smiles shyly. "No."

Before I can stop her though, her mouth is hovering over the tip of my dick and everything just freezes. I swear the world has been knocked off its axis as her hot mouth takes me inch by inch into her mouth. As I close my eyes, my fingers bite into my palms as she moves her mouth up and down my cock. She gags a bit and I want to stop her, but she continues, discovering some more.

"Fucking hell, Amberlyn," I groan out as she swirls her tongue around me, cupping my balls. It's sloppy, and I can tell it's her first time, but it's good. Real. Good.

"Oh my!"

Opening my eyes, I look toward the door where my ma stands as Amberlyn screams and falls off the bed.

"Ma!" I yell, reaching for the pillow near me to cover my junk. I look down at Amberlyn, naked and sprawled out on my floor as my ma utters an apology before slamming the door. Ignoring her though, I go to reach for Amberlyn, and I can see the tears in her eyes.

Fuck me.

eight
Declan

*P*anicked, I reach for her.

"Love, I'm sorry," I say, pulling her up onto the bed and into my arms. "I don't know what she was doing."

She meets my gaze, her embarrassment all over her face as she gasps for breath. "OhmyGodOhmyGodOhmyGodOhmyGodOhmyGod!"

"It's okay, doubt she saw anything," I say to make it better, but I'm pretty sure my ma probably feels like she walked into an HBO porno.

She looks at me incredulously and yells, "Your. Mom. Saw. Me. Giving. You. Head! Declan! OhmyGod."

"Amberlyn, it's fine," I say again, but she is already scrambling off the bed.

"Is she still in there?" she asks, pulling her dress up over her beautiful body. "OhmyGod, can you please take me home?"

"Amberlyn," I say, reaching for her hand, and when I pull her to look at her face, I see that she is crying. "Oh, *mo stór*, please don't cry," I say, pulling her onto the bed and against my chest. "It's no big deal."

"Declan, stop. It is a big deal. She saw me with your dick in my mouth. Not what I want your mother to see!"

"I know," I say, kissing her temple before running my thumbs along her cheeks. Closing my eyes, I beg myself not to laugh. I feel it bubbling in my throat, and I know if I let it loose, she might castrate me. "I'm sorry. I should have locked the door. I just wanted ya so bad."

She hides her face in my neck as she wraps her arms around my shoulders. "I'm so embarrassed. How am I supposed to look at her?"

"In her eyes?"

"You're not funny," she says against my throat.

"Yeah, but it is kinda funny, don't you think?" I ask, and when she pulls back to look at me, I wish I hadn't.

With her eyes in slits, she says, "How is your mother seeing me with your dick down my throat funny?"

"Eh, I mean," I stutter as I hold in my laughter. I've never been caught with a girl in my bed, so I am sure this is as awkward for my ma as it is for me, a bit. But then again, it really is funny. "It's just our luck, ya know? First time together and we get interrupted."

"I'm sorry, I can't find the humor in this," she says, annoyance coming off her in waves.

"Yeah, maybe not…I'm sorry?"

I move my head to where she can see me and grin widely at her. She doesn't smile, but that doesn't stop me. Leaning toward her, I kiss her bottom lip. "Don't be mad, love." Then the side of her mouth. "I promise, she won't even remember it." I kiss her bottom lip once more. "I love you, so much." Before she can say it back, I capture her lips as a smile starts to form. Like I want, she responds to my kisses, wrapping her arms around me as I do the same to her, lying back in the bed with her on top of me. As we kiss, I run my hand down her ribs to her arse, holding her as our mouths move together. When her legs fall to the side of my hips, I throb against her, wanting her, but then she pulls away.

"I think the moment was ruined."

"Yeah, a bit, but I'm sure we can bring it back," I say, cupping her by the back of the head and pressing my lips to hers. Just as I am about to move my tongue into her sweet, hot mouth, a knock comes to my door.

"Declan, son, I need to talk to ya."

"Fucking shite," I mutter, and when I meet her look of horror, I shake my head. "I'm sorry, one second."

"I want to die," she mutters and I glare.

"Not funny."

She smiles. "You get to joke about things that aren't funny, then so do I."

"Not about that," I say, smacking her arse playfully. She smiles as I slowly set her beside me. I get up, pulling my boxers on before reaching for the door. Meeting my ma's embarrassed regard, I glare as I shut the door behind me.

"Ma, really?"

"I'm sorry for interrupting, but you ran off from dinner. We needed to speak to the both of you about the engagement party."

"Well, obviously we wanted to be alone."

"Sure, but we needed to talk."

"Yeah, but knock next time."

"How was I supposed to know you'd run off to fornicate?"

"Because we are engaged! I don't know, Ma, shite, knock on a door!"

"I said I was sorry. Still, we have lots to discuss."

"Well, I guarantee ya, it won't happen tonight. You've embarrassed the living shite out of her, Ma," I say, pointing to the door. "And me."

"I'll say it again. I'm sorry, but like I said, we have a lot to discuss."

"I don't care!" I yell, and I hate that I did that. I don't raise my voice to my ma. I have way more respect for her than that, but all I see are the tears in Amberlyn's eyes. I'm pretty sure her first time has been ruined. While a part of me wants to go back in there and take her, I know this can't be her first time. Closing my eyes, I let out a breath before meeting my ma's unhappy gaze. "I'm sorry, but Ma, I don't care about planning shite right now. I want to spend time with my fiancée, who is healthy and alive. Please, give us time to be us."

"We don't have time, Declan. It's coming up very fast," she says with a shake of her head.

"Ma, please," I say, rubbing my temples. "You're driving me mad, for sure."

She sets me with a look, but before either of us can say anything, the door opens and Amberlyn appears. Her face is bright red, hell, even her skin is glowing, and she doesn't look my ma in the eyes as she says, "They're right. We don't have much time."

"I understand that, but we're a bit busy, yeah?"

She looks up at me, and I know we might have been, but we're not anymore. Which is probably for the best. "We have the rest of our lives to be busy."

I hold her gaze for a moment and then turn to my ma who is also as red as Amberlyn is. "Ma, we're coming. Let me get dressed."

"Grand, thank you." Thankfully, she leaves, and when Amberlyn goes to pass me, I stop her. Wrapping my arms around her waist, I kiss the side of her mouth.

"You're not mad?"

She shakes her head. "Mad is the least thing I am. Embarrassed and horny is more like it."

I smile. "I owe you busy time."

"You do," she says with a nod. "Soon, I hope."

"Very soon."

And that's a promise.

Now, I gotta find the time and I gotta make sure the damn door is locked.

nine
Amberlyn

"No way!"

I look over at Fiona, a deadpan look on my face. I am still completely embarrassed from the other night. All I see is Mrs. O'Callaghan's wide eyes and her look of utter shock. I never wanted to look her in the face again, but not even twenty minutes later, I was at the table planning my engagement party. It was easy to say, I could not make eye contact without burning with embarrassment. Ugh. The horror. To top it all off, I have to go wedding dress shopping with her and Lena, along with my aunt and Fiona. I'm so excited to see her, I can't stand it.

Not.

"I shit you not! I had his dick down my throat, and all of a sudden, 'Oh, hello, Mrs. O'Callaghan!'"

Falling onto the bar, Fiona loses it. She is laughing so hard, she can't breathe and her face is turning red.

"I don't find this funny."

"Oh my God," she wheezes, smacking her hand on the bar.

"Don't laugh, it's not funny," I say once more, but she waves me off.

"Don't look at me, I can't handle it! Oh my God!" she dissolves in laughter, falling to the floor, holding her gut.

"You're a bitch," I say, throwing my towel at her before going to the back to restock the trays. A grin pulls at my lips as I start to fill the trays. It's not funny, but I love Fiona's laugh. It's so loud and obnoxious but totally her. When I hear her come into the kitchen, I drop my grin as I stuff the tray with cherries.

"But really, how does this happen to you? I mean, you can't get a break. You're either yawning, people walking in, sleeping, or getting shot."

I look up at her and she grins, and I smile back. No one has joked about the shooting, but leave it to Fiona to be the first. "Too soon?"

I shake my head. "Not at all."

"Good, but really, are yous two ever gonna have sex?"

I scoff, shaking my head. It's been a week since I've been alone with Declan, so her question is one I've been asking myself a lot lately. I hadn't been able to talk to Fiona about it because she and Kane went on a holiday together. So we are playing catch-up while we prep. Which is nice as I've missed her. "I don't know. It's so frustrating. He's always working now, like hardcore, because everything is getting transferred into his name. And then when I go for dinner, his mom and Lena won't let me out of their sight. It's driving me bonkers."

"Aye, I can understand that," she says with a nod, taking a knife to cut oranges. "Was what you got good at least?"

I close my eyes, letting out a breath. "I know it was my first time, but my God, he has the mouth of an angel."

She laughs. "Good, if he likes going between the legs, you'll never go unsatisfied."

"Oh, he likes it," I say with a giggle. "And I liked doing it to him, until his fucking mom walked in."

"Why didn't he lock the door?"

I shake my head. "We started making out, and then we were on the bed, so really, no one really thought of the door."

"That's crazy."

"Right?! And he wants me to live there! Are you kidding me? I can't even get laid because his mom is up my ass all the time."

She nods, meeting my gaze across the table. "Yeah, I feel ya, but I told ya about this. They have traditions and expectations. All O'Callaghans live in that house. Together."

I shake my head. "Well, that's gonna have to change. I don't want to live with them; I want to live with Declan, by ourselves."

She shakes her head. "Good luck with that."

I bite my lip as I move to start cutting up the limes. As the knife slices through each one, I play her words over and over again. Looking up, I ask, "Do you think I'm wrong for not wanting to live there?"

"No," she says simply. "I wouldn't want to either, but it's part of the package, ya know? I'm just worried it will cause problems once ya make you sentiments known is all."

"Yeah, his mom was irritated that I didn't want to get married on the

O'Callaghan land and that Declan agreed with me."

She snapped her head up, a look of pure horror on her face. "Fuckin' hell, Amberlyn! They all get married on that land."

I shrug, not the least bit worried that I may have pissed his mom off. It is my wedding. Shouldn't it be my choice? "Yeah, but I want to get married where my mom and dad did, by the lake."

She smiles. "That's where I'm gonna get married. Where my ma and da did. That's grand."

"Yeah, Aunt Shelia is excited."

"Sure, she is. It's fierce."

I smile. "I think so."

We fall silent for a second as we continue to cut up the fruit. We make quick work of the trays, and as we clean, we chat about her holiday. They went camping, which I think is hilarious since Fiona isn't an outdoors kind of girl, but apparently, she had a blast.

"We had sex everywhere, and I mean everywhere. The lake, the dock, the tent, the car, the four-wheeler, everywhere. It was more of a sex holiday than a relaxed one, but then again, I feel great."

I giggle as I shake my head. "Must be nice."

"Oh, it was, so damn nice. Mm. Damn, my man fucks like a dream."

"Ugh, shut up," I groan as I wipe the counter around the trays since the juice leaked some.

"Envy green isn't a pretty color on ya!"

"Oh hush," I throw back at her while she carries on with her laughter. Passing by me, she flips my ponytail up, and I try to smack her with my towel, but she is quicker than I thought. With a grin on my face, I grab the bucket for ice to go fill it. When I come back, Fiona is wiping around the liquor chest, which I've already done, but nothing can be too clean. I dump the ice in the cooler and go to get more when I feel her staring at me.

Looking at her, I ask, "What?"

"Just be careful, okay?"

My brows come together. "About what?"

"With Declan. I know you won't leave him 'cause ya love him and all, and I doubt he'll want to leave ya, but his family is very powerful."

I scoff. "You make them sound like the mafia or something."

"Might as well be," she answers with a shrug. "I'm just saying, be careful. Give a little with the small things, so when you fight for the big things, it won't be that big of a deal, ya know?"

I bite the inside of my cheek as I shrug. "I shouldn't have to give for anything, except with Declan."

"You're right, but his ma has a lot of pull with him. Remember, she is the first woman he ever loved. No one can be his ma."

"But you told me not to let them change me."

"I did, and I still want that, but it worries me, ya know? I don't want you to get hurt."

I nod. "I don't think Declan would allow that to happen."

"Yeah, I don't either, but just be careful, okay?"

"Yeah, I will," I agree just to make her happy, but I know I have nothing to worry about.

Declan won't hurt me and he won't allow anyone to hurt me.

When the door opens, I look up to see Kane walking in in his carefree way. Dressed in a pair of jeans and an O'Callaghan tee, his brown hair is pushed to the side out of his eyes that are trained on Fiona.

Smiling, I glance at her as she squeals, closing the distance between them to kiss her man deeply. I hate that I am jealous of them. I haven't been able to really kiss Declan in what seems like forever. I miss him. Turning so that I don't have to watch the display of love, which is horrible of me, I know, I pull out my phone and text him.

> *I miss you.*
>
> *I miss you. That's why I'm here.*

Confused, I hear the door open. Turning, I find Declan standing there, a grin on his face and a small white flower in his hand. He wears a pair of gray slacks with a light blue button-down shirt and a gray sports coat over it. It fits him so tightly around his shoulders and thighs that I find myself drooling over my fiancé. I can't wait to see him at our wedding. Looking all dashing and all mine.

Grinning, I watch as he comes to me while I lean on the bar, my heart kicking up in speed. It always does that when he is around. It just jackhammers against my chest while my stomach does funny little flops. I pray this feeling never stops. I remember my mom saying that my dad did something to her chest every time he smiled at her. She said it felt as if he was standing there with a sledgehammer, just pounding away around her chest to get to her heart. I always thought it was a scary-sounding feeling, but now that I have Declan in my life, I totally get it.

He does that to me.

As he grins at me, I am completely stunned. I've always thought he was a beautiful man, but he is also very regal. Maybe it's the suit, but my goodness, he owns the room. He's been in meetings all week with lawyers and the other associates of O'Callaghan Whiskey, and I swear, he belongs there. He looks like the owner of a company.

Cupping my face, he kisses me hard on the lips. Parting, he kisses my nose before pulling back to hand me the flower.

"It's sweet, thank you."

"Not as sweet as you, though," he says, lacing his fingers with mine. "Tell me, ya got a bit to spend with me?"

"I always have a bit to spend with you," I say like he does in his thick Irish way.

He grins and gives me a wink as I take my apron off. Glancing at Fiona, who is currently making out with Kane, I roll my eyes. They are so engrossed in each other, it's kinda cute.

"I'm gonna go out with Declan. I'll be back before we open back up."

She waves me off as Kane slowly backs her into the bar. Making a face, I say, "Please don't have sex on the bar. We just cleaned it."

Tearing her mouth from Kane's, she grins at me. "I'll clean it again."

"Ew," I say as Declan laughs beside me. I take his hand and we go out the side door before he pulls me to his side. Ignoring that Casey attacked me in this spot, I cuddle into Declan as we walk toward the lake. It's a beautiful day. The sun is shining, there is a slight, soft breeze, and it's just picturesque out. The best part, though, is being cuddled into his side. He is so thick and smells like whiskey and oak barrels. It's a comforting smell and makes me feel at home.

Reaching the lake, we sit on the bank, our hands joined and my head lying against his shoulder. Watching the breeze on the lake, I let out a long breath.

"What's wrong, my love?" he asks.

"I've missed you," I answer, placing my chin onto his arm so I can look up at him. He smiles as he cups my face.

"It'll only be like this a little longer. Gotta get all the legal shite out of the way," he says, running his thumb along my cheekbone.

"I know, I just hate being apart. And seeing Fiona all over Kane has me a little jealous."

His brows come together as his eyes bore into mine. "Why's that?"

"'Cause I want to be all over you, but we never have time for us."

He smiles. "I mean, we got a bit now, want me to take ya against this bank? Doesn't seem very romantic. Plus, not only can my mom see us, but I'm sure your aunt and uncle could too, shite, everyone."

I laugh along with him as I shake my head. "No, I don't want my first time to be where everyone can see us. I'm just frustrated."

"Sexually?" he says, waggling his eyebrows at me and I nod.

"A lot."

Leaning his head to mine, he runs his nose along mine and whispers, "I've been sexually frustrated since the first moment I saw ya."

I giggle before his lips fall to mine in a gentle assault. I close my eyes and our lips move together in such a sweet but urgent way. Moving his hand up the back of my neck, he slowly lies back, bringing me up against his chest. My heart is out of control in my chest, and I can feel his against mine too. Kissing down my jaw, he nibbles on my neck before coming below my ear as his hand slides up my bare leg to the spot at my thighs when my shorts sit. Squeezing my ass, he kisses the spot below my ear before nibbling on my lobe.

He then whispers, "Sure, I can't take ya here?"

My face breaks into a grin as I shake my head. "I have to face your mom tomorrow, and knowing our luck, she'll see us."

He chuckles against my ear before nibbling some more and saying, "I can't wait to see you under this tree. In a beautiful dress, all mine."

I smile as I close my eyes, leaning my head against his. "I'll be your princess."

Pulling away, he looks down at me, moving my baby hairs out of my face. With a grin on his face, he moves his thumb along my jaw before kissing me softly. Pulling back, he says, "No, Amberlyn, you'll be my queen."

ten
Amberlyn

I always thought when I stood in a wedding dress that my mom would be beside me.

That she would be crying and fussing over how beautiful I looked. That she would hate a dress but love another and ultimately help me choose the dress that was made for me. We would cry and hold each other because we were so happy. Then we would go to lunch and talk about more details, about my groom and how Daddy would have loved him. Since my father died when I was younger, I had accepted that he wouldn't there to walk me down the aisle, but then we decided that mom would.

Now though, I had no one to do it.

I hadn't even thought about that until I looked at myself in the mirror and took in everything I was seeing. The dress is gorgeous; of course, we are in the finest wedding shop in Dublin. So I expected nothing less. Especially as the owner herself picked it out since it was up to O'Callaghan standards. It has more jewels and sparkles on it than the sky has stars. It is a strapless top with a skirt like Cinderella's. It's the twelfth dress I've put on, and it's stunning, but I hate it. I don't know if I hate it because I really do or if it is because my mom isn't here to help me pick out my dress.

Every girl should have their mother with her on the day she picks the dress that will begin her forever.

But I don't.

Coming up behind me, Mrs. O'Callaghan looks me over, taking in every detail as she nods slowly. She's done this with every gown and each one I've hated.

"What do you think, Mrs. O'Callaghan?" the owner, Michele, asks, but why is she asking her? Why does it matter to her? It's my dress! And she hasn't asked me once what I think. I just shake my head and walk away. Meeting Fiona's gaze in the mirror, I can see she shares my sentiments, and I know she is on the brink of losing her shit. She's kept her mouth shut on my account, but even I am getting frustrated. My aunt is on top of the world being able to have tea and talk with Mrs. O'Callaghan; I doubt she even notices that I am upset. And I hate how angry that makes me. Everyone, minus Fiona, is more worried about what Mrs. O'Callaghan thinks than me.

And I'm the bride.

"She has the perfect body for this. I love it. I've loved all the dresses though. The only thing that worries me is her wound. Surely it will be heal by then, yeah? Think we can cover it with some makeup?"

"Oh, yeah, I'm sure so," my aunt says and my blood starts to boil.

"I'm proud of my wound. It's a constant reminder of how much I love Declan."

Mrs. O'Callaghan gives me a sweet smile. "Of course, my dear, but it isn't very pretty."

"So? It's a part of her," Fiona says, and I see my aunt pinch her thigh. "Ow!"

"Shush," Shelia says, giving her a look, but I couldn't agree more.

"They are right, but it doesn't matter if you like it, Ma. It's Amberlyn's dress, her body," Lena says as she crosses her arms over her chest. It's the first time she has been even remotely involved. She's mostly been playing on her phone.

"Oh of course, Amberlyn, my dear, what do you think? Is this the one?"

Meeting her gaze in the mirror, I say, "No, I hate it."

Michele gasps, so does my aunt, while Fiona smirks and Lena shakes her head. Mrs. O'Callaghan looks at me in total disbelief, and I slowly step off the platform, tears stinging my eyes as I go back to the changing room to take it off. Slamming the door behind me, I kick the skirt out of my way and let my hands drop to my sides.

I just miss my mom.

Tears start to roll down my cheeks and I suck in a deep breath, trying to hold them in, but it isn't working. When a knock comes at the door, I know it's Michele coming to help me out of the dress, but I need to be alone.

"Amberlyn, can I come in?"

It's Fiona.

"Yeah," I say, and she pushes the door open before glancing at me. I can see the panic on her face, but she tucks it back in as she comes up behind me, undoing the dress.

"Let's get this frilly shite off ya, yeah?"

I nod, my lip wobbling as she unbuttons the back and helps me out of it. Reaching for my robe, I cover my body before sitting on the bench and covering my face with my hands as I cry. I feel her near me before she wraps her arms around me and hugs me close to her, her lips pressing into my temple.

"You miss your mom?"

I nod as the tears start to come faster. Sucking in a deep breath, I hold on to her tightly, needing her strength. "I didn't think this was going to be this hard," I cry as my heart feels as if it is being ripped from my chest and stomped on.

"Amberlyn, it's all so new, and so much is changing. Of course, this is going to be hard. You're always so positive, but sometimes, ya need to accept that this is going to suck."

I nod, my eyes starting to hurt from rubbing them so hard. I want to wipe away the pain, but no matter how hard I wipe, it is still there, slowly ripping me apart. She's right; I try to be so positive about everything, but today…today sucks.

"I'm supposed to be happy though. I'm finding my dress for the day that will start the rest of my life."

"Yeah, but you are allowing them to pick it out. We came in, had tea, and then came up to the dresses they think are up to 'O'Callaghan standards,'" she says, making air quotes. "You aren't an O'Callaghan yet. You are becoming one, so shouldn't your dress be you?"

"Do you think that's why I want to run and hide in a hole?"

She smiles. "That may be one of the reasons, but I think the main one is your ma, for sure. I know she'd want to be here, and I promise she is, in yer heart."

I nod. "Yeah, you're right."

She kisses my cheek as I slowly wipe my tears from my face. Holding my gaze and with a bright smile, she says, "Why don't we go look and see what we find?"

Looking around the room, I still have three more O'Callaghan dresses, but I have no inclination to put them on. Looking back at Fiona, I nod my head, "Yeah, let's go look."

"Thatta girl. Come on," she says, pulling me up and out the door.

When I come out without a dress on, I can see the confusion on Mrs. O'Callaghan's face. I ignore it as I say, "I'm gonna look around and see if something catches my eye."

"None of the dresses that were brought out for you are good?" she asks me, and I shake my head.

"They're not me," I answer as Fiona's arm links with mine; I know it's for support.

"Sure aren't. I see you in something softer," Lena says, standing up and throwing her phone down. "Can I come help?"

I nod. "Sure."

I can tell that Michele doesn't want me to look, that she wants me to choose one of the dresses that are in the room, probably because they cost as much as a car, but she takes me to where the dresses all hang. Looking around the room, we look at each dress. I find two that are all right, but Lena is convinced they will look better on me than the hanger. I'm not sure, but I agree to try them on. We are about to head back to the dressing room when a soft blue catches my eyes. It's the same color as Declan's eyes, and instantly, I'm drawn to it.

Taking it by the hanger, I bring the dress out and I'm in awe. It's a full tulle skirt, the back in layers with a big embellished gathering of tulle flowers. The strapless top has beautiful swirls of crystals and the back is buttoned with little blue buttons. I've never seen such a gorgeous blue, except when I look into Declan's eyes, and I can't help but need this dress.

"Is that a wedding dress?" Lena asks.

"Has to be, yeah?" Fiona asks looking back at Michele.

She nods. "Yes, it's very rare. The only one we got, but Mrs. O'Callaghan didn't like it."

"It isn't her dress," Lena answers. "What do you think of it, Amberlyn?"

I look it over, a small smile playing on my lips. "Reminds me of Declan's eyes. I love it."

She smiles back at me as Fiona beams. "Try it on then!"

It's the first time all day that I've been excited. I woke up with an icky feeling in my gut, and it just got worse as the day progressed. But now, as I slowly slide the soft blue dress up my body and Fiona buttons the back, I can't contain the grin on my face. The dress looks a billion times better on me than it did on the hanger. The blue is gorgeous on my skin, and with my hair, it's almost magical. Yeah, my wound is showing but I don't care.

I love it.

"This is it," Fiona whispers as she looks over my shoulder in the mirror.

Lena stands from where she was fluffing the skirt out before meeting my gaze, taking me in as I do the same. Slowly a smile comes over her face as she nods. "It is."

"Yeah," I whisper as tears sting my eyes. I can't help but hear my mom say the same thing in my head. Closing my eyes, I suck in a deep breath and say, "Let's go show Aunt Shelia and Mrs. O'Callaghan."

Turning, I head for the door but then pause, looking back at myself in the mirror. The back is even more gorgeous than the front. It's cut low, to the small of my back, with lots of embellishment. I love it. Fiona opens the door for me, and I see the grin on her face as she says, "Ma, this is it."

I hear my aunt shriek in excitement, and then I make my entrance. Michele is grinning, my aunt is almost in tears, but I don't miss the look of complete disgust on Mrs. O'Callaghan's face. Ignoring her though, I go up on the platform as Michele fluffs out the bottom again. Meeting my gaze, she says, "One minute."

I look myself over and can't help but think that Declan is going to love it. It isn't traditional, but it's me. It's gorgeous.

When Michele comes back, she has a white lace birdcage veil and a bouquet full of white and light blue flowers. Handing me the bouquet, she quickly braids my hair before putting the veil on my head, covering my face in such an elegant way. Unblocking my view of myself, she steps to the side and I am stunned by what I see.

I see Declan's bride.

Everyone oohs and aahs as the tears gather in my eyes. I found it. I found my dress.

"Is this for the engagement party?

But then it is ruined with that one comment from Mrs. O'Callaghan.

Looking back at her, I shake my head. "No, this is my wedding dress."

"But it's blue."

"I know, the color of Declan's eyes."

She makes a face before shaking her head. "But it isn't traditional."

Before I can answer that I really don't give two shits, Shelia says, "Actually, it is."

I look over at her as she stands and comes toward me. Tears roll down her face as she takes my hands in hers. She kisses my palms before squeezing my hands. "Back in the old days, all the Irish brides wore blue. It isn't like that anymore because everyone thinks white is the color of purity and all that jazz, but some still try to venture back to those days. I wore blue, not something like this, but it was blue, very plain. But so was your ma's. It was this color, short with cuffed sleeves, and she wore her hair down, blowing in the summer breeze. I remember that day like it was yesterday."

I smile, my heart skipping a beat as the memory of her dress comes back to me. "I remember the picture of them. It was almost like sundress because it was all they could afford."

"Yeah, but my brother said she was the most gorgeous girl in the world, and God bless him, but if he were here right now, he'd say he lied. Cause you, my sweet girl, are simply stunning."

My lip wobbles as the tears start to roll down my cheeks. "Aunt Shelia, I found my dress. The dress I'm going to marry Declan in."

"You did, my love. You did."

Wrapping her arms around me, she hugs me tightly, kissing my cheeks as I cry, but when I look in the mirror, I can see that Mrs. O'Callaghan isn't happy about it.

Too bad, I don't care one bit.

eleven
Amberlyn

"I think you'll like it."

Declan smiles before he trails kisses down my throat.

"I sure I will. It'll be on ya."

I smile. "It isn't traditional."

"Eh, who cares," he says, kissing my neck.

"Your mom hated it."

He scoffs. "Again, who cares? It's your dress, *mo stór.*"

"Yeah," I agree, but I am bursting at the seams wanting to tell him everything about it. We only have twenty minutes before the pub opens, and I figured it was enough time to spend with him. Maybe tell him about my dress, even though Fiona swore me to secrecy. It's just so hard not to though. I want to tell him everything about it, every single detail, and how I feel in it. It's been three days since I picked it, and I wanted more than anything to bring it home, but it needed to be altered.

I really need to keep it to myself. Why spend time talking about my dress when we could be making out or something? It's few and far between that we get moments like this. His work schedule is dumb. That's the only word I can think to describe it. I hate it, but stolen moments like this are kind of fun. As the lightning crashes outside and the rain falls in sheets against the hood of his car, I continue to kiss him, our hands exploring each other's bodies, making us completely and utterly mad for each other.

"I don't like being away from ya. Not one bit," he mutters against my neck as his hands trail up my ribs to my breasts.

"I hate it too," I mutter before his mouth comes down on mine.

Pulling away, he sucks in a deep breath as he looks deep into my eyes. They are as dark as the storm clouds above, but unlike the menace of the storm, I love the color of his eyes. I love how when he gets turned on they darken, and it pleases me to know I do that to him. My inexperience makes me a little nervous, but it's times like this that make me feel like I could maybe drive him crazy.

Taking my face in his hands, he kisses me, drawing the kisses from me in a slow, deliberate way that has my toes curling against my flip-flops.

Tearing his mouth from mine, he smiles. "Want to ask ya something."

"Okay?" I ask, gasping for breath. "Now? We are busy, aren't we?"

He chuckles but backs away when I try to kiss him. "Sure, but I've been waiting to ask this, and I can't wait any more."

"Okay?"

"Yeah, I want to come home to ya, darlin'. I want to hold you in my arms and kiss ya to sleep," he says, moving his hand through my hair. "I don't know if you wanted to wait till we were married, but I don't want to wait any longer. We never have a free moment together, and that could change if ya come live with me."

I blink a few times as he holds my gaze. I was pretty direct when I said I didn't want to live with his family. "Come live with you…and your family?"

He eyes me but then nods slowly. "I showed ya my room; it's huge. We wouldn't see my family unless we go to them."

"So why did your mom walk in on us?"

He sits back, letting my face go as he watches me. "Because she's insane. Hell, I don't know, but it won't happen again."

Wringing my fingers together, I look down and clear my throat. "I don't want to live with your family. I want to live with you."

"I swear, it will be like they're not even there."

"It just doesn't seem right to me. I want it to be us," I say, and when he goes to say something, I stop him. "Yeah, I get that it's a big house and they won't see us, but I don't want to live there. I want our own home."

"But my whole family has always lived there. No one has lived anywhere else but there. They are born there and die there."

I can see that this is about to go badly. His face is changing from turned on to annoyed. Smiling, I shrug as I say, "I mean, when you are ready to die, I'll take you back over there."

He glares as he takes the wheel into his hand. "It's tradition, Amberlyn. It's how my family works."

I look over at him and I'm about to tell him that's not the way I work, but then I remember what Fiona said. Give a little on some things. Maybe this is something I need to give a little on. I got my dress, the location, and no telling what else I am going to want. I can see that this is something he really wants, something that means something to him, but can I live like that? Always worried that his mom is going to walk in on us?

"The door stays locked."

"Always," he agrees with a nod.

I look out the window and take in a deep breath. "And if it doesn't work out, then we have to look at other options."

He doesn't answer me, so I glance over at him, and he holds my gaze. "Yeah, but I'm sure it will."

"That's fine, but in case it doesn't, you promise we'll look into getting a place of our own."

He doesn't nod right away, and I know that he doesn't want to agree, but then he nods slowly. "Okay, yeah."

I smile before leaning over and kissing his lips in a smacking kiss. "Gotta give me a week or so. I gotta figure out how to tell my aunt and uncle."

He nods, cupping my face. "Sure. We can wait till after the engagement party if you want."

It is in a week, which will be great. We would be announced to everyone, so then maybe they would be okay with it. Probably not, but oh well, I'm doing this.

I'm moving into my fiancé's mansion with him.

And his family.

"**ARE YA** sure?"

I nod as I wipe up the beer I just spilled. Look back at Fiona, I shrug. "He really wants this, and you said to give a little."

"Yeah, but, okay, I'm being selfish. I don't want ya to leave," she admits with a grin. "Stay till ya marry."

I laugh as I shake my head. "It isn't like I'm disappearing. I'll still come to work, I'll see you once school starts, and it'll be fine, I promise."

She shakes her head as she passes mugs to three waiting patrons. "You say that now, but ya never know."

"I do know," I say, placing my hand on her arm. She covers my hand with hers and smiles.

"Why don't ya stay until the wedding?"

"We never see each other. I miss him," I answer and she nods.

"I only ask because that's when I'm moving out."

I pause and whip my head in her direction. "What?"

She smiles sheepishly as she comes to me, leaning against the bar. "Yeah, I'm moving in with Kane, but I figured you wouldn't move out till the wedding, so I told him that's when I'd move in."

"Fiona! When did you decide this? That's huge!"

Her face reddens as a genuinely happy grin comes over her face. "Ah, we just decided last night. Gives him a couple months to get use to the idea, but I'm starting to leave things there."

"That's so awesome! Next he'll be begging you to marry him."

She laughs before looking over my shoulder where Kane is sitting and eating. "Oh aye, Kane."

I turn to see him look up before grinning. "Yeah, lassie?"

Cocking her head to me, she says, "She asked when we're getting married."

He laughs and so does Fiona, while I stand here confused. "What?"

"We are too young for that. We're gonna enjoy life first. If, after all that, we are ready, we'll do it. But now, we are going to be young and in love. Try the living together thing out."

He nods in agreement before catching her hand before she walks off. "But I'm sure the first chance I get to make you my missus, I will."

She cups his face, grinning as she says, "I look forward to it."

He taps her ass playfully before giving her a smacking kiss. As I stand watching, I envy them. Not only do they get to see each other whenever they please, but they have time. Declan and I don't have that. Everything seems as if it's in fast-forward mode and we have no idea how to slow it down. We'll be married in a couple months, we'll be living in his home, and he'll be running a company while I bust my ass during school. It kind of scares me. I'm not saying I'm having second thoughts because I'm not, but I am nervous.

To my core.

"When you gonna tell Ma and Da?"

I look over at Fiona and shrug. "I was gonna ask you the same thing."

Her brows come in before taking a step toward me. "What's wrong?"

I let my shoulders sag and shake my head. "I wish I had time like you and Kane do," I say quietly, turning to face the bottles of alcohol so no one can hear me. She comes to the front and nods.

"If you want it, tell someone."

"No," I say, shaking my head. "He'll lose the distillery—"

"And you won't let that happen. Yeah, I got that, but you have to think of you too."

"But it isn't just about me. It's about both of us."

"Sure, I get that, but you are being rushed."

"Yeah, but it's my choice," I say, shaking my head. I turn and reach for a rag.

"I shouldn't have said anything. No worries."

I tear away from her gaze and notice we need more beer. "I'm gonna go get some more beer."

She tries to stop me, but I head to the back to get the beer. With each step I take, I hate that I said anything. I knew what I was getting into when I said yes. I knew that this would be fast, that things would change, and that my life wouldn't be just mine, but Declan's too. I want this. I do. So much, I can feel it in my bones. I want him for the rest of my life. And while, yes, some time to just be us and not worry about everything that is going on would be ideal, we have the rest of our lives for that. Once we get married and all that is behind us, it will be us. We will fall more in love with each passing day. It will be great.

It will be everything my mom ever wanted for me.

twelve
Declan

"Rubbish, is what it all is."

I look across my desk at Kane, who nods in agreement. Looking back down at the newspapers, I want to scream. Each one is nothing but trash, but still, the people of this town read it. This is one of the parts I hate about being who I am. The part that comes with having the name O'Callaghan. A part of me wants it all to stop, but this is who I am. It worries me, though, because I'm bringing Amberlyn into this. I can't shield her from these people, hell, I can't even shield myself, so I have to ignore it. But it's so fucking hard.

Reading each one, I shake my head. It's complete bollocks!

Will Casey Burke go away for life or will his plea of insanity break him free?
What will the O'Callaghans do if that happens?
Will the Whiskey Prince be there to support his bride?
When is the wedding?
Will she marry the man she took a bullet for?
The Whiskey Baby due early next spring!

Glancing back to Kane, I say, "I'm so tired of it all. I wish they'd all go away."

"Ah, it's been like this since you were born," he answers and then he laughs. "Remember when we took your car and went joyriding? We were drunk, drugged up, and had the devil in us according to the papers."

I smile. "The devil part might have been true."

Kane laughs. "Yeah, for sure, but still, it's all shite. We know the truth. Casey is going to go away for life. Amberlyn will make sure of that while you are there, and no one, outside of who was invited, will find out when the wedding is. No baby is coming though, right?"

"Be real. No. We haven't even done it yet."

He smirks. "Oh yeah, can't close, huh?"

I glare. "Not when my ma is walking in every five seconds."

He laughs as he shakes his head. "Eh, it will happen. But in the meantime, ignore all this shite, yeah?"

I nod. "Yeah, it makes me nervous though."

"What does?" he asks, his brows coming together.

Meeting my best mate's gaze, I ask, "What if he does get off?"

I can see in Kane's eyes he has thought the same as I have. Casey is claiming that my family caused his distress and that we drove him to do what he did. My da says it's all crazy and he doesn't have a leg to stand on, but it does worry me a bit. My da had offered to pay him to leave, every time we were in a room together I was ready to kick his arse, and Kane did hit him. I don't know much about legal stuff, but nonetheless, I'm a little nervous.

I just want it all to go the fuck away.

I don't want Amberlyn to have to sit in the courtroom and testify against him. I don't want to be there either. I want to be far away from that gobshite for the simple fact I'm not sure I can keep my cool. I know I'm supposed to forgive him, but it's bloody hard. He almost killed the one I am devoted to. That's not something I can forgive. Who could forgive that? Yeah, Amberlyn has, but she's a fucking angel!

Kane shakes his head and waves me off. "No, he's gonna go to jail. He won't get away with this."

"Yeah, hopefully, you're right."

He scoffs. "I'm always right."

I chuckle as a knock comes to the door, and it opens to reveal my ma. I want to make a face of distress, but that'll upset her, so I smile instead. "Howya, Ma."

"Hey, honey. Kane."

"Hey, Mrs. O'Callaghan," he says as she kisses the top of his head.

"What are yous two up to?"

"Reading rubbish," I say, throwing the paper in the trash. "Don't want to speak about 'em though. What brings ya by?"

"That it is," she agrees, shaking her head. "Everyone wants to know the date, but we are being very tight-lipped."

"Fantastic."

"Yeah, so anyway, I wanted to talk about the engagement party."

Fuck me.

Kane hides his grin, probably due to my expression as my mother goes on.

"Everyone is coming, and I mean everyone. Everything is pretty much taken care of, but we need to get with you and Amberlyn about the cake."

I make a face. Amberlyn is working as much as I am. I doubt she cares about a damn cake. So I tell my ma that, despite her dismay. At this point, we don't even want the party. We just want to get married and be done. All this hoopla is getting to be a bit much. We want to start our lives together, not prance around for people to make up more rubbish about us.

"Well, I need to know what you want."

Letting out a long breath, I say, "Kane, what kind of cake?"

"Chocolate, of course."

Looking at my ma, I say, "Chocolate it is."

I can tell she doesn't approve of my decision-making but I don't care. I am over everything. I am stressed out about work, about this fucking party, and then most of all, having sex with my fiancée. I know it's dumb to be stressed out about something that everyone does, but it gives me the willies. What if all the interruptions are a sign that I'm not supposed to be with her, or even be inside her? Ugh! It's completely mental, but still, it's got me a tad nervous. Okay. A lot nervous.

"Fine, chocolate," she says and I smile. I fully expect her to leave, but no such luck. Looking over at me, she says, "Also, I need to tell ya something."

My brow cocks up. "Yeah?"

"You know that I'm good mates with the O'Malleys, yeah?"

My stomach drops. Please Lord. No. "Yeah, why?"

She laces her fingers and looks away, which tells me that my suspicions were correct. "Well, I invited them to the engagement party, but they RSVP'd back with Keeva as a guest too."

Kane shakes his head as I lean on my forearms. "Well, tell them she isn't invited."

She makes a face. "I can't do that!"

"Why not? It's my party! I don't want her there."

"Declan, son, please, it's been years since you dated her."

"She used me for my money, Ma! She's the scum of the earth!"

She waves me off. "Please, I doubt you'll see her. Just wanted to let you know. Warn Amberlyn about her, maybe."

Pinching my brow, I say, "No, you disinvite her. I don't care how that makes ya look with the O'Malleys. I don't want Keeva at my engagement party."

She lets out a breath, and when I look up, she nods. "Fine."

"Thank you. I got work to do, Ma, anything else?"

She sets me with a look. "Yes, when is Amberlyn moving in?"

"After the engagement party."

She nods. "And when is she quitting the bar?"

I make a face because I haven't thought about that at all. "I don't know? Probably after we marry."

She again doesn't like my answer. "Hm. Well, people are saying we have no money and that she has to work to help you get by."

Kane and I let out loud hoots of laughter. "Ma, if we were poor, would we be throwing these lavish parties? Be real. I am done with these fucking papers and people talking shite," I say, and then I throw my arms up. Looking up at her, I point at her before saying, "New rule. No one from the media is allowed at any more of my parties."

"Attaboy! Fair play," Kane exclaims in agreement.

"Declan, be real. And don't encourage him, Kane."

Kane smiles up at my ma and says, "But it's true. They are all causing so much drama. It isn't about anyone but Declan and Amberlyn, yeah?"

"Yes, that is true, but still, they are needed so that we make the papers."

Slamming my hands down, I say, "I don't want to be in the papers, Ma! I'm done. No more. I am about to be the head of this estate, and that's my decision."

She eyes me and then shakes her head. "I'll be speaking with your father about this."

I nod. "Be my guest. Would you like me to come too?"

She glares, and I may have crossed the line there. "I don't care that you are about to marry or even that you're in your twenties, but I'll take ya over my knee and wear your arse out. You watch your tone with me, Declan."

My face reddens as Kane chuckles, that is until she says, "Same goes for ya too, Kane."

Meeting her gaze, I nod. "Yeah, Ma, sorry. But I'm so irritated with it all."

Her eyes soften a bit as she smiles. "Yeah, I know. It will all be over soon, and you'll start a new adventure with that sweet girl at your side."

A smile comes over my face as I nod. "I can't wait."

We share a smile, and I hope that my eyes tell her I'm not joking around. I'm done with it all. I have the power to stop it, and I'm going to. Instead of parading for the damn media and hoping to make a show like my family does, I want to stay private. Like Kane said, nothing matters but Amberlyn and me. That's it.

"I'll see ya at dinner. Bye, Kane."

"Yeah, have a good day, Ma," I say as she heads out the door.

"Bye, Mrs. O'Callaghan," Kane says as the door shuts.

Letting out a breath, Kane laughs. "Well, it's always so much fun with your ma."

I chuckle. "Sure is. She's mental, I swear."

"Indeed," he agrees as he leans back, kicking his feet up on my desk. A comfortable silence falls upon us as he plays on his phone and I work. Being the boss of the malting room has its perks. Kane is able to sit in here and hang with me most of the day. But when he works, he works; that's why I don't mind it all. I like it. It's good to bounce ideas off him, and he is always there for a good laugh.

As I click through emails, out of the corner of my eye, I can see him grin as he texts wildly on his phone. Must be talkin' with Fiona. Taking a pull of my water, I clear my throat and ask, "How's things with Fiona?"

He looks over at me and shrugs. "Good. She's moving in."

One brow goes up. "Oh yeah?"

He nods, letting his phone fall to his lap. "Yeah, she was leaving shite all the damn time, and then she brought up yous two getting married. And I was like, whoa, not ready for that, but how about you move in? And she agreed."

I smile. "Don't act like ya don't want it. I know you do."

He shrugs one shoulder, not looking at me as a grin pulls at his lips. "Maybe so, but I sure as hell ain't ready to be married though."

I roll my eyes. "Yer already married in a sense. Lord knows you aren't going anywhere and neither is she."

He doesn't say anything for a moment and then waves me off. "Eh, shut up with ya."

I laugh as he goes on, "I'll ask when I know that she meant what she said—that I was enough as just a malter. She's gonna start school and make loads of money, while I'll still make the same, ya know? So we'll see."

I don't like this side of Kane. The part that was damaged by his real ma. No one really knows that his ma ran out on his dad when he was four. Only I know because I watched it happen. She didn't like the life they had, but there was no changing it. Then his da met Kane's stepmom and she took Kane as her own. She was the ma he needed, but still, sometimes, this part of him comes out. I'm usually the insecure one he helps pick up; never are the roles reversed. But I guess some things don't ever go away, and his real ma is someone that still rears her ugly head to hurt Kane.

Clearing my throat, I say, "She'll still love ya and you know it. She isn't like your real ma, Kane. She isn't going to run."

He nods. "She says that too."

Shocked, my eyes go wide as I hold his gaze. "You told her?"

Kane doesn't tell anyone about that. Maggie is his ma, and that's all there is to it.

Shaking my head, I say, "See, you know it's true. You wouldn't have told her that if you thought she had a foot out the door, yeah?"

He shrugs again and bites his lips. "I was drunk when I told her."

I laugh. "Liar."

Kana laughs too but then stops when he looks over at me. "I love her and I pray she doesn't leave me, but I know it could happen."

Holding his gaze, I say, "That's the scary part about love. You're all in and pray that they are too."

Kane nods. "Love expert now?"

I smile. "Eh, fuck no. But I know that we both picked some top birds, for sure."

He smiles as he nods. "That's the damn truth."

When my email dings, I look back at the computer and see that it's an email from my da. "Fuck, guess my ma went straight to talk to my da."

"Really? Jeez, it's not that big of a deal, I think," is Kane's opinion as I open the email. Reading it quickly, I find that I was wrong to assume what I did. It isn't about what I discussed with my mom.

It's about my whiskey.

"He approved it," I whisper, shocked. I really don't know why I am because I am about to own this company, but I thought I would have to wait to do it myself. I sent the email to get beta testing done on a whim, in hopes he'd agree.

And he did.

"What'd he say?"

Looking over at Kane, a grin pulls at my lips as I say, "Cathmor is going into beta testing."

Kane's face breaks into a grin as he exclaims, "Fuck yeah! Awesome, Declan, congrats!"

I can only nod as I reread the email. I still can't believe it, but it's there, in black and white. Glancing back at Kane, I ask, "Wanna go to the pub?"

Kane nods as he shares a knowing look. "Yeah, let's go."

Standing up, I can't wipe the grin off my face. Before, I would throw one back with Kane to celebrate, but there is now another person I need to make this moment a billion times better. The only person who matters.

Amberlyn.

thirteen

Declan

When the door slams behind me to the pub, my brows shoot up to my hairline, I'm sure. Standing before me is my fiancée, but not dressed the way she normally would be.

"Don't laugh," she says, running her hands down the front of the flowy gold dress she wears. It has a big flower embellishing the front of it with sheer sleeves, and it's very form-fitting. It's something my mother and sister wear on the daily. Her hair is done very elegantly and her makeup done just as well. "Your sister sent it over," she informs me when I am done drinking her in before meeting her gaze. Her eyes are not as bright as I like them to be, and I can tell she is completely uncomfortable.

And then I remember that she has tea today with my sister, Ma, and the Fadmish ladies.

"Love, I wouldn't laugh 'cause there is nothing to laugh about. You're beautiful, of course."

She makes a face, obviously not believing a word I say. "I look all old."

With my brows pulled together, confused, I ask, "Old? How?"

"She thinks the dress is something an old lady would wear," Fiona supplies.

I nod as I close the distance between us. Taking her by her hips, I smile, kissing her nose. I don't think that at all. She looks distinguished. Like an O'Callaghan, but cute as a button. With the heels she's wearing, she's as tall as me, and I enjoy it more than I'd like to admit. Kissing her nose again, I say,

"You're stunning, *mo stór*. Don't think that."

She brings her lip between her teeth and shakes her head. "This isn't me."

I smile, holding her chin in my thumb and hand. "Then go take it off. Go as you please."

She looks away as she lets out a breath. "I can't. I can tell it cost money, and Lena called to make sure I liked it. I couldn't bring myself to tell her that I would never wear such old-looking stuff."

"I told her she looks nice. She fits the part of an O'Callaghan going for tea," Fiona says, leaning on her hand as Kane drains a pint, the least bit entertained by my fiancée's drama.

Meeting Amberlyn's gaze, I nod. "Ya do."

She looks down and lets out a breath. "So I should get used to this? Being dressed like this?"

I lift her chin. "No, love, you pick your own clothes, design your own stuff. Don't allow my sister or ma to do it for ya. Be you."

A smile pulls at her lips as she nods slowly. "But what about your mom?"

"What about her? You are my fiancée. I want you to be comfortable."

She smiles shyly before wrapping her arms around my neck. She then kisses my jaw and the side of my mouth before saying against my lips, "I am now."

"Good," I say, kissing her nose one more time. Then her cheek and her neck, before kissing her lobe. Softly, I whisper, "I'd love to peel this dress of ya."

She lets out a girlie giggle as her arms tighten around my neck. "I have tea with the Fadmish ladies in an hour. I need way more time to get ready."

I chuckle as I kiss her lips once more. "Rain check, then?"

She laughs as her shoulders slump. "We are one big rain check," she says sadly, and I hate that she is right. Also, that look on her face. The one of complete disappointment. I haven't had a free moment with her, but I know that'll all change once she moves in. Only a couple more days.

Kissing her lips, I pull away and ask, "Are you packed to move in yet?"

She shakes her head. "A little, but I haven't told my aunt and uncle yet."

I set her with a look. "Think ya should, yeah?"

She nods. "Yeah, I'll get to it. Tomorrow, for sure, since I'll be moving in Sunday."

"Yeah, I gotta tell them about me too," Fiona says as my lips press against Amberlyn's again.

"Might want to wait a bit. Let her leaving die down," Kane suggests as I cuddle Amberlyn into my side.

Stroking her jaw with my thumb, I watch as she yanks at the sheer fabric on her shoulder and says, "It itches."

"Change then. I'll tell my sister."

She waves me off. "No, I'm fine, but I'm picking my own clothes from now on."

"Sounds good to me," I agree, kissing her temple. "Hey, why don't I come over after tea, and we'll have dinner with your aunt and uncle and tell them?"

She eyes me. "You want to be there for that?"

I smile. "Of course."

She grins back at me and nods. "Yeah, I'd like that."

"Grand," I say, kissing her temple once more as Kane stands up, raising his pint.

"Fiona, love, get three more pints for me."

She eyes him and asks, "Why?"

"I want to make a toast."

"Okay, ya weirdo," she mutters as she gets us all pints. Amberlyn looks at me questioningly, and I shrug as Kane clears his throat.

"Okay!" Kane says with the biggest grin on his face. "My best mate, Declan O'Fucking-Callaghan is the shite. Not only is he about to marry the bird of his dreams—"

"I really hate that you call me that," Amberlyn says with a laugh. "I'm not a bird."

"Shh, you," he says, laughing before raising his pint up more. "He is getting his distillery and things are going to be grand, but today we found out that his whiskey is going into beta testing, which is fucking awesome!"

"Oh my God!" Amberlyn gasps, hugging me tightly. "That's amazing, Declan. Congratulations!"

She kisses my lips hard as Fiona cheers, "Fair play! That's awesome, Declan."

I grin against Amberlyn's lips and hug her tightly to me. It's funny though. Because, out of all that Kane says, all I really care about is the fact that I am about to marry the bird of my dreams. I am extremely happy that the distillery is almost in my grasp and that my whiskey will soon be enjoyed by the world, but the most important thing, the one thing that gives meaning to my life, is that I'm about to marry Amberlyn.

As I stare into her aquamarine eyes, I can see our whole life together. It will have ups and downs because she isn't one to be strong-armed into something. Though I would never do that, I have a feeling she and my family will butt heads. Through the years, the men of my family have always married quiet women who were to accent them in public and reproduce. It has been drilled into me since birth to find a woman who will stand quietly and do as I say, but I never wanted that.

I wanted someone like Amberlyn. Someone who will stand up for herself against me, or anyone else, for that matter. She isn't a pushover, and I believe that all the pain and loss she has been on the receiving end of has made her tough as nails. Something she'll need if she's going to be my wife. It won't be easy, but I believe that our love will overcome the obstacles that may arise. All we have to do is get through the next couple months. Once we are married, nothing else will matter. It will be her and me, and that's it.

As her eyes sparkle with love and pride, I know we have it all wrapped up. We are meant for each other. Two halves of a heart. My Amberlyn. *Mo stór.*

"I am so proud of you," she says, her fingers tickling the back of my neck.

I smile as I brush my lips against hers. My cheeks burn with color. I don't like the attention on me, but when I'm in her arms, I don't have the desire to take off and run. I don't want to be anywhere but where I am. Kissing her lips, I melt against her as she holds me tight.

Backing away, she grins at me as I whisper, "Grand 'cause I want to be a man who you are proud of."

"Well, Mr. O'Callaghan, you have that in the bag."

"So do you, future Mrs. O'Callaghan."

Her lips curve as she leans into me, looking deep into my eyes. "I love the sound of that."

Closing my eyes, I lean my forehead against hers as I take in the same air she breathes. "As do I, *mo stór.* I can't wait till it's for real."

As she cups my face, I open my eyes and she smiles. "Not too much longer."

"I'm counting the hours."

"I'm counting the minutes," she counters.

"Fine, the seconds are what I'm counting," I tease back, kissing her nose.

"I wish it would just happen so both of ya will stop all this ooey gooey counting shite! Jaysus," Kane supplies before looking over at Fiona. "I refuse to be like that."

She laughs before looking over at us. "Don't let him fool ya a bit. He's as ooey gooey as a melted slice of cheese, that one."

That has everyone laughing, and as Amberlyn laughs in my arms, I pull her closer.

I live for moments like these.

Just holding her and feeling her laugh against me.

I almost lost her.

These moments.

That is something I'll never forget, and because of it, I treasure her.

Completely.

fourteen

Amberlyn

" And this is my future daughter-in-law, our soon-to-be Whiskey Princess."
Six pair of eyes cut to me as I stand awkwardly near Mrs. O'Callaghan and Lena. While I am dressed like them, even look as if I could be one of them, I feel so out of place. Both of them are very slim, long legs, and long, flowing blond hair. Their dresses make them look like a billion bucks, and while mine is obviously by the same designer, I'm pretty sure I look frumpy in it. I never really cared for tea dresses; I don't like the length or the look of them, but apparently everyone who is in the world of upper society loves them.

Declan assured me that I looked great, but I am sure I could wear a paper bag and he'd think that. By the look of the ladies around the table, I don't look great, I look stupid, and I want to go home. Wringing my fingers together, I wish that Declan were here. He'd assure me that the Fadmish ladies aren't looking at me like I don't belong. That they aren't stuck-up people but very sweet ladies, but he is nowhere to be seen. He drove me over here and said he'd take me home afterward. I'm pretty sure he's out playing with his horse.

Lucky duck.

I want to stop being nervous, but I don't get what I wish for. Smiling, like I assume I'm supposed to be, I walk with Mrs. O'Callaghan and Lena into the gazebo before taking my seat between them. Everyone falls into fast conversation while I sit there and try to keep up. Some of the ladies' accents are very thick and I try to understand them, but it's hard. Lena and Mrs. O'Callaghan keep up with no issue at all, not that I thought they wouldn't, I just wish I could. I've been here almost six months; shouldn't I be a little more fluent in the Irish manner of speaking?

I'll catch on. Hopefully. Looking off to the left, I watch as two bluebirds play carelessly in the bird bath. I'd love to be one of those birds right now. It's a gorgeous day. Fall is coming and you can feel the cool in the air, but still it's beautiful. I love the weather here. It's so crisp and instantly makes you feel happy. It isn't just weather though, I've realized since being in Ireland. No, it's a part of you. The way the air brushes your hair off your shoulders or kisses your cheeks. It's poetic almost. I just love it here.

Leaning back in my chair, I cross my legs but soon Mrs. O'Callaghan is tapping my ribs. "Sit up, my love," she whispers, and I almost think she isn't talking to me until she sets me with a disapproving look. My brows come together as I sit up like I'm asked to. I'm not sure why I do that, but I do. Crossing my hands on my knee, I keep smiling as one of the ladies and Lena talk about Micah. From what I hear, she is a friend of Micah's family.

"And you'll go with him?" she asks Lena.

Lena smiles as she shrugs. "I'm considering it. I just don't know what I'd do without a straightener or my phone, even!"

Everyone laughs and I smile attentively. I feel someone looking at me, and when I glance over at the lady who was talking to Lena, she's smiling at me. She then asks, "Would you go if our sweet Declan were leaving for Africa?"

I clear my throat before saying, "I'm sorry, I didn't catch your name."

Everyone smiles and I know it's because of my accent. My non Irish-speaking accent. "Considering I didn't throw it, I'd doubt ya would." I try not to be offended as she says, "My name is Rhonda."

"Nice to meet you," I say with a grin, one that is totally fake, of course. "Yes, I would go."

"Yous wouldn't be scared about not having a straightener? Or other things we women need?" Another of the ladies asks with a look of horror on her face. "I wouldn't go! I'd wait like a good wife would."

Everyone nods in agreement and even laughs softly as I shrug, running my finger along the rim of my teacup.

"I'd have Declan. What else would I need?" I say simply, a small grin pulling at my lips. I'd go anywhere Declan was. We'd figure out a way to be happy wherever we are.

"A phone? Makeup?!" Lena laughs.

"Who would I need to call? Declan is there. I would call my cousin and family when I could. They'd understand," I answer and receive nothing but looks of surprise. "And as for makeup or even nice clothes, Declan loves me no matter what. I don't have to get all glammed up for him to be attracted to me. He's seen me at my worst and my greatest, and thankfully, he still loves me. As I do him," I say, and then I feel like I've said too much. Lena is looking at me like I've grown two heads within the time it took for me to say all that. The other ladies just look skeptical of me. Maybe it did sound like I was trying too hard? Trying to prove that I was good enough for their beloved Whiskey Prince.

Lena lets out a laugh and then covers my hand. "I guess my love isn't as strong as Amberlyn's, then."

I know she meant it as a joke, but there is some truth in her eyes that I see before she looks away.

Rhonda looks back at me and smiles. "Well, she did take a bullet for the lad. He is obviously important, yeah?"

I nod. "More than anyone would ever realize."

Reaching for my cup, I take a long pull, but when the tap comes to my ribs, I almost spit the tea out.

"Love, don't slurp, sip," she says to me, and I blush before swallowing what was in my mouth.

"Didn't realize I was," I say, but that rewards me with looks of disdain from my future mother-in-law. Abandoning my gaze, she looks across the table.

"They are quite in love," Mrs. O'Callaghan says, and when I glance over at her, I see that she drinks with her pinkie up. I always through that it was in stories, but nope, she is rocking the one pinkie up as she sips her tea. "I worried that she was only in it for the money, but she didn't even know who we were."

"No?" Rhonda asks, shock visible along her wrinkled eyes.

I smile. "I'm from America; I had no clue who the O'Callaghans were. I never drank whiskey, and I'd only been here two months maybe before I met Declan."

"You stay with the Maclasters, yeah? They didn't tell you?"

I nodded. "Yes, with my aunt and uncle and cousin. Fiona had told me about it, but it didn't seem like a big deal to me. I don't consider someone royalty like you guys do because they are rich."

A few ladies gasp as Mrs. O'Callaghan laughs. "It's more than that," she informs me.

My brows come together as I meet her affronted gaze. "I didn't mean to offend you. Sorry if I did. But what I mean is that I've met rich folks, even some famous ones, and still, they don't get treated the way you guys do here."

"It's a different way of life here," Lena says with a smile. "Our family has been around since the formation of County Mayo, even then we were what people held the standard to."

Mrs. O'Callaghan nods. "We are the bar. The high bar in society. Everyone wants to be us because of how we carry ourselves. We are not only rich, as you say, we do a lot for the community, we make the best damn whiskey in the world, and that's why we are considered royalty, as you say."

I can tell I've pissed her off. I'm not entirely sure how to fix that, so I only nod, tucking my hands in my lap. An awkward silence falls on the table before Mrs. O'Callaghan clears her throat, lifting her cup from the table. Looking at the ladies, she smiles. "Declan adores her."

I feel as if she said that a tad offhandedly, kind of like Declan is crazy to adore me, but then I think maybe I am being paranoid or even feel a little guilty for what I said. So I don't say anything as the ladies nod in acknowledgment, grinning at Mrs. O'Callaghan.

"That's wonderful. He deserves to be happy," one of the ladies says. She is younger. My age, even.

Meeting her gaze, I say, "What was your name? Sorry."

She waves me off. She is very pretty, long brown hair to her butt, built like Lena, and, of course, she is rocking her dress like she's on a runway and not at a tea party. Meeting my gaze, she smiles widely at me as she says, "Keeva O'Malley. It's wonderful to meet you."

"You too," I say, a little perplexed. Glancing at my mother-in-law, I ask, "I thought everyone's last name was Fadmish?"

She smiles, tapping the back of my hand. "No love, we are the Fadmish ladies. A tea group."

Oh, 'cause that's cool, but I smile just the same.

"We've been doing this since before Noreen was born. I was friends with Ivor's parents. It's an old tradition around the O'Callaghan estate."

"Wow," is my thought, but who am I to think it is stupid? They probably think I'm stupid for not liking their little tea party.

"Have you gotten your dress for the wedding yet?" Rhonda asks me.

I grin as I nod my head. "Yes, it should be ready by the end of the week. They had to take it in some."

"Do ya have a picture?" someone asks and I reach for my phone, but Mrs. O'Callaghan stops me.

"Sure, she does, but it's a surprise. We aren't showing anyone."

Rhonda rolls her eyes before waving at Mrs. O'Callaghan. "Ya sly dog, you just don't want to show us 'cause you don't like it."

I look over at Mrs. O'Callaghan expectantly, and she laughs in a very stuck-up way. "That isn't true. It is a surprise."

"I didn't know that it was," I find myself saying. "But you don't like the dress?"

Mrs. O'Callaghan doesn't meet my gaze. Instead, she sends a look at Rhonda before looking back at me. "It isn't what I would have picked for you."

Which was a nice way of telling me she hated it.

"Oh well, I love it," I say proudly.

"I do too," Lena agrees, squeezing my hand. "It will blow Declan away, for sure."

"Which is all that matters," I add and everyone smiles at me.

Rhonda nods as she says, "This is true. From what I heard, it's blue. A blue wedding dress is very traditional. I like your style, my dear."

I smile. "Thank you."

"I can't wait for the wedding. It's gonna be so much fun," Keeva says. "Seeing both of you all dolled up and pretty. It's gonna be great."

"Yes, it's gonna be gorgeous, for sure," Lena agrees. "I'm gonna be a crying mess!"

I send her a grin as Mrs. O'Callaghan says, "So will I. I can't wait though. Declan is so happy with you, Amberlyn. She's good for him. "

"He is," Lena agrees and it warms my heart, but when I look at the ladies, I don't think they feel the same as my future in-laws. Especially Keeva, which I don't understand at all.

"Well, let's hope it lasts a lifetime!" Rhonda cheers, holding up her teacup to me.

"It will, don't worry," I inform her with a grin.

"You are very young," Keeva says. "Only twenty, yes?"

I nod. "Yeah. I'm one of the lucky ones to find her soul mate so young."

"I couldn't say it any better myself."

I turn quickly at the sound of Declan's voice as he climbs the stairs, a grin on his face that is only for me. He holds himself so regally and handsomely. Placing his hands on my shoulders, he kisses my temple before squeezing my shoulders tightly.

"Ladies, good afternoon," he says and they all beam at him. Except for Keeva. She is just staring at him. My brow comes up before I look up to see that he is looking at her in a distressed way. What the hell? Looking down at me though, the look goes away and he smiles. "Having fun, *mo stór*?"

I grin at my nickname from him but then lie, "I am."

"Grand. I was coming by to see if ya was done. Figured we'd go for a ride."

"I'd love that," I say excitedly.

"They don't go long without each other," Mrs. O'Callaghan says with a grin.

"Ya can tell they're very much in love," Rhonda says and Declan grins.

"She's it for me. Ready, love?"

"I am," I say, standing up and cuddling to his side. Looking out at the ladies, I say, "Thank you. I had a wonderful time."

It's a lie, but then again, it wasn't that bad.

"You'll have to join us every week, so we can get to know ya better," the lady who sits next to Keeva says. She looks like an older version of her, so I assume she must be her mother. Keeva is still looking completely distraught as she stares up at Declan. I'm not sure what that is about, but I know that coming to another one of these is the last thing I want.

It may have not been that bad, but I still feel like they don't approve of me. No matter how much I love Declan and he loves me.

But instead of saying no, I say, "Sure, if I have time."

I wish I could say no, but it just worries me. I feel like they don't think I am good enough for Declan, or at least that is the way they are looking at me. Maybe I can convince them before the wedding. I don't know why I want their approval. As pathetic as it is, I find myself wanting it. Don't ask me the reason; I'm not even sure why.

Looking up at Declan, I smile when he grins down at me and I know why. For him.

fifteen
Declan

"Is your dress ready for the engagement party?"

I look over at my bride and meet her playful gaze. She is sitting on my sister's horse, Belle, and looks like a vision. I had Fiona meet me so I could get Amberlyn some jeans and a tee, something she is completely comfortable in. I think I like her more in jeans anyway. She doesn't hold back when she is in jeans; she is happier, and I like her that way. I know that it isn't what O'Callaghan women wear, and I'm sure I'll get an earful from my ma, but in a way, I don't care.

I won't dim this girl's light. Not when the world has been out to dim it at any passing chance.

"Yeah, I think Fiona picked it up with hers."

"I heard it's very scandalous," I tease.

She giggles. "Who told you that?"

"My ma."

"Yeah," she says with a shake of her head. "Your mother does not like anything I like."

I smile. "She probably never will, either."

"I think she wants me to be like Lena. All proper and pretty and I'm not that girl."

"I think you are," I say as our horses trot alongside each other. The sun is bright in the sky, kissing her skin in the most beautiful way. Her hair is down, brushing along her back as she bounces in the seat. Of course, I notice her breasts that are hidden behind the T-shirt she wears, and I want to tear the shirt off, but I feel like we are both waiting until our first night living together. Or maybe we just don't have the time, and she is too scared to do it anywhere but in a bed. Which really, who am I to ask for anything else? I should probably have candles and soft music playing.

Ha.

She sends me a grin, pulling my gaze away from her breast as she says, "Well, that's all that matters, I guess."

"No guessing about it," I say with a wink, reaching out to take her hand. "Is the dress a surprise?"

She shakes her head, squeezing my hand. "No, it's glittery and backless."

I give her a sexy grin. "Scandalous for sure."

She laughs. "Maybe. But I went with blue because of my wedding dress."

I perk up in my seat. "It's blue?"

She nods but looks a little sheepish. "I thought you knew that."

"Nope."

"Yeah," she says, smiling sweetly at me. She lets go of my hand and cups my face, our legs knocking into each other from how close we've brought the horses, not that we mind. "It matches your eyes."

I lean over, kissing her quickly before pulling back to better see her. "I can't wait to see it."

"Me either," she says, sending me a grin I know is just for me. Her grin is so refreshing and honestly makes me day.

As we ride, we discuss the engagement party and how my ma is making a circus out of it all. I want to get the damn thing over. I am tired of waiting to marry this girl. I know I wanted to give her time before, but now, I'm just tired of all the hoopla.

"My ma tried to invite the blogs because she said they weren't the papers," I say as I dismount my horse before helping her down.

She laughs as her arms come tightly around my neck. "Why does she want people there other than friends?"

"'Cause it's all for show, don't ya know?" I say, shaking my head as she cuddles closer to me.

"I just want it to be us," she says against my neck. "Do we have to stay long?"

I chuckle against her hair. "Believe me, the first opportunity I have to pull ya away, I will."

"Promise?" she says, a little sex-kitten look on her face, her eyes burning with desire.

"On my life," I state before giving her a suggestive look. "I can even take ya right here. You tell me."

She grins as she looks around and I do the same, even though I know where we are. We're off pretty far from the estate, and I doubt we'll be bothered, but even I know that it doesn't feel right. As much as I want to be buried inside of her with no cares in the world, I also want to it be perfect. Memorable.

Looking back at me, she holds my gaze as she shrugs.

"I mean we could…" she says, her voice trailing off. I can feel her heart pounding against her ribs, vibrating against my chest.

"But it doesn't feel right," I supply since I can sense the "but."

She smiles shyly. "Yeah, it doesn't feel right."

I smile back at her as I wrap my arms tightly around her, almost making us sway in the cool air of the day. Staring into her eyes, my heart kicks up in speed. It always does. There is something so magnificent about this woman that just does it for me. Lacing our fingers together, I pull away and then lead her to a flat area for us to lie. Spreading out the blanket I brought with us, I sit down first before she comes down to sit beside me. Lying back, she cuddles into my side, her fingers dancing along my ribs with the sounds of our horses grazing around us.

Closing my eyes, I turn my head so that my nose goes into her hair before taking a deep breath in. This feels so right. So perfect even, and I honestly still can't believe that I get to do this for the rest of my existence. Curving my hand along her hip, I smile as she cuddles deeper into me. I know that we'll do this a lot. Just the two of us. Lying back, I let the sun warm my face as we both relax in the warmth. Along with the noises from the horses, I can hear the fish flopping out in the pond, and I have the urge to go out there. Maybe take Amberlyn out.

"Do you like to fish?"

I feel her shrug against me. "Yeah, it's okay."

"We'll take my boat out soon."

"That sounds relaxing and fun," she mentions and I nod.

"Yeah, it will be nice. Get away a bit in the boat I made."

"You made a boat?"

"I did. Kane helped."

"And it still floats?" she teases and I laugh, my hand tightening along her hip.

"Yeah, it does! It's in top shape, thank you."

She giggles beside me, and my face breaks into a grin when her nose tickles me along my jaw. "Let me know when."

"Will do," I agree. "It will be soon."

"So you'll be able to get away?"

I smile. "I'm gonna fucking try. I've never worked this much."

"I know," she agrees. "But it's okay. Once I start school, I'll be busier too."

"Yeah," I say, and I can't help but think of what my ma said about her job and how she needed to quit.

While I don't agree—I feel she can do what she pleases—I know that the expectations of my family are different. Amberlyn is to marry me, and we must try for a baby as soon as possible like an O'Callaghan should. I'm sure she doesn't feel that way, and I should probably be honest with her, tell her the expectations, but that's only what they are. They aren't rules; they are what we have to do, but these expectations have been pounded into me since birth. I adore my family's ways, and I do want to do what the men of my family have been doing since the beginning, but not at the expense of losing the love of my life.

"Do you know Keeva?"

My eyes shoot open, the sun blinding me. I close them once more before looking over at her and rubbing them gently. "What?"

"Keeva O'Malley? She was at the tea thingy, and you two were looking at each other weird."

I clear my throat before opening my eyes again to look at her. Honesty is the best way here and I nod. "Yeah, I do."

"Who is she? Why were you two looking at each other like that?"

Looking down at her lips, I gather my words. I've always heard of women being insanely jealous of exes, but surely Amberlyn is above that. "We dated for almost a year."

She shoots up and out of my arms, looking down at me. "What?!"

Okay, maybe not.

"I used to date her."

"Keeva? Really?"

Coming up on my elbows, I nod. "Yeah."

"For a year?"

"Yeah," I say again.

"She's very gorgeous, runway pretty."

"Eh, she's all right, but she's a horrible person."

"Really?"

"Absolutely. Broke up with her 'cause she was using me for my money."

"Oh wow. What a bitch," she decides and I laugh.

"That's how I felt about her most of the time. She was always asking me for money and shite. Drove me mad."

"I bet. I'd never do that."

"Oh, I know," I guarantee her, squeezing her above her elbow. "She's still in love with me apparently, but I don't want anything with her."

Amberlyn looks down, bringing her bottom lip between her teeth. She's always so cute when she does that. Reaching up, I press down on her chin, releasing her lip from her teeth. Grinning at me, she asks, "Are you sure?"

I scoff. She has no reason to ask that.

"Yeah, very sure," I say very forcefully. Maybe a bit too harshly by the look on her face. "I promise ya, Amberlyn, I love you. Only you. She doesn't add up to you in any way. I promise ya that."

A little grin comes over her face before she leans down, pressing her lips to mine. Taking her by the back of her head, I don't allow her to go anywhere as I deepen the kiss, plunging my tongue into her mouth to taste her. I crave the taste of her. So sweet and perfect. When her leg comes over my body to where she is straddling me, her hot center burning against my cock, I gasp against her lips.

Taking her by her hips, I hold her in place as she devours my mouth, taking over the kiss and blowing my damn mind. We play, tease, and even bite a bit, her mouth so hot as she kisses me over and over again. When she starts to move against me, I swear I am having a heart attack. My heart feels as if it is gonna come out of my damn chest right here! Stopping her, I pull back, looking up into her flushed face. She has those sultry little sex-kitten eyes, and I know I'm in danger of keeping my control intact.

Pulling in deep breath, I manage to say, "My God, *mo stór*, what the hell are ya doing? Driving me insane, yeah?"

"I want you," is all she says before she takes my mouth with hers.

Unable to comprehend what she is saying, I allow her to kiss the hell out of me, but when her hand comes under my shirt, her fingers dancing along the muscles of my stomach, I can't breathe. Pulling away once more, I look up at her, completely hanging on by a thread.

"Amberlyn, love, what are you doing?"

"I want you," she says again against my lips, her fingers still sliding along my hot skin.

"Here?"

"Here."

"Now?"

As she grinds against me, her eyes dark with desire, she nods slowly. In a husky way, something I've never heard come from her sweet lips, she whispers, "Right now, not a second later."

Ah, shite.

I'm a fucking goner.

sixteen
Amberlyn

As soon as the words leave my mouth, I watch as his eyes widen, and I'm surprised I said it. I just want him so bad. My whole body is on fire; my heart is pounding so hard, I am worried it is gonna crack my ribs. My breathing is labored and I feel as if I've run a thousand miles. I am dripping with arousal for this man and I am ready. We've been playing this little game of wanting each other for way too long, and yeah, we are in a field with horses eating some grass, but honestly, I don't care. I know his mom or anyone could walk up on us right now, but those thoughts couldn't be further from my mind.

It's time.

Before anything else can leave either of our lips, he rolls us over, coming down solidly between my legs. He is so hard, and I love the feel of him. I can't wait for him to be inside me, and by the feel of it, I'm not going to have to wait much longer. Going onto his knees, he throws his shirt up and over his head and onto the grass. I take in his strong chest, the abs, and the little trail of blond that leads down into his pants. Good God, he is gorgeous.

Lifting me up, he pulls my shirt off then my bra, but just as his mouth is about to drop to my breast, he pauses, looking up at me, his mouth a breath away from my nipple. "Stop me now, love, or I won't be stopping."

"Don't stop," I pant, pressing my breast into his mouth.

His hand takes ahold of my other breast as he sucks my nipple into his mouth, his other hand holding it in place as he feasts on me. Closing my eyes,

I let my head fall back as he sucks and nibbles on me in the most delectable way. I'm not sure if it is my arousal or the heat from the sun, but I am burning up. When he leaves my right breast for my left, I cry out from the breeze hitting my breast. My pussy clenches in response, my whole body shaking with anticipation of him inside of me.

I'm scared. I'm excited. I'm freaking out, but I don't care. I need him. I need this.

I lie back and he kisses down my stomach, pausing where my jeans start. Sitting up, he unbuttons my jeans and pulls them down with my panties. Kissing my center, he dips his tongue inside me. Opening me, he buries his face between my wet lips and ruthlessly flicks his tongue along my clit. I squirm under his mouth, crying out and digging my fingers into the blanket, needing something to hold on to before I rocket off the damn blanket. When his fingers enter me, I almost scream from the sheer feeling of something inside me. It's the first time he's done that, and soon he is fucking me with his fingers, my whole body shaking out of control. The pleasure is unbelievable, and it's not long before I am writhing under his mouth, crying out his name as he licks up the length of my pussy, his fingers slowing inside me. My body shakes from the aftershocks of my orgasm as he stands, tearing his jeans off and then his boxers.

He is erect and I'm breathless at the sight. While I had it in my mouth not even a week ago, there is something about him standing above me, his cock hard and long, the blue sky behind him, and the sun glistening against his sweaty skin. He sure is a sight to see.

"You're beautiful," I whisper and he smiles, his skin dark red in splotches on his body. I can see where my nails dug into his shoulders, and I worry I might have hurt him, but his face shows nothing but want.

"I was thinking the same thing," he says as he comes down on top of me. Lying against me, he kisses my jaw, my chin, and my mouth as my heart just pounds out of control.

It's about to happen.

I'm about to lose my virginity.

Closing my eyes, tears sting as his mouth moves with mine. When he pulls away, I open them to watch as he sits up, his hand coming behind my knee, opening me wider to him. He sends me a grin and asks, "Ya ready, *mo stór*?"

I don't say anything; I bite my lip as I nod. Holding my gaze, he smiles again, taking my face with his other hand.

"I love you."

That eases some of my panic and I smile back. "I love you too."

Leaning down, he kisses me, long and with so much passion, I almost cry. He loves me so much, and Lord knows, I love him too. When he pulls away, I want to beg him to come back, but then he is putting a condom on, his hands shaking. I want to smile at the sight of him but I, too, am shaking with lust. I watch as he takes his cock in his hand and he directs it inside me. Closing my eyes, I listen as he groans while I take him inch by painful inch. My body feels as if it is being ripped apart from the inside. I want to push him out, but I know it's tough the first time. That it gets better. So I bite my lip as my body goes taut. I'm worried he won't fit, but soon he is completely inside me, filling me in ways I've never been filled, and I can feel his hard breath against my jaw as I gasp for my own breath.

"My God," he breathes before he pulls out and then slowly enters again. It doesn't hurt that bad this time, but it still stings. Still biting my lip, I dig my nails into the back of his arm as he moves back out of me. But when he enters me again, he stills, a strong grunt coming from him and his cock pulsating inside of me.

"Damn it."

I wait for him to move, but he doesn't, and soon he is pulling out of me. Confused, I open my eyes to look up into his gorgeous face. Sweat is dripping down his temple, but he won't look at me. Running his hand down his face, he takes in a deep breath and shakes his head.

"That's it?" I ask, and I wish like hell I haven't once the words leave my lips. "Wait! No, act like you didn't hear that! I'm sorry! Ah!"

He laughs, but I know it isn't from his heart. He is hurt I said that, and I couldn't hate myself more.

Way to ruin it, Amberlyn!

Still laughing, he shakes his head. "I'm so embarrassed."

Internally I scream before coming up on my knees, crawling over to him and wrapping my arms around him, kissing down his jaw.

Quickly, I say, "No, it was perfect."

He scoffs. "I couldn't even last. My God, you are so damn tight."

"It's okay, I promise. I just thought it was supposed to feel good."

He cuts me a look. "So ya didn't even enjoy it?"

Fuck me!

I know my face says it all, and before I can even try to lie, he shakes his head and looks away. "Fucking hell, I'm a fucking wanker."

"No, you are perfect," I say, trying to make it better, but I'm sure I am making it worse.

"Ah, hell, Amberlyn, let me wallow," he says, shaking his head. "Don't lie to me."

Closing my eyes, tears leak out the sides as I lean my head on his shoulder. "I'm sorry," I whisper.

He laughs, again soulless. "What for? I'm the one who failed ya."

"No, not at all," I say, looking at the profile of his lovely face. "It was the first time. I'm sure the second time will be good."

He looks down, moving his hand along his naked thighs. "The first time was supposed to be memorable. Now when ya think of this, you'll think of me coming after two pumps in ya."

I close my lips tightly to keep from laughing. This. Is. Not. Funny. But soon, I am sputtering with laughter, and it's not long before he is too. Looking over at me, he wraps his arms around me and we lie back on the blanket. Cuddling into his side, I hook my leg over his hip before meeting my lips to his. Holding me tightly, he moves his mouth with mine, but then he pulls back.

"I'll rock yer world next time."

"Of course you will," I say with a nod, and then I smile sheepishly. "Did I hurt your feelings? I'm sorry."

He shakes his head. "Ya have that diarrhea of the mouth, as Fiona calls it. Plus your face tells me everything you are thinking. It wasn't good, but it will be next time. For sure."

"I do love you," I say as I run my finger along his jaw, looking deep into his eyes. "So much. I wouldn't have wanted my first time to be with anyone but you."

His eyes fill with passion as he nods. "I wish it had been my first time too."

I press my lips together to keep my retort in, but I swear he reads my mind because he says, "Which, the way I came, might as well have been."

I giggle uncontrollably beside him, and he wraps his arms tightly around me, covering my mouth with his and silencing me. Playfully, we kiss and just laugh at the sheer perfection that is us. I wouldn't change a thing about this. It was a hot mess, but our hot mess. When my phone starts to sound, I pull away because it's Fiona calling.

"Sorry," I say as Taylor Swift sings about shaking it off. "Fiona is calling."

"Yeah," he says as I lean over him, getting my phone out of my pants.

Hitting the talk button, I say, "Hello?"

"Hey, where are you?"

I pause. "Riding with Declan."

She laughs. "Riding him or a horse?"

I giggle and she screams, causing me to hold to phone out. "Ah, Fiona!"

She apologizes before giggling like a little girl. "I want all the details," she says closely into the phone, and I just laugh.

"Yeah, yeah, why'd you call?"

"Dinner with Ma and Da? I'm not surprised ya forgot."

"Shit! I'm coming."

"Are ya now?" she asks suggestively, and I just shake my head before hanging up on her. "We gotta go. We are supposed to be at dinner."

"Oh shite," Declan says before hopping up, but when he does, I see that there is blood all over his stomach.

"Oh my God! What happened?"

He looks down and shakes his head in confusion, but when he looks back at me, he points at me. "You're bleeding."

I look down to see that I am, in fact, covered in blood from the waist down. "This was a train wreck."

He laughs as he pulls me to him. "Yeah, but who cares?" he asks, and I smile. Winking at me, he says, "I love ya."

I cup his face as I nod. Looking deep into his eyes, I feel so well loved. Yeah, this was a train wreck, but I'd take a train wreck and feel completely in love over the perfect first time and for it to end in a month.

This is forever.

Train wreck, rain checks, and all.

Kissing his lips quickly, I pull back and say, "I couldn't agree more."

seventeen
Amberlyn

After going back to Declan's room to clean up and to change—thank God, I had that ugly darn dress—we rush back to my aunt and uncle's. The table was already set and everyone was seated when we got there. To my surprise, Kane was seated too. He never comes for dinner. Eyeing him as he gives me a look, I give him one back, which results in us both snickering. Declan pulls out my seat for me and I sit down, sending him a grin before he sits down beside me, both of us apologizing for our lateness.

"He stole me away from tea, and we went riding and lost track of time. I'm so sorry," I say, sending a shy grin to my aunt. I am probably grinning like a fool, and I'm sure the whole room knows I've just had sex.

But thankfully, my aunt waves me off and says, "It's fine, honey. We just sat down. Kane and Michael were discussing something with some kind of compressor. We had no trouble waiting."

I smile, but when my gaze meets Fiona's playful one, I turn bright red. I hope that my eyes are conveying the fact that I will kill her if she says anything, but I guess they don't because she says, "I'm sure that isn't the only thing you lost."

Declan looks up and then at me before looking over at Fiona and chuckling as he shakes his head. Kane is holding back his laughter, a sinful smirk on his face while my poor aunt and uncle are in the dark.

Thank God.

Glaring, I reach for my cup and shake my head as my aunt asks, "What did you lose, honey? Did you find it?"

When beer spurts out Kane's nose and Declan starts to choke, I swear I am going to kill Fiona. Even as she grins at me, her face glowing and looking beautiful, she too is fighting to keep it together, her eyes dancing with laughter. But I know I might have to end my cousin.

"Jesus, Kane, ya all right, lad?" my uncle asks, and Kane coughs in between laughing.

"Yes, sir. Goodness," Kane sputters as he wipes his face and shakes his head. "You're evil, ya know," he mutters at Fiona before kissing her cheek.

"That she is," I say, and I feel bad since my aunt and uncle have no clue what is going on. Declan is still snickering but trying to hide it as he holds his cup up over his mouth. I am burning with embarrassment, but I can't say I don't expect it from her. It's classic Fiona. She lives to embarrass me.

"I don't know what is going on, but how's everything coming for the wedding?" my aunt asks.

I smile as I sit straighter, ignoring the laughter of my cousin, her boyfriend, and mine. "It's going great. It's going to be very nice."

"Still going through with it, then?" my uncle teases, and I nod as Declan grins.

"Yes," I say as Declan's fingers lace with mine. "Very much so."

"Good to hear," he says, and I believe that he is genuine when he says it. Grinning at him, I lean into Declan and let out a contented sigh as the conversation is brought to a new topic. Whiskey. I always enjoy listening to Declan talk about his business. He is very passionate about it, and it's easy to tell that he knows everything there is to know about it. I'm very impressed when Kane starts talking, though. Like Declan, he is very savvy in the business and keeps up like a pro. While my aunt, cousin, and I only eat and pipe in when we can, my uncle is up to speed with them, and I think that surprises Declan.

"You're retired, yes?" Declan asks, his eyes trained on my uncle.

"I am. Been for a couple years," he answers, a playful grin on his face. "Was glad to go."

"I didn't know you were retired," I say before Declan can go on. "I thought the B&B has always been your job."

Looking over at me, my uncle shakes his head. "No love, this was my ma and da's, but I got into the whiskey business with Jameson Whiskey and worked for a very long time. I was finally able to work at home, which was good since my da had long passed and my ma was heading that way." Taking ahold of my aunt's hand, he smiles. "Shelia ran this without me for a while, raising Fiona in my absence. Then I decided it was time for me to be home all the time and quit, but we say I retired since I did so many years. Best decision, I think, but I do miss the business."

"And we love having you home," my aunt says, and I can see that Fiona agrees. I do too; I couldn't imagine him not being here all the time.

"Ya know, Mr. Maclaster, I'd love to pick yer brain sometime when you have time," Declan says, his eyes still trained on my uncle. "My whiskey just went into beta testing."

"Fair play, congratulations," he says, nodding his head to Declan. My chest burns with pride as Declan grins sheepishly. "What's it like?"

Grinning at Declan, I listen as he explains each flavor in his whiskey, the slow burn, and the splendor of it.

"I've had it. It's good," I add, and Declan grins at me as my uncle nods.

"You'll need to bring me a bottle."

"I'll do that tomorrow."

"Grand, but yeah, after dinner we'll break out my favorite bottle and we'll talk the legs off a donkey, yeah?"

"Grand," Declan says, and I can tell he's excited. I'm just glad they're getting along. I want my uncle and aunt to like Declan since I plan to spend the rest of my life with him.

Glancing over at me, he smiles as he reaches for his mug, taking a pull of his beer as Fiona says, "Great, so we'll clean while you three drink. Seems fair."

My uncle grins as he tips his drink to her. "Training ya for wifehood."

When my aunt's hand comes hard into his chest, I'm sure he regrets that comment. If he didn't, he sure does when the next sentence leaves her lips. "Oh yeah? Let me say this, you go and get piss drunk, but by the morning, that kitchen will be clean."

My uncle's face turn a bit red, but his grin doesn't give anything away as he nods. "Yes, love." Leaning over, he kisses her and then glances at Declan and Kane. "And that, my lads, is how it is being a husband."

That has everyone laughing as we continue to enjoy our dinner. My aunt's cooking will be one of the biggest things I'll miss once I leave. Surely though, I'll have time to come for dinner when I please. If it comes down to home cooking with my aunt or tea with his mom, I'll have no problem choosing. If she'll even have me. I'm not sure how it will go once I tell her I'm moving out. I feel like she knows it will happen, but she is hoping that it will be after the wedding, like Fiona had hoped. I really don't want to leave, but then again, I do. It's bittersweet. I'd rather not leave them, but the thought of coming home to Declan every single night and waking up to him every morning sounds almost a magical as Disney World.

Once cake is brought out for dessert, I nibble on my piece as Kane and my uncle go back on the subject of the compressor in the beer chest. Declan's fingers dance along my wrist, and when I glance back at him, he is grinning at me. Leaning forward, his lips go to my ear as he whispers, "You are so beautiful."

My mouth pulls at the side as I lean into him, his lips still pressing to my ear. I love him so much.

"When are you going to tell them?" he whispers again and I close my eyes.

"Ugh, get a room," Fiona groans, and Declan's laughter tickles my ear as he pulls back. "Or a field," she notes, sending Kane into a fit of laughter as Declan chokes on the swig he has just taken.

"I'm gonna kill you," I threaten, and she laughs along with Kane as my aunt and uncle look at us like we have all lost our minds.

"What is going on?" my aunt asks, and I shake my head.

"Nothing," I answer before Fiona can. "She's lost it."

"Oh, I'm not the one losing anything, but you sure have," she teases some more, and now Declan is laughing and I feel like I'm gonna catch fire with my embarrassment. Leaning into Fiona, Kane almost falls out of his seat as his body shakes with laughter. I glare over at Declan, and his laughter turns to coughing as he reaches for his water, looking away.

Glancing over at Kane and Fiona, I glare as I say, "We are no longer friends."

Fiona scoffs. "Ah, if only it were that easy. I'm not going nowhere and neither is he," she says, cocking her head to Kane.

"Whatever," I mutter, but it's true what she says.

Glancing at my confused aunt and uncle, I grimace as she says, "You guys are havin' da craic for sure."

"They are. I am not," I say, shaking my head as the laughter stirs up again.

"Well, forget them then. When do you go for your final dress fitting?"

"In a month. We'll get Fiona's dress then too. I think I want her to wear a creamy white color."

My aunt nods and Fiona makes a face. "I thought you said orange?"

I shake my head. "I don't want orange anymore; I think it'll clash with my dress."

"Shouldn't you wear the cream though?" Declan asks, and I know he isn't trying to be funny, but of course, Fiona and Kane take it to a whole new level.

"Yeah, she can't wear white after today," Fiona mutters, and I kick her swiftly in her knee.

She hollers out as my aunt cries out, "What in the world?"

"She kicked me."

"She is teasing me!" I holler back.

"How old are you two?" my uncle asks, and you would never believe we are in our twenties by the way we stick our tongues out at each other. "My goodness, bunch of wee lasses in the room, yeah, Shelia?"

"For sure, wouldn't believe one is getting married soon."

I glare over at Fiona and she glares back. "I think you broke my knee."

"You deserved it," I spit back before looking over at my aunt. "She might not be in my wedding," I decide, but instead of scoffing at me, Fiona laughs. I try to hold in my own grin, but it doesn't last long, and soon I am shaking my head as laughter sputters from me. As I meet Fiona's playful gaze, she reaches over and takes my hand in hers, squeezing it tightly as she smiles. She drives me crazy, but she is mine, and I wouldn't have anyone but her stand beside me at my wedding.

"Declan, who will stand up with you?" my aunt asks, bringing our attention to her.

"Kane, of course," he says nodding his head toward Kane as he reaches for another piece of cake.

"Aw, how sweet," she says and we all smile.

It kinda is, I guess. As long as those two stay together.

"When will you be moving out, Amberlyn? Before or after the wedding?" my uncle asks, and I whip my head to look back at him. I fully expected to be the one to bring the subject up, not the other way around.

Clearing my throat, I feel Declan's hand on my knee as I smile. "I was actually gonna tell you guys tonight that I'm moving out after the engagement party."

Silence falls around me and I suck in a deep breath, holding it as I wait for the yelling, the telling me I'm crazy. But unlike I expected, they both just nod and my aunt actually smiles.

"We hate to see ya go, but it's a part of life," she says, and my uncle smiles as he cups Declan's shoulder.

"To the estate, I assume?"

Declan nods. "For the time being. Amberlyn doesn't really want to live there, but she'll try it for me."

I blush as all eyes fall on me. "Yeah, I want us to have our own place, but his whole family has lived nowhere but there, so I figured I'd try."

"Grand, you should. You may love it," my aunt says.

I want to disagree, but I smile instead. I don't want them to worry about me. No matter what, Declan will make sure I am happy. He's proven that over and over again.

"Well, you're next, Fiona, love," my uncle says with a grin.

Fiona looks up, surprised, before glancing at me, probably suspecting I've said something but I haven't. "What, Da?"

"You're next to move out and get married," he says and then he grins. "Make sure you ask for her hand, Kane."

"Oh, uh," Kane stutters and Fiona shakes her head.

"We aren't ready for marriage yet, Da," she says before elbowing Kane.

He clears his throat and says, "But when we are, I will, sir, for sure."

"Good. Declan forgot," he teases, looking over at Declan.

My sweet fiancé's face reddens as he nods. "I did, but I made up for it."

"He did," my aunt says as she looks back over at Kane. "But don't forget."

"I won't," Kane promises. "And I know she wants to wait to tell ya, but she's gonna move in with me after their wedding."

My eyes go wide at Kane's announcement as Fiona's mouth drops. Quickly I look over at my aunt and uncle, and they are both just staring at Kane.

"Oh shite," Declan mutters and I elbow him. I'm not sure if we should take cover or not. My uncle's face is turning a bit red and my aunt's eyes are filling with tears, I think. Oh goodness. Poor Fiona.

"Is that right?" my uncle asks finally, glancing at his daughter.

Fiona doesn't say anything right away, she only holds his gaze as her fingers lace together. "Yeah."

"Why after the wedding?" my aunt asks. "Do you want to go now?"

She clears her throat as she shrugs. "I do, but I don't want both of us to leave ya."

It is easy to say that this day has been full of surprises because my aunt doesn't start to cry or even yell, she laughs, and soon my uncle joins in with her.

"We aren't senile! If ya want to go, go, my love," my uncle says, shaking his head. "We will be fine."

"Really?" Fiona and I ask at the same time.

"Yes," my aunt says with a grin. "We've raised ya right, Fiona, and we've done well with ya, Amberlyn. Yous two are ready for the world. So go and know, no matter what, this will always be yous' home."

Leaning into Declan, I look over at where Fiona is staring at her parents before glancing over at me.

"That was a little too easy," she decides and I nod.

"I know," I say before glancing back at them and then meeting her gaze once more. "Maybe they are senile?"

Soon the room is full of our laughter, and I can't believe this is my life now. It used to be only my mom and dad and me, and while it was always loud and fun in my home, I never felt like I do at this particular moment. I'm looking around at the faces of my family. My aunt, my uncle, and cousin. Kane who has wiggled his way into my heart and then my love—my Declan. I'm complete. It's weird, but it also makes me feel like I am doing everything my mother wanted me to do. She wanted me to live and I'm doing that.

Declan eighteen

I want Michael Maclaster to work for me.

He is very clever when it comes to flavors and ways of brewing whiskey. I always knew that he had worked for Jameson, but I didn't realize how close he was to the inner workings of the distillery. Hearing him talk about it is like talking to my grandda, and it's refreshing. I'm thoroughly enjoying it and want nothing more to bring him on to my team, but as soon as I bring that up, he shoots me down.

"Ah, Declan, I'm done with that."

"Never," I try, but he is already shaking his head.

"No, I am. With Fiona moving out, it gives me and Shelia time to ourselves. I can't get a job now."

Leaning toward him, I say, "I'll pay ya whatever ya like."

He smirks at me as he shakes his head. "Declan, lad, when you marry Amberlyn, you'll learn very quickly that being wealthy is having that girl look at ya and smile. I don't need money; I need the time back that I lost with Shelia 'cause I didn't know then what I know now." He leans back in his chair, taking a shot of his whiskey before setting me and then Kane with a look. "Listen to this old man, lads. Don't work yerselfs to death 'cause at the end of the day, she'll love ya no matter what."

I want to convince him otherwise, but I can see in his eyes it's no use. As I climb the stairs to Amberlyn's room, his words play over and over in my head.

I've been so giddy to start working hard to make O'Callaghan's a success on my own, but maybe that's wrong of me. I already work too much as it is and hardly get to see my love. I could see the regret in Mr. Maclaster's eyes for the years he spent away from his daughter and wife, and I just can't do that.

I have to be mindful.

Amberlyn comes before my work.

No matter what.

Reaching Amberlyn's room, I push open the door to find her on her bed. Her knees are brought up to her chest with a book on her knees. She has changed since she isn't wearing the dress any longer, only a pair of sweats and a T-shirt. Her hair is piled on her head and she is sleepy-sexy. I want to lie down next to her, nuzzle my nose into her neck, and fall asleep with her breath on my cheek. This is my bride. My life.

Looking up at me, she smiles. "Come here."

I come to her without question, crawling into bed with her. She cuddles into my chest and opens the book along our legs. The first thing I see is a small Amberlyn. I know it's her from first glance. Her cherub cheeks and bright aquamarine eyes. She was as stunning as a child as she is now.

"This is me at nine."

I smile. "Gorgeous, of course."

Turning the page, it's her again with who I presume is her da. She has his eyes, his lips, and the shape of his face. He was a happy man from what I can see. His arms are tight around Amberlyn's small frame, grinning at the camera. I can almost hear the laughter. On the opposite page is one of her, her da, and her ma. I thought she looked like her da, but she is her ma made over. Simply stunning.

"This is my mom and dad."

"You look very happy."

"I was," she answers and slowly she turns the page. Each picture is her with her parents at various spots, their home, on vacation, and at sporting events. They were happy, very happy. When she pauses at one picture, her fingers come along the face of her da and she sucks in a deep breath. They are both wearing Mickey Mouse shirts, standing outside of a gate. "This was three days before he died. I was twelve."

"Where were you guys?"

"Disney World," she answers, smiling. "We left that day; it was the most magical trip of my life. We had so much fun. My mom always said we'd go back, but we never did. I think it hurt her too much."

Snaking my arm around her, I kiss her temple. "We'll go, yes? Me and you, fly to the States and do it again."

She glances up at me, her eyes watering a bit as her bottom lip wobbles. "Really?"

"Yeah, for sure. Wanna go before or after the wedding?"

"Probably after. We have so much before."

"Sure, but I don't care. You tell me and we will go."

She cuddles into me and my heart aches in my chest. I want her to be happy. I want to fill the hole she has in her, and I pray that I am doing enough to help. To make this life one she is proud of. One her parents would be proud of.

"I love you, Declan."

"I love you," I whisper as she turns the page again. We don't say anything as she slides each page over, and I watch as her ma gets skinner and skinner. When the last picture appears, one of her mother lying in a bed with a scarf around her head, her face sunken in and her eyes dull in color, I have to swallow back my own tears. I can feel them falling from Amberlyn's sweet face, but I know I have to be strong for her.

"She died that night," she says softly, biting her lip. "I knew it was going to happen. I felt it in my heart. I kissed her over and over again, telling her how much I loved her, and she kept saying it back to me. She didn't want to leave; I know she didn't."

"Who would ever want to leave you, Amberlyn?" I ask. "I couldn't fathom it. I couldn't imagine my life without your love, and I know that it had to be so hard for your ma and your da. But I know they are watching and they are so fuckin' proud, *mo stór*. So proud."

Burying her face into my neck, she cries. Her whole body shakes against me as she sobs for the death of her parents. I place the book beside us and hold her, allowing her to get it all out. I knew before I even realized she had my heart that there would be days like this. When she would lose it because of the loss she has suffered. I hate that she is in so much pain, that her parents aren't here to watch her grow and live her life. If I could, I'd give it all back. Meeting her, loving her, and ultimately being allowed to marry her if only she could have her ma and da back, or hell, just her ma. I know I'd find her. I would because she was made for me. We were made to be together. No other way, just us.

Kissing her temple, I whisper how much I love her and she just cries against me. I want to comfort her, but really what can I do? How do you mend that kind of loss? I just don't see it happening. As much as I want to believe I do comfort her, I know that it can't be enough. Time will heal, and hopefully, I'll help a bit. When she pulls back, her eyes full of tears, she cups my face, running her thumbs along my jaw as her eyes search mine.

When her lips curve up in a shaky grin, it honestly guts me. She is so beautiful and so fuckin' strong. It kills me. I wish I were a quarter of what she is. To go through so much pain but still love with all ya heart is saintlike almost. She is my angel. My sweet, gorgeous angel.

"I swear, Declan, you are my salvation," she whispers, tears rolling fast along her cheeks. "I wouldn't be as happy as I am without you. I try so hard to be happy, to make other people happy, and to just be the person everyone wants. But when I'm with you, I only have to be me. Sometimes that's a hot mess of tears, but I know you'll always love me."

"I will," I promise. "No matter what."

Her lip starts to wobble, and when her eyes close, I want to gather her in my arms, but then she sucks in a deep breath before glancing at me. "I'm not saying this to hurt your feelings, but you'll never be what my parents were—"

"I know that—" I say, but she shakes her head, cutting off any further words.

"And I know you don't try to be. You are Declan, only Declan, for me, and that's all I need. I miss my parents, I do, and I know that over the years, the pain will dull, but I just want you to know that I wouldn't make it without you. I'd put on a front, I would, but I would never experience life the way I am now that you are in it."

Smiling, I cover her hands with mine. "And to think, we have so much more to do. Our wedding, honeymoon, and then our life. No matter what, I'll be beside you."

"Good 'cause I don't believe in divorce."

"Nor do I. This is it. Me and you, *mo stór.*"

"That's how I want it."

We share a grin before pressing our lips together. Gathering her tightly in my arms, I deepen the kiss, hoping to portray how much love is in me for this woman. How my whole life is devoted to her. That is until a knock comes at the door.

Parting quickly, I let my legs hang over the bed as Amberlyn says, "Come in."

In comes Mrs. Maclaster with a sullen look on her face. "Sorry to bother ya, but I just got the mail and this was in it."

She crosses the room and hands the letter to Amberlyn. I want to mind my own business, but the look on Shelia's face has me nervous. Glancing over, I see who the letter is from and soon my blood is boiling.

Casey Burke.

"How can he send this to me?" she asks as she tears it open.

"The inmates can send post if they like," I answer as Shelia sits down in a chair by the bed. "Can I read it?"

She nods before clearing her throat. "I'll read it out loud."

My dearest Amberlyn,

I hope that all is fit with ya. That you are happy and healing well.

I first want to apologize for everything that I've done to you. I should have never touched you or hurt you in any way.

I always felt like ya was seeing me and not what everyone said about me. It was intoxicating; you are intoxicating, that is. I can see why O'Callaghan is so in love with ya. You're special. That being said, I never meant to shoot you. I know ya love him, but he has done nothing but hurt me over and over again. His family has run my name through the dirt. His sister broke my heart, his da tries to pay me off to leave, but I can't. My ma is sick and needs me. She is dying, Amberlyn, and if you testify against me, she'll die without my care. I have to be there. Please, don't testify. I know you can turn this letter in and it'll have me rotting in jail, but I'm hoping you'll find it in yer heart to help me out. If not for me, then my ma. Please.

Find it in yer heart. Please.
Casey

As the words leave her lips, I hate them. I hate every single word, and I want nothing more than to stuff them all down that eejit's throat. They are all lies. All of them. But when I go to tell Amberlyn that, her eyes are full of tears and she is shaking her head as she slowly folds up the letter.

"Well, then," Mrs. Maclaster says.

She chews her lip before looking over at her aunt. "Do you know where his mom is? Is she still at home?"

Mrs. Maclaster nods. "Yeah, she was in a home, but there was no money coming in, so now she has a friend who comes in to care for her."

Looking over at me, Amberlyn meets my gaze. "I'm still gonna testify against him, he has to pay for his crime, but his mom shouldn't pay for his mistakes."

"I mean, she did raise the gobshite," I say, but she tsks me.

"Declan."

I look away as I shake my head. "It's true, though," I say, and even Mrs. Maclaster agrees with me.

"This is true, but I can't help put her son away knowing that she'll die without proper care."

Again I shake my head, knowing exactly what she is doing. "Ya have a heart of gold, Amberlyn."

"And you love me for it," she says and I nod, kissing the side of her mouth.

"I do and I'll have my assistant call tomorrow to get her put back in the home, fully paid for."

She shakes her head. "No, I'll do it with my money. I don't want to make your dad mad."

Taking her hand, I kiss her palm before meeting her gaze. "Don't ya worry about my da, I'll deal with him. But, Amberlyn—"

Her eyes start to water again. "Yeah?"

"My money is your money, my love. Don't ever forget that. And if doing this for that wanker's ma will make you happy, then it's done."

When the brightest grin comes across her face, I remember that I may never love her the same way her family did, but I'm going to try my hardest to love her even more.

nineteen
Declan

I've never seen anything so beautiful in my whole life.

I feel I say those words at least a dozen times when Amberlyn is in the room.

But tonight, it can't be because I'm biased and completely in love with her. No, it has to be because she is the sun, shining on us all. Blessing us all with her beauty. I mean, she's fuckin' sparkling.

As she slowly comes down the stairs to meet me, I drink in every single detail. The way her hair is down to the side in a soft, loose braid that I know must have taken some time. There are little flowers throughout it, in the perfect spots to accentuate the braid. The dress she wears is formfitting, showing off all her curves and the parts of her that have me out of my mind for her.

The dress is a color I've never seen on her before. The bodice is almost a soft pink rose color, very pretty, and has her skin glowing. It's covered in stones and dips down lower than I know my mother would approve of along her breasts. It hugs her to the middle of her thighs and then the skirt is made of cream ruffles. It is a very stunning dress, but again, not something an O'Callaghan woman would wear.

I like that though. I want her to have her own personality. She wasn't born into this life, she is joining it, and I want her fun, quirky style to add in with the classic one of my family. I think she is gorgeous. Even though she is wearing more makeup than I like, it's done very dramatically, but it works. She needs to stand out. I want the whole room, everyone, to know that my fiancée is downright magnificent.

I hold my hand out and a grin pulls at my lips as she takes it, a small smile pulling at her light, nude-colored lips.

"Dazzling, my love. Simply breathtaking," I whisper before pressing my lips to the side of her mouth. She is so soft and smells like heaven. Pulling back, I look down into her grinning face and can't help but fight for my next breath.

"Thank you," she says, lacing her fingers with mine. "I really like you in a tux."

I chuckle, liking that she approves of my attire. I can see the desire swirling in the depths of her stunning aquamarine eyes, and it takes everything out of me not to check the time. I'm giving this party an hour. After that, she is mine.

Sucking in a deep breath, I tuck her hand between my ribs and bicep before letting it out. "Let's go before I take ya against the wall, yeah?"

She lets out a breathy laugh before saying, "I would applaud you for doing that, considering this dress is tighter than a little coat on a fat guy."

I laugh, loving her reference to one of my favorite movies, but then I set her with a look. "A dress doesn't come between a man and his woman."

Grinning at me, she says, "Duly noted."

"Grand, now let's go get this party over."

She hesitates and then glances at me. "I really don't want to go."

The party is loud, not with music either, but with voices. It's very intimidating and I don't want to go either, but we both know we have to.

"Me neither, but my ma would have both our heads if we don't."

"I know," she says, letting out a breath. "She has been schooling me on how a proper lady acts at her party. It's been insanely boring. I may not be an O'Callaghan-raised woman, but I doubt I'm gonna get shit-faced and hang from the chandeliers."

I scoff. "You should for the show," I say with a wink. "I love ya the way ya are. Ignore her, and let's have us some fun for an hour before the real fun starts."

"Which is?" she asks, but we both know what I'm talking about.

"Me peeling that dress off ya and making up for the first-time disaster."

She giggles, which sets my nerves on fire. I love her sexy giggle. "I love our first time."

"Bollocks, it was a disaster."

"Our disaster," she says fondly before leaning her head against my shoulder. "Nonetheless, I'm counting down the next sixty minutes."

I cuddle in closer with her before kissing her temple. "Ah, me too, *mo stór*. Come on. Let's get this over with."

She lets out a small sigh as we start to move to the door of the party. "Are there gonna be a lot of people?"

I nod and I can't chance looking at her. I know she doesn't want to deal with people like I don't. If we had our way, we'd send out a nice little announcement. But that isn't the way the things are done in my family. Lena's engagement party was so big and over the top, but I'm pretty sure mine is putting hers to shame. The estate was in full party-mode all day. The last time I saw this many people come in and out, setting stuff up, and moving things was for Lena's party, and that was hell. So I've already prepared myself for a jammer. Poor Amberlyn, though, she has no clue.

When we reach the door, Jimmy bows before smiling at us. "Ready, yous two?"

"As ready as we'll ever be, I guess," I say, squeezing her hand to receive a small smile.

"Yes, sir," he says before pulling the doors open. From what I can see, the room is filled to the brim.

Amberlyn takes in a sharp breath before saying, "My God."

"Yup."

"Well, let's hope there is a chocolate fountain."

I send her a grin and wink. "I made sure there was one."

"You are the best soon-to-be husband ever."

I lean down, pressing my lips to hers as Jimmy clears his throat.

As we part, I smile and whisper, "I love ya, Amberlyn."

"I love you."

Then with a bellowing voice, Jimmy yells, "Presenting Mr. Declan O'Callaghan and his fiancée, Miss Amberlyn Reilly."

With my head held high, I walk with my woman beside me inside the crowded ballroom as they all stand, clapping for us. I want to say that everyone is smiling, happy for my engagement, but I can't. Each face has a different expression. They're either smiling or scowling at us. They are jealous, of course. They want to be Amberlyn, or even me. While it's very disconcerting, I ignore it. How can I care about anything when my soon-to-be wife is the only thing I see?

She wears a large smile, her face bright and intoxicating, but I can see the nervousness in her eyes. She hates this stuff as much as I do. As I lead her to the dance floor, because it is customary for the couple to dance first, almost like they do at a wedding, I take her hand, standing away so everyone can drink in the beauty that I get to enjoy for the rest of my life. She smiles shyly as me, covering her mouth with her hand as the applause goes up an octave. When "Unbroken Promises" by Erick Baker starts, I turn her into my arms and grin at her as her arms come up and around my neck.

As I hold her, you couldn't slide a piece of paper between us, we are so close. Her eyes hold mine as we slowly sway to the music. I love feeling her this close to me; I love looking into her sweet eyes and knowing that she loves me with every fiber of her being. I've waited my whole life to be with a girl who would love me, all of me. And I would have never imagined that it would be a beautiful American girl who has been through the wringer.

While it wasn't what I wanted, I thought I'd marry some snotty, tea-drinking, money-blowing girl. One my ma picked out for me. I wouldn't love her, but she would do. I needed someone to be my companion. I was easy to get along with, anyone would do, and I was worried it would come down to that if I didn't get out of the house and find myself a girl. As much as I wanted to find the love of my life, I didn't believe I would. But that all changed when I set eyes on the girl across the lake who loved to read and had winter-bright skin.

My Amberlyn.

As people watch us or continue to what they were doing before Amberlyn and I came out, I wish we were anywhere but here. I hate being put on display, and as I gaze into her eyes, I find myself saying that.

She nods, a grin pulling at her lips. "Me too. We should elope," she suggests with a wink. I know she wants to come off as joking, not to disappoint me, but I can see it in her eyes. She wants just that.

"My ma would kill us."

She nods, tangling her fingers behind my neck. "I know, and plus, I want a huge wedding."

"Yeah, I know," I say with a nod. "But not this big, right?"

She looks around as a nervous laugh escapes her. "No way. I don't even want a fraction of this."

I look around and I agree. "I'll talk with my ma."

She smiles as she cuddles into my chest. "You make me so happy, Declan."

"As do you, *mo stór*."

As her lips touch mine, the song ends and the expected applause comes. Taking her hands in mine, I kiss each one before leading her off the floor to where Fiona and Kane are standing. Like her cousin, Fiona is stunning in an orange dress that hugs her tightly. I can tell my best friend enjoys the view since he doesn't even take the time to greet me, his eyes trained only on his beautiful girlfriend.

"You look great, Amberlyn," Fiona says, kissing her cheek. "Way hot."

Amberlyn's face reddens as she waves her off. "Oh hush, you are the hot one."

"Well, duh, but so are ya," she throws back at her, and I laugh as my arms snake around her waist.

When drinks are presented, I take one for each of us as Fiona and Amberlyn fall into easy conversation. They are very comical and soon have both Kane and me laughing along at whatever they are speaking of.

"I got everything packed by the door, and my da decides that's when he wants to freak out on me," Fiona explains, shaking her head as Kane chuckles. "I mean he is crying, Amberlyn, full out-cryin', and I'm so confused that I haven't a clue what to do. I look at Kane and he is just standing there!"

"I had no clue what to do! I don't do good with tears, ya know that!" Kane says in his defense.

"I know, but still. He said to go if I please, so I'm going!"

"I was there; he did say that. He got misty-eyed with me this morning, but it was more Aunt Shelia who was crying all over me," Amberlyn explains, and I feel bad that I wasn't there this morning. I had some work I had to finish before the party, and she guaranteed me she was fine bringing everything over. When I came home, she was there, in my, er, our bed, reading a book. I was about to crawl on top of her to make up for my poor performance before, but like always, a knock came at the door. Then my ma floated in with her makeup team, and I didn't see Amberlyn until the moment she walked down the stairs.

Looking over at my soon-to-be bride, I wouldn't mind slipping away and then slipping into her.

But like always, my ma ruins it.

"Declan, Amberlyn, come now. We have to greet everyone."

Rolling my eyes, I groan loudly as Amberlyn laughs, holding my hand as my ma drags us from family to family, introducing Amberlyn to all of her friends. I just stand there, hoping I don't look too bored, but apparently, I don't do well, because Amberlyn elbows me in the ribs, scolding me with those sexy aquamarine eyes. I know she thinks she doesn't really fit into my life, but as I watch her go from family to family, starting conversations, I know she is wrong. She's a natural, and I can't describe how excited I am to spend my life with this woman.

When we get to the O'Malley family, I want to go the other way, but Amberlyn and my ma are already talking about the party and how excited Amberlyn is for the wedding. I nod my head to them as her hand slides into mine, pulling me closer.

Leaning her head to my shoulder, she says, "How are you, Keeva?"

Looking where she is, I am surprised that I didn't notice Keeva in her runway-ready black dress, her hair falling down her shoulders with her lips painted red. When I send a dark look to my ma, she looks away, and I have every intention of having a talk with her later.

"Grand, thanks. You look beautiful tonight."

"Like always," I say, holding her closer as she grins up at me.

"Thank you," Amberlyn says before looking back at her. Keeva goes to say something, but her ma cuts her off.

"Not to disrespect ya, Amberlyn, but..." She then looks at Keeva and me. "I always thought that yous two was gonna get married, yeah?"

Keeva glances at me longingly while I scoff. My ma laughs, waving her off, and I go to tell her otherwise, but Amberlyn beats me to it.

"I bet you did, but good thing Declan has a good head on his shoulders or the O'Callaghans would go broke."

I sputter with laughter as everyone else stares at us in utter disbelief.

"Amberlyn," my ma scolds, but I gather my girl in my arms, kissing her lips.

Pulling away, I say, "Her humor and her honesty are what have me head over heels for her. Good seeing ya, but I want to go dance with my almost-wife."

Laughing, we head to the dance floor and I can feel them staring a hole in my back, but I don't pay them any mind. "Ma is gonna be pissed tomorrow."

"I know. I don't care though. I don't like Keeva since she hurt you."

"How sweet. Defending your man's honor and all."

"Always," she promises as I swing her around before pulling her close into my arms. Dropping my head down, I take her lips again, dragging sweet kisses out of her as we slowly sway on the floor to the soft music. She tickles the back of my neck with her fingers, and I smile against her lips as we slowly part.

"I love you," she says, her eyes glittering with the promise of our future.

"I love you," I promise, holding her tight. "We have ten more minutes and then we are gone."

"What in the world could pull you from this amazing party that is celebrating us? I mean, we haven't even hit up the chocolate fountain."

I smile. "A repeat performance, of course," I tease, my eyes bright with laughter.

She laughs. "A repeat performance. That sounds like a party, but so does that fountain."

"I'll have them bring the damn fountain to the room if ya want, but I will have ya naked in my bed in twenty minutes tops," I say, squeezing my arms around her.

Her body shakes in my arms as she throws her head back, her laughter loud and so happy. Looking up at me, she cups my face, her thumb caressing my jaw as she searches my eyes.

"I love you like this. So happy, no cares."

I nibble at her thumb as I hold her near. "Oh, I have cares, *mo stór*. I care what you feel, what you want, and what makes ya happy." She smiles as her face warms, her eyes glazing over a bit. "But the reason I'm like this is because of ya. You've changed me. Bewitched me with your love and outlook on life. I want nothing more than to give ya everything and anything you might need."

It's like she doesn't even process what I say, but then she has to have because she says, "All I need is you."

Holding her close, I kiss her nose before falling into the depths of her sweet eyes. "Ya got me."

twenty
Declan

*I*t isn't as easy as I'd like to pull her away.

As much as she says she didn't want the party, she seems to be enjoying herself. She talks up everyone at the party, ignores the questions about the trial that is in a couple weeks, and even all questions about her wedding dress. I don't get what's the big deal about her dress, but it seems every lady we talk to, they want to know. I, for one, just want the damn day to get here so all this hoopla can be behind us for sure.

Especially the trial.

Every time I think about her sitting up there, reliving that night, I swear I want to come out of my skin. I don't like the thought, not one bit, but she seems to be ready for it. I thought she was mad to wanting to pay for that gobshite's ma's housing, but I can tell it makes her happy. That pleases me, it does, but it's not only that. She makes me proud. She has such a big heart. It's one of the things I love most about her. While I could care less about helping that family, it does feel good to do something for someone who didn't have control over her wanker of a son. Like Amberlyn said, it wasn't her fault.

I still won't forgive the arsehole though.

Sliding my hand down the inside of her arm, I lace my fingers with hers before kissing the spot by her ear. She looks up at me, and I can see the desire in her eyes. She is finally ready to leave. Taking her hand with my other, I let go of her fingers and place my hand at the small of her back as we head for the exit.

But in true fashion, my ma stops us.

She looks regal tonight, not that she ever looks any different, but tonight she really does look like a queen. Her hair is up in a huge bun, her whole body glittering with diamonds. Her dress is big and puffy, a light pink color. All she's missing is a crown.

"Where are you going?"

"I'm dead on my feet, Ma, ready for bed," I explain, my hand sliding against Amberlyn's bare back.

"But the party isn't over."

"For us it is."

"But you were late!" she all but yells.

"So? It's our party. We're ready for bed," I say before reaching out to squeeze her shoulders. "Goodnight, Ma."

"Goodnight, Mrs. O'Callaghan," Amberlyn says as we step around her and into the hall. I'm surprised she doesn't follow us but thankful too. I want to take my fiancée to bed. Walking closely together, we head toward the stairs, saying goodnight to all the people who pass us. It wasn't that bad, I guess, but still I'd rather be in bed than prancing around this damn party.

"It wasn't that bad," Amberlyn says and I laugh.

"Funny, I was thinking the same thing," I tell her, holding her close. "Yeah, it was bearable."

"I had fun."

"Grand, me too," I agree. "But it did bother me that everyone brought up that wanker and the trial."

She shrugs as we turn the corner, taking the next set of stairs. You'd think that my family would invest in an elevator, but when Lena and I suggested that, our parents told us we were mad. Something about keeping the original bones of the house, and while I agree, I swear it feels like I am climbing the stairs of Hogwarts or something.

"It's really no big deal. I'm not nervous at all," she assures me. I look over at her to see if her face says something else, but she looks confident. "I'll go in, tell the truth, and he'll go away. It's pretty cut-and-dried. There are three witnesses who saw what happened. He has to pay for his crime, and the attorneys say there is no other way it can go. He'll go away, which is what is best. Can't go around shooting people 'cause you are upset."

"Especially the woman I want to spend the rest of my life with," I say, kissing her temple.

"Are you nervous?"

I shake my head. "No, like ya said, it's cut-and-dried. The lawyers think they'll try to bring up the fact that we don't like each other, but still that doesn't give him the right to shoot me. I'm worried for Lena though."

"Yeah, me too. They'll more than likely bring up their relationship."

"Yeah, even though it won't do anything. Their breaking up doesn't give him the right to shoot you."

"Absolutely," she agrees as we finally reach our room. Wrapping my arms around her waist to keep her from moving anymore, I run my lips up and down her neck, nibbling at her ear and neck before sinking my teeth into her shoulder. She gasps out, her hands grasping mine as she leans back into me, lengthening her neck for me.

"Mm," I whisper against her neck as my hands travel up her body, cupping her breasts through the fabric of her dress. "Let's take this off."

"In the room," she gasps out, her ass pressing against my growing cock.

"Yeah," I agree, walking with her, our bodies pressed together as we head into the room.

Shutting the door behind me, I lock it before turning her in my arms, meeting her lust-filled eyes. A small grin sits on her lips as I slowly run my hands down her bare arms, lacing my fingers with hers. Pulling her to me, I capture her mouth with mine. As we slowly kiss, teasing each other with our teeth and tongues, I let go of her hand and find the zipper to her dress before slowly pulling it down. She pulls back from our kiss, looking up at me as I catch the front of her dress. With her eyes on me, I slowly bring the dress down her body, replacing the fabric with my lips, kissing her in various spots as her dress hits the floor. Stepping out of it, she kicks it to the side as I slowly undo the straps to the gold heels on her feet. Taking each of them off, I kiss her ankles before trailing kisses back up her thigh, stopping at the spot between her thighs.

Kissing her through her lace panties, I take the fabric at her hips and slowly bring them down, meeting her gaze as I pull them off.

Cupping my face, she smiles. "I love you."

My heart knocks in my chest, my body shaking with the anticipation of being with this gorgeous woman once more, but most of all, I just feel complete. She does so much to my heart, and I hope I never stop feeling like this. Like I'm on top of the world.

As I kiss her wet lips, she jerks against my mouth and I look back up at her and say, "I love you."

Opening her to me, I flick my tongue against her taut nub, her cries of pleasure filling the room as she jerks and thrashes against my mouth. I can feel her legs about to give out, but I like her standing like this. Digging my fingers into her arse, I bury my mouth in her center, getting my fill of her beautiful pussy. She tastes like something I've never had. Something that is all mine. Something I'll crave for the rest of my life.

When her fingers dig into my shoulders, she cries out, my name falling off her lips as she jerks against me again.

But I'm nowhere near done.

Still on my knees, I lead her back onto the bed, her head falls back on the pillows and she looks up at me, confused. Opening her legs wider, I slide my fingers inside of her as I find her clit again, flicking my tongue against her and driving her mad. Her moans are loud and her body is shaking as I take all of her. She arches into my mouth, and I hold her up as I bury my tongue deep inside of her, replacing my fingers with my tongue. Sucking up her arousal and climax, I press my thumb into her clit, sending her rocking up into my mouth as she cries out, begging me to stop.

"Declan!" she cries, thrashing underneath my mouth.

Moving my fingers inside of her tight, beautiful pussy again, I run my tongue along her clit and suck it while fucking her with my fingers. Soon she is squeezing me with her climax, and she is screaming so loud that I swear I'm about to blow my own load. Lifting up, I look down at her and love what I see. Her whole body is flushed, her hair in a fan along our bed. She looks like a well-loved woman, and I am just getting started.

Standing up, I remove my bow tie, my eyes trained on her as I slowly pull it off and throw it to the side. Next is my jacket, and with each piece of clothing I remove, her eyes get darker and darker. I love the aquamarine of her eyes, but this storm blue is breathtaking too. When I push down my pants, my cock springing up, her eyes get wide as she sits up.

"My turn?"

I shake my head. "No baby, I want to be in you," I whisper before reaching for a condom and sheathing myself.

Her tongue comes out, wetting her mouth as I slowly crawl on top of her, taking her by the back of her knee, opening her up. Directing myself into her, I push into her, watching myself disappear inside of her. She gasps out, her fingers digging into my bicep as I completely fill her. It's a tight fit but a glorious one, one I've craved every second of the day.

Once I am completely inside her, I fall onto her. Moving her hair out of her face, I kiss her mouth, her nose, and cheeks as a small grin pulls at her lips. Bracing my hand beside her head, I push her leg back and slowly pull out before thrusting back inside her, causing a sound of pleasure to leave her lovely lips. Meeting her hooded gaze, I do it again and again, her fingers biting into my biceps as mine dig into the sheets of the bed. She is so tight, so fucking perfect, and all mine.

Knowing I need to change positions or I am going to come hard inside of her, I push up onto my knees and bring her up, holding on to her ass as I kiss her hard. She wraps her arms around my neck, her legs doing the same around my waist as I kiss her, my tongue exploring her mouth as she does the same to mine. Unable to take it any longer, I pull back and start to pound into her, holding her by her ass to keep her from sliding. Her breasts bounce against my chest, her cries filling my ear as I thrust into her, not holding back. I feel her squeezing me with another orgasm and I can't restrain myself anymore, letting go inside of her. I still as my head falls back, my whole body going taut as I unload in her hot, tight, little body.

Her fingers dust along my jaw as she trails kisses along my neck before taking my mouth with hers. Falling on top of her, we continue to kiss, our bodies in a tangled heap, and I feel as if I can't get any closer to her. Holding her as tightly as I can, I kiss her bottom lip before looking deep into her eyes.

"Much better, yes?" I ask even though I can see it all over her face.

I rocked her world.

She smiles as she nods. "So much better," she whispers as she nuzzles her nose into my neck. "When can we do it again?"

I chuckle against her ear as I place a kiss there. "Gonna have to give me a bit."

She giggles before pulling back to look at me. "Can I ask you something?"

I nod. "Anything."

"Does it feel different without a condom? I heard it did."

I shrug. "I don't know; I've never done it without one."

"Oh," she says, her brows coming in. She then looks at me, moving her fingers down my throat. "How many people have you been with?"

I bite my lip as I hold her gaze. "Do you really want to know?"

"Yeah, I think I do."

Swallowing loudly, I think for a moment. I don't want to answer her, but I also won't lie. Sucking in a deep breath, I meet her gaze and answer, "Seventeen, now eighteen."

When she looks away, I don't know what to say. Maybe I should have lied? "I'm sorr—"

She shakes her head, meeting my gaze again. "Don't apologize. That was your life before me. Now though, I'm it," she says with a wink.

I grin at her, holding her face in my hands. "You're fuckin' right."

Her face reddens a bit as she holds my gaze. "You are my first and my last. I like that."

"Me too," I agree, and I can't express how much I actually do like that. There is something special about my being her one and only. Knowing that I'll be the only one who's ever been in her body, to make her come, and have my name fall from her swollen lips. She is completely and utterly mine, on every single level there is. There is something very frightening about that too. Will I be enough? When she starts to dust her lips along my jaw, she pulls back, biting her lip before she grins at me.

"Wanna go take a shower, maybe we can start something in there? I really want you."

I like the way she thinks and even more that she wants more of me. The question from before quickly evaporates from my brain. I have nothing to worry about; I am enough for her. Dropping my lips to hers, I hold her gaze.

I'm not saying I want to kiss her, because I always do, but I want her to see in my eyes how much I love her. Her sexy grin falls, replaced with a sweet one as her fingers tangle in my hair. Our love is suffocating, but I'll die a happy man if she is the last I'll see.

She's waiting for an answer, and I have no problem doing what she asks. Kissing her quickly, I grin before saying, "Yeah, let's go."

twenty-one
Amberlyn

For the last two weeks, the only time we've gotten out of bed is when we have to go to work. I love it. I do. Being wrapped in Declan's arms, completely lost in the love he provides me with is just amazing, really, but something is bothering me.

I don't feel like we are adults.

I feel like we should be making a home for us. Making dinner—it's delivered at six every night or we go eat with his parents, doing laundry—again, done for me and delivered by noon the next day, and cleaning—done for me. I can't decorate because the house is already decorated! The only thing I do around here is have sex, read, or watch TV with my fiancé. I mean, don't get me wrong, it's great, but I kinda feel as if we are kids, hiding out in his room from his parents.

But we can't even hide well.

I swear that Mrs. O'Callaghan has a book with all the reasons to come to talk to me and Declan. Let it be a subject that deals with the wedding, the distillery, tea time, or anything that comes to mind, she is knocking on our door. It's insane and is honestly driving me up the wall. What bothers me the most is that Declan seems to be completely satisfied with everything. I know that he has lived his whole life only working when it comes to the distillery, but I've worked for everything I've wanted my whole life, and I feel like I'm a blob. Living off him almost.

It's a scary feeling, and every time I want to bring it up to Declan, something comes up or his mom knocks on the damn door!

And right on cue, there is a knock on the door as I pull my blouse on, buttoning the top button. I flash him a dark look and he shrugs.

"Yeah?"

The door opens and she comes in, a little grin on her face. "Just checking to see if yous were ready to go."

We are going to an elementary school today to give book bags full of supplies for all one hundred kids. I am superexcited about it, but I kinda wish it were only Declan and me going.

"Yeah, Ma, we are getting ready now. Be down in a few."

"Okay!" she says as she flutters away, shutting the door behind her. Looking over at Declan, I see he's laughing quietly.

"It isn't funny," I snap at him, and he smiles.

"I know but still. You're cute with that little cross face of yours."

"Watch out, buddy, before it's directed at you," I warn, and he shakes his head, still chuckling.

"I just don't get it. She finds any reason to come up here. I think she is realizing that I've grown up, or at least that's what my da says. She doesn't do this shite to Lena."

I didn't think of it that way, and I can understand the realization of your son being a man, but still, it's annoying. "That's fine and dandy but, Declan, we are hardly ever alone! It's driving me up the wall," I say, way sharper than I intended.

His brows come in as his hands go to his khaki-clad waist. "What would you have me do, then? Ask her not to come up here?"

"That would be a start. Or maybe, get our own place. I just don't—"

And another knock comes at the fucking door!

Clamping my mouth shut, I glare as he reaches for the door. "Ma?"

"Sorry, I forgot to tell you to make sure you wear blue with your O'Callaghan pin. Oh! You have it on. Here is Amberlyn's. She may not be an O'Callaghan officially, but I feel she is."

I roll my eyes. I want to believe this woman is genuine, but come on. She's probably sitting outside the door, snickering that we are fighting.

"Thanks, Ma, we will be down in a few," he says quickly before shutting the door and then looking back at me. Coming toward me, he reaches out with one arm, snaking it around me to pull me to him. As he looks deep into my eyes, all my anger washes away as his mouth pulls up at one side. "Don't be upset with me."

"I'm not," I say, fingering the lapel of his shirt. "I just don't feel like we are adults. Everything is done for us."

He chuckles. "Because that's my life, Amberlyn. You've worked most of your life for what you've wanted. You've been through some hard stuff. Embrace this. It's your life now. People are paid to make sure we are taken care of so we can focus on each other. What more could you ask for?"

"To cook my own dinner, maybe? Or do my own laundry? I feel like a blob, Declan!"

He smiles, letting me go to pin the crest of his family on my shirt. It's a white pin with an armored helmet with green flourish coming out of it and a stallion underneath it. I don't know why, but the butterflies in my gut go crazy as he runs his finger along the pin before meeting my regard. "You're not a blob, Amberlyn, you're an O'Callaghan. My soon-to-be wife. This is how our life is. We don't do those things you mentioned; we have people who do and make good money doing it. For the time being, all you have to worry about is loving me, going to school, and working at the pub. After we get married, I'm sure you'll fall right into place."

"Fall into place? What do you mean?"

His brows come together as he holds me close. "That my ma will leave us be and that you won't worry about cooking your own dinner or mine. You'll embrace this because this is what we are."

"You don't want more?"

"More? No," he says, laughing. "I don't want to do laundry or yard work. I have you and the distillery and one day, our children. Let our staff be responsible for all that mundane stuff."

"Wow," I say, shaking my head and backing out of his embrace.

Reaching for my jacket, I put it on as he asks, "Wow, what?"

Looking back at his confused face, I hate that I think what I do, but how can I not?

"This is the first time I've ever thought of you to be a snob."

He looks at me like I've hit him. "A snob?"

"Yeah. Mundane stuff? That's all I did when I was growing up, caring for my sick mother. It isn't mundane. It's what adults do!"

His confusion leaves his beautiful face, and compassion replaces it as he nods. "I'm sorry, that was rude of me."

I shake my head, anger still coursing through my body. "It's fine. Let's go, your mom and dad are waiting."

I go to leave, but he stops me, wrapping his arm around my waist and cupping my face so that look at him. "Declan—" I say, but before I can finish my sentence, he is shaking his head.

"Amberlyn, it isn't fine. I can tell you are still upset, and please allow me to apologize."

"I accept your apology," I say, and I do, but it doesn't mean that I'm not still upset over it.

"Sure ya do, but let me explain," he says, still not letting me go. Reluctantly,

I look up at him, and I know he sees the fire in my eyes. It isn't okay what he said. Setting me with a look, he goes on, "This is how I was brought up. A silver spoon in my mouth, and thankfully, I don't have to live any other way. If ya want to do dinner, fine, I'll make arrangements for you to cook when ya want to. Want to do the laundry? I'll have a washer and dryer put up here. Anything you want, you tell me and I'll make happen."

He is too good to me, but he isn't listening to me. That's not what I want. I mean, yeah it is, but I want more. "I want our own place. Somewhere where we can be alone and not worry about someone waiting on us hand and foot. Or your mother walking in on us."

I know he doesn't want that. I can see it in his eyes, but he nods his head anyway. "I've been here my own life. I had plans to carry ya over that threshold, to bring our babies home here and to grow old here. Me and you."

"I can understand that, and I want those things too, minus this house."

I can see the gears moving in his head as his eyes stay trained on mine. Letting out a long breath, he asks, "Can you give me till the wedding? If by then you still want that, then I'll make the arrangements."

That is only two months away.

Can I last that long? Maybe I'll start to like it. This way he lives. Or, I'll drive myself completely insane. I know I will put up with it because I love him.

"Yeah, I can wait."

"Grand, love, thank you. C'mere," he says, bringing me to him for a long, lusty kiss. The issue is still there, like a big fat elephant in the room, but at least we've come to a compromise.

One I can live with.

Once in the car—which is basically a limo—I lean on Declan's arm as we drive through the country to the school that is outside of Mayo. It's almost an hour away, and I am dreading the trip. I'm excited to get there, but being stuck in the car with Mrs. O'Callaghan means that I will not get a word in edgewise. I guess I could nap, but as soon as I close my eyes, she starts to talk to me.

"Amberlyn, honey, did you approve the seating chart?"

Opening my eyes, I look at Declan, confused. "Did we do that?"

He smiles as he nods. "Yeah, Ma, we did."

"Grand," she says with a nod, but then she lets out a sigh. "I hate that we have to do this today. I have my whole day planned doing wedding things."

"I'm sure the wedding won't suffer," I say with a smile. "We will all be there, bells and whistles, no matter what. These kids won't have school supplies without our help."

An awkward silence falls as Lena nods. "She's right, Ma, the wedding isn't tomorrow. Let's enjoy helpin' the community, yeah?"

Folding her hands, Mrs. O'Callaghan makes a face like something stinks and nods. "Yeah, sure."

Declan looks over at me and kisses my nose. "Not mad still, are ya?" he asks in a whisper.

I shake my head. "No, not at all."

"Grand."

"What's wrong? Did I do something?"

I want to roll my eyes, scream at her to stay out of our business, but I know that would be frowned upon. Plus Declan's dad still scares me, and he is staring at me as Declan shakes his head.

"No, Ma. Amberlyn isn't used to having everything done for her. It's all an adjustment."

"It is," Mr. O'Callaghan says with a smile. "Which is why we usually only marry people like us."

That was rude, right? I feel like that was rude. Looking at Declan in disbelief, I see he is rolling his eyes. "And most of the time, they aren't really happy, yeah?"

I notice Lena look away from Micah, biting her lips as his parents glare.

"I'm marrying for love. True, perfect love. She'll adjust," Declan says, wrapping an arm around me.

"I didn't mean to offend you, son," his father backtracks, but Declan shakes his head.

"But ya did and you probably offended her. Let's drop it, yes? This is supposed to be a good day of helping people who don't have the advantages we do."

That shuts everyone up, and I am impressed with how Declan holds himself. He was so shy before, but now, he is so noble. I've enjoyed watching him grow over the last couple months, and I like to think I've helped get him to the man he is.

My future husband.

As everyone talks about whatever they do, Declan and I cuddle into each other, playing with each other's fingers and just enjoying being near each other. It never gets old, the feeling of him near me. I crave it, the nearness of him, making me feel complete. It's a beautiful feeling, and I know it's one that my mother would want me to have.

Smiling, I realize something. "I haven't had that dream of my mom in a while," I whisper to him and he nods.

"I know. I don't go to sleep until I know you are asleep, not dreaming. You've been quiet."

"So you stalk my sleep, weirdo," I tease and he laughs.

"I don't want you to sleep poorly. I worry, ya know."

"I know; it's sweet," I say, kissing him. "But yeah, I miss her."

He gathers me in his arms, kissing my jaw. "I know, I'm sorry. I wish I could make it better."

"Me too," I admit. "But I doubt anything can."

"Yeah," he agrees, kissing me again.

"But thank you for trying," I add quickly and he smiles.

"Always, *mo stór*, always."

twenty-two
Amberlyn

When we arrive at the school, I am bouncing in my seat against Declan. I am so excited to get out and do this. I love kids, and knowing that I am helping make sure they have a good school year is very rewarding. Hopping out of the car first, I grin as a very tall blond-headed lady comes toward us, matching my grin. She is huge, almost the same height as Declan, and soon I'm realizing her grin isn't for me, but for him.

"Mr. and Mrs. O'Callaghan, so good to have you again," she says in her thick Irish brogue. We all shake hands, and Declan introduces me after giving her a tight hug.

"Is this your bride-to-be?" she asks with a grin.

Declan grins. "It is. Amberlyn, this is my friend Amy. We grew up together."

She sends me a full grin. "We did. I've been waitin' years for Dec to get married. Too bad he ain't my type, huh?"

They both laugh at this, and I feel as if it is an inside joke. They have a very easy demeanor to them; it's refreshing to see Declan like that with someone else other than me. I'm surprised I don't feel the least bit jealous either since Amy is a very pretty girl. Huge, but pretty.

I smile as I hold my hand out, taking hers. "It's wonderful to meet you. I'm excited to marry him."

"I think ya both are!" she says, giving me a side hug, and I don't pull away. She's very easy to like. "Okay, well, let's go. The kids are excited for all their new stuff."

"I am excited too," I exclaim, but I notice that other than Declan, everyone else does not look very excited.

That soon changes once we get inside with all the book bags. Kids are everywhere, and it's so much fun passing the bags out to watch them tear them open to see what's inside. For the first time, I see a true smile on Mr. and Mrs. O'Callaghan's faces as they suit the kids up and listen as they talk of whatever they are thinking of. It's a lot of fun and I can't contain my excitement. Lying on the floor with three kindergarteners, I feel so amazing. This is what I want to do. I want to be a teacher. While a part of me wants to work with high school kids, it would be just as great to work with these sweet-faced little kiddos.

Either way, I want to teach, and I want to have a whole bunch of my own kids. I was an only child because my mom and dad were worried they couldn't afford me, so why would they have more? It was a tough decision, they told me, because they loved having me so much, but I respect their decision. Plus, I enjoyed being spoiled by my parents, though I did miss having a sister or brother. Thankfully, I have Fiona now, but I plan on having a bunch, at least two, maybe four, tops.

Looking across the room, I find Declan on a play couch with a tea hat on as two little girls clank their teacups with his. He has this big, beautiful grin on his face as he plays animatedly with the sweet girls. As he meets my gaze, his grin grows surprisingly large and I smile. He is going to be a great dad. I chose well. When I blow him a kiss, the little kids I'm lying with all let out groans of disgust before we all dissolve in laughter. And soon I'm rolling on the floor like I am a five-year-old too.

Soon it's time to go to another classroom, and for the next two hours, we go to each classroom, playing and visiting with each class. It's so much fun, and at one point, I have to push my emotions down to keep from crying. All the kids are obviously not from money or else we wouldn't be here, but I didn't realize how bad off they are until now. Some don't even have matching shoes on or clothes. I want to take them all home, but I'm sure that couldn't happen. But there has to be something more we can do.

"We should do a clothing drive next," I say to Declan as we head to the next classroom. "Or bring jackets and shoes. I can order a whole bunch from Target and Walmart back in the states."

He nods. "Yeah, we will set it up."

"That can cost a lot," Mr. O'Callaghan says and I nod.

"Maybe, but I'm sure we can make it happen."

"Yeah, maybe we can use the money from your pub job, yeah?" he says, and I don't miss the acid in his voice.

Setting him with a look, I cross my arms as I say, "Yeah, I have no problem using my own money for it."

"We'll talk later, yeah?" Declan says, wrapping his arm around my shoulders.

I smile sweetly at him, but I don't miss the look of annoyance his dad sends me as we reach the next room. While I want to get on the floor and play, Amy stops me at the door with a friendly grin.

"You are really great with kids," she says, crossing her arms and leaning against the door jamb as Declan and his family pass out book bags. "Declan chose well in ya."

"Thank you."

"You'll make a great ma."

"I hope to," I say, my cheeks burning a bit. "I also want to be a teacher though."

"Oh, really?"

"Yeah, maybe high school, teach literature or something along those lines. I'd love to be a librarian, read all day to the kids."

She smiles as she nods. "I wish we had that here."

Whipping my head to her, my brows come up. "What do you mean? You don't have a library here?"

She shakes her head. "No, this school is new. They just built it, but they ran out of money along the way. They had to choose between the library and a gym. They went with a gym and said to put books in each classroom."

"You're kidding me," I say, completely stunned. "Can they even do that?"

She shrugs. "I guess so since they did. Someone said that they'll come back once the funds are raised, but I don't see that happening anytime soon."

"That's insane."

"It is," she agrees. "But that's the age we live in. Money rules everything. I see our after-school activities going once we run out of funding for the teachers or equipment. It's a hard business, this education. The kids you wanna help, you can't, and they get lost in the system, when all they need is some love and help along the way. It's heartbreaking, but at the same time, there are times I can help and it works, ya know?" With a determined nod, she says, "We'll get our library, and then maybe we can hire ya as our librarian, yeah?"

I smile, my heart breaking for everyone in this school. "I would be honored to."

"That is if they let ya out of the estate to do more than just make babies and be Declan's arm candy."

I don't think she means to offend me, but I suspect my face gives me away. She quickly backtracks, saying, "That came off a bit rude. I didn't mean to offend ya."

"No, it's fine. Apparently everyone has the same idea of what I am going to do once Declan and I are married, but the truth is, it isn't like that. He is very sweet and cares what I want. We decide together what we will do. It's really great, and I know he'd support me to work as a librarian."

She nods as she looks across the room, smiling when her gaze settles on Declan. "He really is," she agrees in almost a whisper. Looking back at me, she says, "I came out to him first. He thought I was in love with him, but really, I wanted to be like him. He was strong, popular, and a great guy all around. When he tried to kiss me once, I quickly told him I liked girls and wanted to be his mate instead of his girl. It was funny; we laugh now, but then, it was scary. He has cared for me no matter what, even when my family wasn't supportive or even his." She clears her throat, and I can't believe how hard my heart is pounding in my chest for this woman I've just met. "So yeah, I get what ya mean and know that you're right. He would support ya no matter what. The thing ya might have an issue with is that family of his."

Noticing where she is looking, I nod. "Yeah, they've been somewhat of a problem, but we are considering getting our own place."

When she laughs, I look at her, surprised. "He isn't going to leave that house. He was born there, he's gonna die there with his bride and kids living there too."

I bite the inside of my cheek. "So you're saying I'm stuck."

"I mean, he loves ya, and he never expected to find someone he would love when he got married. He was surrounded by so many fake birds, ones out for his money, and now that he has found someone who loves him for him, he might change his ideas a bit. But I wouldn't hold yer breath."

"That does worry me because I can't stand it there."

She laughs. "Who could, but them? Even Micah doesn't like it there. Every chance he gets to leave, he does, but then Lena doesn't really love him neither. She puts on a good front, but he isn't what her heart wants. She wanted the wanker you're testifying against."

Again I whip my head toward her in complete and utter shock. "What?"

"Oh yeah, she loved him something insane, but once he raped her—and he did it because that girl was saving herself for marriage and he couldn't take it— it all went downhill. Ya don't come back from the person ya first love, especially when they hurt ya the way Casey did. He not only raped her, but he broke her heart by not being the man she thought he was."

"Oh my gosh," I say, shaking my head as I watch Lena and Micah interact.

"But she'll marry him because it's what her parents think is right, and she'll grow to love him. Hell, she may by now, but I know when she first agreed to marry him, she didn't."

"Wow," I say, still in disbelief. "She's such a sweet girl."

"Yeah, and Micah is twenty times the man that Casey is. Which, by the way, don't hold back. Make sure that wanker stays locked up, yeah?"

Meeting her gaze again, I bite the inside of my cheek. I want Casey to pay for his crimes, and I've already decided he will, but all I keep seeing is his ma crippled in her bed, thanking me and Aunt Shelia over and over again for paying for her housing. I didn't tell her who I was, but when I walked out, I considered not testifying against Casey so he could be there for his mom. But then, how is that fair? He has to pay for his mistakes. He does. That's all there is to it.

"Yeah, he will," I say as Declan comes toward me, smiling as he wraps his arm around me.

"Gossiping with my lady, yeah, Amy?"

She laughs as she waves him off. "I don't gossip."

He laughs along with her. "Ya daft cow! Don't lie to my face."

That has them laughing harder as I stand there completely confused since being called a cow isn't very nice, but I chuckle along, not to be left out.

"Whatever. Hush you," she says, shaking her head. "But for real. I like her a lot."

Declan grins as he holds me close. "She's amazing, yeah?"

"Perfect for ya."

We share a smile, and I can see the love shining in his eyes. He really is the best thing that ever happened to me.

Soon it's time to leave, and as we hug Amy, I'm sad to go. I hug her once more as she says, "When I get that library, I'll be calling ya."

"And I'll report the day it opens," I say as we part and Declan takes my hand. We head to the car and I lean into him, feeling so empowered by today. Which is good. I need something to make me feel good. The trial is starting soon and I am dreading it, but when Declan's lips press into my temple, I know that it is all going to be okay.

Turning my face, I press my lips to his and smile. "Can I ask you something?" I say as we take our seats next to his dad.

"Of course."

"I want to buy a library for the school."

A grin pulls at his lips as he cuddles me into his arms. Before he can answer though, his dad says, "First clothes for these kids, now a library? Ya said she wasn't after ya money, Declan."

"I'm not," I answer, but Declan holds a hand up to me, stopping any further words.

"If she were asking for me to buy her cars, clothes, and stuff, then yeah, she'd be after my money. But wanting to help people is different," he says very sternly. "So please, don't disrespect her like that."

His father doesn't say anything, but I can see in his eyes that he is not happy. "I apologize."

"Thank you," Declan says before glancing back at me. He then holds my face as he strokes my lip with his thumb. "Ya want a library for the school?"

I nod. "I do. Don't you think it would be great for them?"

"I do, and when Amy told me, I thought it."

"Really?"

"I did."

"I thought so too," Lena adds. "Poor kids."

"It could cost a lot though," Mrs. O'Callaghan says with a shake of her head. "But I do agree, they need a place to dedicate to the written word."

"They do," I say. "It would be so beautiful to do."

"Then we will build one," Declan says with a nod. "In your ma's name too."

Tears spring to my eyes as I fight to breathe. I never thought to do it for my mom, but how genius is that? It would be perfect. As I reach for him, a stray tear runs down my face and I can only breathe his name, "Declan."

"Let's just say it's an early wedding gift, yeah?"

If that is my wedding gift, then I don't know what he'll give me when we are old and gray, celebrating our fiftieth anniversary. Nothing I can say would remotely sum up how I feel for this man or how he has just made my lifetime. He said that he doesn't know how to make losing my mom easier to cope with, but giving me a library for her is one way to do it. He is the most amazing person on earth, and by some grace of God, he is mine. Dealing with his shitty family I can live with as long as I get to wake up to this gorgeous, generous man. Not everyone would think to include their fiancée's deceased mother in something they want, but Declan did. Holding him tight to me, I nod my head as I meet his gaze. Then with a watery smile, I agree in a whisper, "Thank you."

twenty-three
Declan

I don't like seeing her up there.

It gives me the chills and has my heart pumping in my chest.

I already went, already told my side. Of course, the defense tried to attack me, saying that I had some kind of hatred toward the wanker. I didn't lie either. I told the truth, saying, yeah, I hated him, but he still had no right to try to shoot me or get Amberlyn instead. After I said that, they backed off a bit, and I didn't even try to hide my disgust for him. I looked him right in the eyes, and he was the one to look away, like the fucking coward he is. But Lena won't look at him. Her eyes are trained on her hands and her voice is soft. It's killing me.

When Amberlyn's hand slides into mine, her fingers lacing with my own, I look over at her to see that she is watching intently too as the defense asks Lena questions. Questions that I know are hard for her. You can read it all over her. She is tense in position; she's almost pale and on the brink of tears. I want to rush up there, cover her with my body, and shield her from the questions she thought she'd never have to answer again, but I can't. This has to happen and then Amberlyn will go next.

If it's this hard seeing my sister up there, I don't know how I'll handle the love of my life.

Beside me, my ma is tense. She is picking at her nails, and I can hear her labored breathing. My da is the same, all of us so nervous and scared for the woman whom we see as our sweet little girl. A girl that that fucker ruined.

"So you had a relationship with Mr. Burke, yes?"

Lena swallows loudly as she nods. "Yes."

"You were in love?"

"I was with him, but not the other way around."

"Why do you say that?" the defense attorney asks. He is a small man, kinda round, but very young. I thought I had recognized him but wasn't sure. Maybe I saw him on the telly or something. Either way, I hate him. I don't like the way he is talking to my sister or the way he spoke to me. He's an arse.

"Because he never told me so."

He nods as he leans on the stand. "You were fifteen when you started dating Mr. Burke? He was eighteen?"

"Yes."

"So is it easy to say that he didn't tell you, though very much felt those feelings, but he was worried since you were so young?"

"Bullshite," I mutter as Lena shakes her head.

"No, I told him countless times and he just nodded, saying one day he'd feel the same."

"But still, he did tell your father he loved you."

"Yeah, so that we could marry, but he never told me," she says, finally looking up at the man. "He was after my money and broke my heart in the process."

"Is there proof of that?" he asks sharply, and I want to rip his fuckin' face off.

"Yes."

My brows come together as I wait for the proof. I wasn't aware there was. "Please enlighten me, because I've read over your file many times, Ms. O'Callaghan, and I haven't seen anything that gives credence to that statement."

"Did you read in the file where I was left outside my gate with bruises up my thighs, my dress ripped, and my body covered in bite marks?"

An eerie silence falls over the courtroom, and my ma quickly takes my hand as my eyes well up with tears. Like I had so long ago, I want nothing more than to hop up and beat the shit out of that fuckin arse. He broke my sister, raped her, and then almost killed my love. How dare he have the right to stand trial to walk in this world? It almost doesn't seem fair.

"I did read that."

"Well, what it doesn't say in that file is that before that, I asked him if he loved me. He told me no. I asked him why did he tell my da that then, and he said because he wanted to marry me before someone else could. I didn't understand; I was young and stupid. I fell for his charm, but then he said not to worry my pretty head about it anymore." Her eyes start to fill with tears, and I close my eyes to hide the view I see. But I can still hear. I wish I couldn't, but her words rattle my soul as she goes on. "That my da wouldn't let us marry, so we'd just have fun. Again, I didn't understand, and he started to take my shirt off. I said no, that I was waiting for marriage. So he said, such a child's answer, but I understand. Then he said, let's drink. I didn't want to seem like a child like he said. I wanted to be a woman, one he would love, so I drank. I got so pissed that I couldn't even have told ya my name. I passed out, and when I woke up, I was almost frozen and hurt everywhere," she cries, her tears falling in streams. "You've apparently read all this. So please, explain to me how he loved me? I was his responsibility that night, and he basically left me to die after getting me drunk and then raping me. If that's love, then I want none of it."

The defense attorney turns from her and heads to the table where Casey sits. Lena looks out at us, and I manage a weak smile to show that I am here, but I know it doesn't help. When she looks to Micah, I hope that he can comfort her, but I find that he is playing a game on his phone. Letting go of my ma's hand, I reach over Amberlyn, smacking the phone out of his hand. He looks up, shocked, and I glare.

"My sister is up there, going through something no one should have to live through twice, and you're playing on yer fucking phone?" I whisper loudly.

His eyes are wide and his mouth is moving, but no words are leaving his lips. Sputtering, he reaches down for his phone, muttering an apology before tucking it back in his pocket. Rolling my eyes, I sit up as the attorney turns to look at my baby sister.

"It's okay," Amberlyn whispers in my ear, kissing the lobe. "She's so strong, Declan. She has this."

I want to believe her, but my sister looks so frail, so little. Even though she is dressed like a million bucks, not a hair out of place, she still looks like a baby. My wee sister.

"You were there with Mr. Burke the night he allegedly shot Ms. Amberlyn Reilly."

"He didn't allegedly shoot her. He did."

"That hasn't been determined yet."

"Only because Amberlyn hasn't been up here. She has the scar from where she saved my brother."

I feel Amberlyn move, and I look over to where she is rubbing the spot above her heart. Where a thick scar sits. It's a constant reminder of what happened, something that has been hard to let go of. It still hurts when I see it. I just want to kiss it away or take it off and put it on me. She is forever scarred, and when I said that to her the other night, she told me it was a badge of honor. It was a sweet way to think of it, but I wish she didn't have to wear it.

"Why did she 'save' your brother? Because he physically and mentally abused Mr. Burke?" he says, and my annoyance grows quickly.

"No, Declan never abused him in any way. They don't like each other, with good reason. Casey gave more than he took."

"Okay, can you please explain to me what happened again?"

"I already did for the prosecution."

"I know, but I want to ask some questions and I want to hear it again."

Sucking in a deep breath, Lena lets it out before looking back down at her hands. "He texted me. First time in years and it said that he had to speak to me. Told me where he was and I went. Like an idiot, but I did—"

"Why?"

"I don't know."

"Because you still love him?" he supplies.

She scoffs. "Not in the least."

"So you didn't tell him you still loved him out there in the alley?"

Her brows come together as my heart starts to pound louder. "No, I did not. I told him I care for him and probably always will, but I don't love him."

"Caring for someone is a form of love," he states, and Lena looks up, glaring.

"Sure it is, but so is wanting to kill someone. So are you stating that Casey Burke loves my brother, but he could never love me?"

"She's a spitfire," Amberlyn observes, her face breaking into a grin. "She's giving him a run for his money."

"That's not what I'm implying at all."

"Okay, then please don't imply that I still love the guy who raped me and almost killed my brother, but instead shot my future sister-in-law."

Looking down, I can see the frustration on the attorney's face. Amberlyn is right; Lena is driving him mad.

"So you went outside in the alley with him?"

"Yes, and he asked me if I still loved him. I said no, that I care for him and his ma. He asked again, and I told him no, that I don't feel anything for him. I'm getting married next summer; my fiancé is the only one I love," she pauses, shaking her head before glancing up at the attorney. "He became very upset, yelling at me, telling me to tell my da to back off since my da was trying to pay him to leave due to the fact he causes havoc everywhere he goes. He couldn't leave though because of his ma, and I understood. But I wasn't going to tell my da to stop because I believed he needed to pay for what he did to me or leave me be."

"But he had left you alone. He hadn't contacted you in years."

"No, he hadn't, but when he saw me out, he made it a point to come to me, talking to me about how we should be together and all. But each time I shot him down."

The attorney bites his lip before waving her along. "Please continue."

"My brother Declan came out with his fiancée, and then everything went mad. They were yelling at each other for Casey to get away from me, and Casey was accusing Declan of ruining his life, and then the gun was pulled. It was his grandda's; I had gone out to the field with him once and watched him fire it. It has a very noticeable big stag on the side of the handle. I shouted for him to put it down, but he didn't. He shot it off, and I screamed as Amberlyn jumped in front of the bullet, taking it above her heart. He intended to shoot my brother; I saw it with my own two eyes."

The attorney pinches his nose before turning to the table. "That's all I have."

"Judge, permission to reexamine Ms. O'Callaghan please?" the prosecution lawyer asks, and the judge nods as the lawyer rises up, heading toward Lena.

"With your two eyes, ya said?"

She nods. "Yes."

"So Casey Burke shot Amberlyn Reilly but was aiming for your brother, Declan. Do you think he wanted to kill him?"

She looks out at me, and I hold her gaze as she sucks in a deep breath. I watch then as she looks dead-on at Casey and nods her head. "Without a shadow of doubt, Casey Burke wanted to kill my brother. I could see it in his eyes."

"See what?"

"The rage. The hatred. He hates us, and his last words before he pulled the trigger were, 'I'm going to ruin your life, like ya have mine' and then he shot."

"Do you think he was in his right mind?"

"Yes, I do."

"So his insanity plea—"

"Is him trying to cover up his mistakes. He does that a lot."

The prosecution lawyer nods his head. "Thank you, Ms. O'Callaghan."

And I know we have it in the bag. As long as Amberlyn does as well as Lena has.

The prosecution lawyer doesn't sit down as Lena comes down, heading toward us. Instead, he reads from his paper and says, "Your honor, I call to the stand Ms. Amberlyn Reilly."

She looks at me and smiles before my lips meet hers. Pulling back, I smile as she cups my face and heads up to the stand. Taking her spot is Lena, and I wrap my arm around her, kissing her temple.

"I love you," she whispers and I smile.

"I love ya more," I answer, holding her tight to me. I notice that Micah hasn't moved an inch and hasn't even tried to hold her hand as Amberlyn is sworn in. Once she is seated, I listen as she replays the night over again. Her story equals up to Lena's, and I'm not surprised when she tells all.

"Declan tried to take me home to hide the fact that he was embarrassed that his dad had just informed me of his deadline of marriage. That's why we went out the side door. We were in the middle of our argument when we heard Lena and Casey arguing too."

She continues to tell how it all went on and my heart just beats for her. She is so strong, sitting up there completely confident as she tells her story. She is dressed in a pantsuit, her hair in a high bun, looking exceptionally beautiful.

"So you are sure he meant to shoot Declan and not you?"

"Yes, he aimed right for him, and I couldn't let him kill Declan. He has so much to live for. I only have him to live for, so I did what any other girl in love would do. I protected my man."

A collective aww goes through the courtroom as the lawyer nods. "Thank you, Ms. Reilly."

She smiles a thanks as the defense lawyer stands. "You dated Mr. Burke, yes?"

"Briefly."

"Why didn't it work out?"

"Because I was in love with Declan."

"So Declan stole you from him?"

Amberlyn laughs, and I can't hide my grin. "If you know anything about Declan, you would know he is very honorable and would never steal someone's girlfriend. He may have wanted to, but Declan wouldn't do that. He instead stood to the side and told me that he'd wait. Since I didn't feel what I felt with Declan when I was with Casey, I told Casey I couldn't see him anymore. Casey proceeded to get very angry and put his hands on me, forcing me to kiss him. I had to fight him off and knew that I would never ever trust him again. He tried to speak to me many times after that, but I always tried to get away. He doesn't do well with rejection, I've noticed."

That must have derailed the lawyer because he turns, reaching for a piece of paper, his brows drawn together.

"Counselor?" the judge asks and the lawyer turns, nodding his head.

"Excuse me," he says before sitting down. "That's all I have."

"Judge, can I please reexamine Ms. Reilly?" the prosecution lawyer asks and again the judge agrees as he rises up, heading to Amberlyn.

"I neglected to ask you the same question I did Ms. O'Callaghan," he says with apology in his voice. "Do you think Mr. Burke was in his right mind when he pulled the trigger?"

"Yes. He was angry, but he knew what he was doing."

"Do you forgive him?"

Amberlyn looks up and I smile. She is such a beautiful soul. "Yes, I do."

The room collectively gasps, and some people start to whisper as the lawyer goes on. "Should the jury forgive his crime?"

She then shakes her head. "No. He needs to pay for the pain he has caused me and my family. Everyone was so distraught 'cause I could have died. While he may not have meant to shoot me, he did mean to shoot my fiancé and ultimately kill him. I, for one, do not want that kind of person walking the same streets I do, or even drinking at the pub I work at."

"Thank you, Ms. Reilly."

"Thank you," she says, and as she comes off the stand, I rise, waiting for her. When she reaches me, I pull her into my arms and press my lips to hers.

"I think I told ya once that my life would have no meaning without ya."

She grins as she holds to me tighter, her fingers biting into my shoulder blades. "Yeah, I think you did before you asked me to marry you."

"I did, and those words are still true. I love ya, Amberlyn."

"Good," she says with a wink. "Because I still and always will love you."

twenty-four
Amberlyn

*I*n the crook of Declan's arm, I listen as Mr. O'Callaghan boasts about how the trial went. It did go well, but I'm not going to lie and say it was easy. I was a wreck when Declan was up there and they were attacking him, basically saying he caused Casey to go off and try to kill him. Like the man he is though, he kept his cool and didn't falter at all. When Lena got up there, though, all his strength was gone. He was a nervous mess and I tried to comfort him, pointing out that Lena could hold her own, but the poor guy didn't see that. He saw that his sister was under scrutiny, reliving the horrible events she went through, and of course, he wanted to save her. Can't blame him though. I, too, wanted to pull her down and just hug her.

I just couldn't imagine.

I had such an easy life, shielded from all the bad people. But then again, while I didn't have to battle the demons Lena does, and even Declan does, I have my own. Stupid drunk drivers and cancer. Two things that I have no power getting rid of.

"That gobshite will go away, no doubt about it. Good show, yous did wonderfully," Mr. O'Callaghan says, sending us big, happy grins. I look toward Lena to find that she is looking out the window, completely ignoring her father's happiness.

"I loved the part where Amberlyn talked about your honor, so sweet."

"And true," I say, taking my gaze from Lena. "Everything I said was true."

"Still so beautiful!" she coos with a wave of her hand.

"So tomorrow, Burke gets on the stand—"

"Probably lie through his teeth," Declan adds and Mr. O'Callaghan nods.

"Of course, and then the jury decides. After today though, there is no way they wouldn't go in our favor."

I look out the window and let out a breath. I feel good about today. I told the truth and believe he should go to jail, but looking into his eyes really did gut me a bit. It was like he was reading his letter out loud to me, begging me not to testify, but I couldn't let him get away with this. His mom will be fine, and surely he won't do too long. Hopefully, time in jail will fix him, and he'll come out a good, upstanding citizen, meet a sweet girl, maybe have some kids, and grow old. I can only hope, but still, I feel bad for his mom.

Leaning on my shoulder, Declan kisses my cheek. "Ya okay?"

I nod. "Fine, just a lot."

"Yeah," he agrees, gathering me into his arms and kissing my cheek again. Cuddling into him, I look to where Lena is staring out the window, Micah silent beside her. Usually he is playing on his phone, but he hasn't touched it since Declan knocked it to the floor. Maybe he broke it?

When the car stops, the doors open and we file out. I assume we are heading inside, but Declan stops me, pulling me to him and in the other direction.

"Declan, honey, where are you off to?"

Glancing back his mom, he says, "We're gonna go on a walk, clear our heads a bit."

"Oh, you don't want to eat?"

He shakes his head but then looks to me. "Ya hungry?"

I shake my head. "A walk sounds great."

"Grand, we're good, Ma. Be back later."

Lena looks at us longingly, and I can't help but feel that she'd rather walk with us than go inside. Since I'm not sure why Declan wants to go for a walk, I don't say anything as she heads back inside while his mom says, "Okay, see ya later."

He puts his arm around me and we head out toward the lake, walking in a comfortable silence, the warm sun shining down on us. When we don't go where I thought we would, the dock, I look up at him.

"Where are we going?"

"Just walking," he explains as he holds me tighter. "You were amazing today, my love."

Wrapping my arms around his waist, I smile. "You too."

"I'm sorry ya had to get up there and do that. You shouldn't have been involved at all."

Rolling my eyes, I let him go and look up at him. "Even if I wouldn't have stepped in front of you and taken the bullet, I'd still have to testify because I saw what happened."

He shrugs. "Sure, but still. I wish none of this would have happened."

He hasn't said anything like this in a while, and I know it's because I told him to let it go. It was bound to come back up with the trial and all.

"It's not your fault."

"Eh, I don't know. I sometimes feel it is."

"It isn't," I remind him. "I made my own choice. Took my own risk to save the man I love."

He smiles down at me and nods. "Yeah, but I should be doing the saving, ya know?"

I grin back at him, wrapping my arms around him. "But you have. You have saved me in every way possible."

"How so?" he asks, confused.

"I could be a puddle of tears, doing nothing but crying and being sad because I'm an orphan," I say, holding his gaze. "But instead, I'm happy and I'm excited for my life. You bring out all the good in me."

"As you do for me," he answers, kissing my nose. "I do love ya."

"I love you too," I say back as we reach a hill that a large stone building sits on. "Oh wow," I gasp, taking in the beauty of it.

"Yeah, this is the old church that most of my ancestors got married in. It was built in 1790. Pretty, yeah?"

I nod as he leads me in through an entrance that I'm pretty sure had a door at one time. Everything is very old, but it has good bones; I feel like they could still hold a service here. It's beautiful, but the windows are gone and there is only one pew.

"Why doesn't it have windows and a door? It could still be used."

"Eh, no one has kept up with it. The only reason it isn't infested with animals and dirty is 'cause my ma has people to come clean it out every other month."

"Why, though?"

"She was born here."

"What?" I ask, my eyes wide.

"My ma's ma worked on the grounds and was pregnant but didn't want anyone to know because she'd gotten knocked up and wasn't married. So she worked all through her pregnancy, had every intention of leaving my ma in the church for someone to come save or something, but she looked into my ma's eyes and couldn't do it."

"Oh my goodness," I say, covering my mouth. "That's so crazy."

"Yeah, so she raised my ma the best she could, very poor, but my ma was and still is a very pretty lady. My grandma used to say she was born on this land because she was meant to rule it and more shite. She married my da and here we are."

I smile. "That's sweet that she keeps the church clean."

"Yeah, it makes sense. I come up here some, just to sit and to get back to me," he says, and then he falls into the pew, looking up at me. "After Lena was found, they couldn't locate me for hours 'cause I sat in here, crying and throwing myself a blaming party. It was bad, but I dusted myself off and went back, ready to stand by my sister."

I sit down next to him, taking his hand in mine. "You are the most amazing person I know, Declan," I say, kissing his palm.

"No," he says with a shake of his head. "Ya know yourself, right?"

I grin but shake my head. "I'm not that amazing."

"You're right," he says, cupping my face. "You're damn well spectacular, yeah?"

He kisses me as my heart just flies out of my chest and into the clouds. Wrapping my arms around his neck, deepening the kiss, I fall onto him. Holding me, he devours my mouth, both of us playing and enjoying the great splendor of kissing each other. When his hand goes up and under my shirt, I arch my back, wanting his hands on me. Trailing kisses down my throat, he nibbles at the valley of my breasts before slowly pulling away, looking at me with those intoxicating blue eyes.

Pushing my jacket down my arms, he takes my shirt off before kissing my neck again, my chest, and then very slowly trailing kisses along my bra. Tangling my fingers into his hair, I let my head fall back as my bra slips down my arms and his mouth is on my breast. Swirling his tongue and nibbling at my nipples, he has me crying out and arching into his mouth. Squeezing my eyes shut, I hold on to him with everything inside me as he slowly marks his mouth down my tummy to the button of my pants.

Pulling his head up, his eyes burn into mine as he stands, removing his jacket and then his pants along with his boxers.

"Take your pants off," he demands, and I don't question him or even protest. I stand up, pushing them down my legs along with my panties before standing bare-ass naked in front of my fiancé. A grin pulls at his lips as he reaches for me, cupping my breast, his eyes scalding as he drinks me in. "You're stunning, *mo stór*."

I'm breathless as he takes me into his arms, our mouths meeting in a hot embrace. I am humming with awareness of his hot, hard body against my soft one. His fingers dance along my skin, molding and kneading me as his mouth just drives me out of my damn mind. When he bends down a bit, taking me by the back of my thighs, I hold on as he lifts me, sitting himself down before bringing me down on his lap.

His dick presses against my belly, my wet center dripping for him as he continues to kiss me senseless. When his fingers find my wet spot, swirling his finger along my clit, I cry out against his mouth, riding against his finger, wanting my release. Holding me by the back of my neck, he kisses me intensely as he flicks my clit, sending me into space. Soon my body is trembling, shaking, and I'm sure I'm going to spontaneously combust.

This man gives me everything my body was missing before, and I have the rest of my life to get my fill of him.

Closing my eyes, I ride my orgasm as he nibbles down my neck, whispering how much he loves me. When he pulls back, I look at him through hooded eyes as he smiles.

"Love, can you reach my slacks? I don't want to move ya," he says softly, his hand molding my breast.

I look behind me and I'm sure I can reach them. Leaning back, him holding my hips, I take ahold of his pants, but as I'm about to come up, his mouth is on my vagina, and I go languid. He holds me and my head dangles as he sucks my clit into his mouth and I cry out, my heels digging into the pew.

"Oh God," I cry out, and I'm sure that is wrong on so many levels.

But I don't have time to think of that before I am flying on pretty little pink orgasm clouds, my body seizing up before I go completely limp, my vagina throbbing with want for this man. Pulling me back up by my arm, he takes my mouth with his before he takes his pants from me. I really don't know what happens next, but soon, he is lifting me and then I'm coming down onto him. He fills me completely, my whole body squeezing him as my fingers dig into his shoulders before he starts to move my hips, showing me how to ride him.

"There you go, my love. A little faster, yeah," he coaches in my ear, holding me tightly as I move my hips faster, his dick going in and out of me, deeper and deeper with each stroke. "Fuck yeah, love, yeah," he says, his fingers biting into the small of my back until he takes control. Or maybe loses it because he takes my hips and thrusts up into me, his body slapping into mine, his dick going so deep, it takes my breath away. Holding on the best I can, I cry out with each thrust, loving the feeling before he stills, gathering me close before he slowly thrusts inside me. When he stops, he squeezes his arms around me before nuzzling his nose into my neck.

I suck in deep breaths, trying to breathe, but I'm sure that won't even happen. He's taken it all. All of me. Every single bit. When he pulls his face out from my neck, he looks me deep in the eyes and smiles.

"Ya blow my mind, *mo stór*. Completely, ya know that?"

I smile back, running my finger down his shoulder to his elbow. "I don't even think I can breathe right now," I admit, and he laughs.

"But ya are," he says, pressing his lips to mine.

I get lost in his kisses. I don't have to think when I am kissing him. I can just vanish.

Pulling away, I cup his face, loving him with every fiber in my body. A grin pulls at his lips before he presses his lips to my chin. Still smiling, I ask, "Do you think we are going to hell for having sex in a church?"

He laughs, pressing another kiss to my bottom lip. "After that, I'd take a one-way ticket, as long as I get to do it again," he says before kissing me again. "And again," he whispers against my lips before kissing me once more. "And then some more. I can't get enough of ya, and I'm not going to try."

"Please don't," I beg as he lays me down on the pew, kissing down my throat. "I don't ever want you to try to."

twenty-five
Declan

ike we all knew he would, Casey fuckin' lied through his teeth.

With my fist clenched at my side, I hold Amberlyn's hand with the other as I listen to the complete bullshite that comes out that wanker's fuckin' mouth.

"I did love Lena, very much," he claims. "I never raped her. We didn't even lie down that night. I took what she said to heart; I'd figure out how to marry her another way. I dropped her off at the gate like I always did and drove off, like I usually did. The next thing I know, I'm being accused of raping her, and from then on the O'Callaghan family has had it out for me. Always putting me down, running my name through the mud, coming at me in public and trying to ruin me."

"Did you feel threatened?" the defense asked.

When a scared look comes over that fucker's face, I want to smack it off, especially when he claims, "Yeah, of course. They are rich. They have ways of making people disappear."

My da scoffs as I shake my head; even Lena rolls her eyes.

"Have they ever tried to have you disappear?"

He nods. "Yeah. Old man O'Callaghan has offered to pay me off many times. Told me to leave town or he'd open the case about Lena again. I'm innocent, but they keep on with it. No charges were ever pressed, so why they feel like I need to burn for that is beyond me."

"What happened that night you allegedly shot Amberlyn Reilly?"

He shakes his head and I want to laugh at his theatrics. It's downright pathetic. When the tears well up in his eyes, it takes everything out of me not to stand and call him on his bullshite. It's just completely insane!

"Fuckin' wanker," Kane says from behind me and I nod, completely disgusted by him.

"I didn't mean to hurt her. I love Amberlyn."

Amberlyn looks at me and I roll my eyes. Love? This bloke has a different notion of love.

"We dated and we were happy. She says that Declan didn't steal her from me, but he did. He swooped in, his money waving in her face, and she was a goner. Of course, she'd go for a rich guy, the damn prince of this county instead of a struggling artist."

Kane scoffs and I have to agree. This dude is out of his damn mind.

"I was heartbroken, distraught even. I tried to win her back, but she wasn't having it," he says before pausing to wipe his face. Sucking in a deep breath, he looks at his lawyer and with the most pathetic expression ever, he says, "I never stopped loving Lena, still do love her. I figured out I was using Amberlyn as a rebound, so I reached out for Lena and she came. We professed our love for each other, and we were gonna run off together, and then Declan comes out, telling me to go. And like Lena always does, she listens to her brother and is leaving me. Amberlyn is standing there, looking at me like I'm worthless, and something inside me snaps. I didn't even have control of myself. I would never try to kill someone. I would never do that. Never," he pleads with his hands up. "I don't even know what happened next. I woke up at home and then the police came, saying I shot a girl. I would never do that," he cries. And when he looks at Amberlyn, I swear, if looks could kill, he'd be dead. "I would never."

"But they say you did."

"I wasn't there. Mentally, it wasn't me. I was out of my mind," he cries, and then he just breaks down. Crying so damn hard that if I didn't know he was a full of shite bastard, I'd believe him. Looking at the jury, I see that some are wiping their tears, and I want to scream that they are dumb. He is playing them all. Wake up! He is a fuckin' liar!

"So you are the victim?"

"I am. I'm sick in the head from where they have ruined me," he pleads, and all of us are in disbelief.

Is this really happening? Handing him a box of tissues, the lawyer pats his shoulder before looking at the judge. "I have nothing more."

The prosecution lawyer stands automatically and tucks his hands in his pockets before looking over at Casey. He is excited about something, and you can tell that this isn't his first trial.

He is ready to pounce.

"Explain to me, Mr. Burke," he says and Casey looks up, his eyes red as he watches him. "You say that you were in love with Ms. O'Callaghan and Ms. Reilly, yes?"

"Yes. Lena is the best thing that ever happened to me."

"Hmm, why didn't you ever tell her that?"

"I did, all the time."

"So she's lying?"

"Yes, that what that family does. Lie and deceives."

"Hmm, that's mad because I've known this family a very long time. When they aren't working hard to make their whiskey great, they are helping the community. They have parties and invite everyone. They are generous. Last I heard, they are building a new library for Brighton Elementary. They also paid for your ma to be housed in the home, so I'm sorry, but I don't see them as being liars or even deceivers."

Casey's mouth drops at hearing about his ma, but he recovers quickly, shaking his head "Probably out of pity, to make them look good!"

"Hmm, maybe, but still," he mutters but then quickly starts another sentence, probably because the defense was about to object. "You said you don't remember pulling the gun out or even pulling the trigger, right?"

Casey looks up and something inside me tells me this is it. This is what the prosecution was excited about.

"No, I don't."

"Why did you have the gun? Your grandda's old pistol?"

"Um," Casey says, pausing. My da smacks my leg and Kane squeezes my shoulder. Amberlyn is beside me, sitting on the edge of her seat as we wait for him to answer. "Um, for protection, of course."

"Protection for what? It's not common to carry a gun in Mayo. I don't have one for sure, and I put bad guys in jail. It kind of makes people mad."

The courtroom laughs as Casey looks wildly at his lawyer. The prosecution stands in his line of sight, smiles, and asks again, "So please, tell me why you went to the O'Callaghan estate with a gun. Did you plan to use it?"

"No," he blurts out. "It was for protection. I forgot I even had it."

The prosecution doesn't say anything for a second, but then he puts his hands back in his pockets. "If it was for protection, what made you want to use it, do you think?"

"I don't know; it wasn't me."

"Hmm, but you said you forgot about it. Why do you think you pulled it out and shot an innocent girl?"

"I don't know."

"Could it be because you hate Declan O'Callaghan, and you didn't have the gun as protection from everyone else, but actually in case Declan came out so you could kill him? And wouldn't that mean your actions were premeditated? That you took the gun with the intention to do harm?"

"No, never," he says.

"Or maybe it was actually to kill Lena? Maybe with her out of the picture, all the rape accusations would be gone and you could live your life. Because, like I said, no one really carries guns in Mayo, so in order to carry one legally, it would have to be registered. Your grandda didn't have his gun registered because it was so old, so in turn, no one could trace it back to you. Am I correct?"

Whoa. I never thought of that. Looking at Lena, I can see her eyes filling with tears as she looks down at her lap. Amberlyn moves her hand into hers, and Lena gives her a watery smile.

"I didn't think he could do that. Any of this."

Amberlyn nods. "Me neither, but he did."

"Yeah," she says with a nod before wiping her face to look at Casey.

Looking back at the stand, I see that Casey is just staring at the lawyer, his mouth hanging open, his eyes wide. You can see the guilt all over his fucking face. He was gonna kill my sister if she didn't agree, or maybe me, who knows. But that wanker wasn't out his mind; he knew what he was doing. He's a fuckin' psycho.

"I'd never," Casey promises. "I love her."

"Sure ya do," the prosecutor says. "I have nothing more."

WHEN WE all walk out of the courtroom four hours later, we are elated.

Not sure what the jury was doing, eating cake or what, but they were unanimous.

Casey Burke was guilty.

The show he put on as they took him out of the courtroom was almost comical. He thrashed around, screaming and crying. For someone who loved my sister, he never looked at her or begged her for forgiveness like a normal human, but we all know he's a liar.

Riding in the car, we are all smiles except for Lena and Micah. I don't know what happened, but during the break while we waited for the jury, they went off together. When they came back, he sat behind us while she sat beside Ma. I don't see them fight much, but they usually make up quickly, and I hope that's the case this time. He can be an idiot, but he's a good guy.

Once we get back to the house, we gather in the sitting room for drinks and dessert. My ma, Mrs. Maclaster, Amberlyn, and Fiona are sitting by the window, talking animatedly while my da, Mr. Maclaster, Kane, and I sip whiskey and talk more about the trial. I believe that if it wasn't for the prosecution picking up those small details, Casey might have gotten off. I wanted to kiss the guy, but instead I shook his hand, promising him the biggest bottle of whiskey before he walked away to do the interviews that were waiting for him.

"My son tells me that we need ya here in the distillery," my da says, and Mr. Maclaster laughs.

"I told Declan it isn't going to happen. I don't have time."

"Maybe part-time, then?" I ask relentlessly.

A wide grin brightens his face as he shakes his head. "Let me talk to my wife, yeah?"

"Better than no, I say," my da informs me. "I heard Cathmor is almost done with beta testing. All is well."

"It's a damn good whiskey. I feel it will sell well," Mr. Maclaster says, and I'm stunned to silence.

"I agree. He's gonna do great things," my da says, sending me a confident grin.

"Yeah, he will," Kane adds, toasting his drink. We all meet our cups to each other's and I nod thanks before we swig, but I pause when I hear my ma say something that catches my attention.

"Not anytime soon," Amberlyn says with a laugh. "We want to live a bit, just us."

My ma laughs as she waves Amberlyn off. "Ivor and I married, and two months later, I was pregnant with Declan. We have babies quickly around here."

With my brows pulled in, I step over to where they are, placing my hand on Amberlyn's shoulder as she says, "Well, we are gonna wait. I want to finish school first."

"Uni? You're going to the uni?"

"Ma, let it be," I say, not wanting to have this conversation with everyone here, not that it is any of her business anyway. "We are gonna wait a bit, like she says. We want to enjoy each other."

"Well, how long?" she asks, her face full of disappointment. I hate that look, but I shrug.

"Not sure. When we are ready. We aren't ready yet."

"Maybe you will be by the time the wedding comes."

Amberlyn laughs. "That's in a month and a half. I doubt it. I want to finish school first."

My ma glances at me and I hold my palms up. "Those are her wishes and I'm good with them. I want to be able to give my kid attention. Let us find our place in the world before we bring our kids into it."

"Well, then," she says, shaking her head, and when she gets up, I squeeze Amberlyn's shoulder, causing her to look up at me.

"I think I made your mom mad again," she whispers and I laugh.

"Won't be the last time, yeah?"

I lean down to kiss her just as someone takes my hand. Tearing my mouth away from hers, I turn to see that Lena is there, tears in her eyes. She shakes her head quickly, stopping my next sentence before she nods her head to the left, indicating the library.

"Excuse me, love," I say, kissing Amberlyn once more before following Lena out of the room. Once the door shuts, she turns and the tears start to rush down her face. "Lena, what's wrong?" I ask, taking ahold of her arms. "Are you hurt?"

"No, that's the problem."

"What?"

"I broke it off with Micah."

Stunned, I shake my head before asking, "Excuse me?"

"I told him to leave, that I wasn't gonna marry him."

Swallowing the lump in my throat, I squeeze her arms. "Why? Please don't say ya still love that wanker and you're going to wait for him?"

She laughs as she shakes her head. "Hell no!"

"Oh, thank God, then why?"

"I don't love Micah."

Confused, I ask, "What? Really?"

"No, I don't even think I ever did. He was just an easy out, and now, I don't want the out. I want to live the life I want. I want the love you have with Amberlyn. The one I would die for. I don't want to marry someone because it's convenient for me."

"That's never a good reason," I agree, but I have to ask. "Are you sure?"

"Yeah."

"Then I support ya," I promise and she smiles.

"Ma is gonna flip."

"Oh yeah," I say with a laugh. "She's gonna try to talk you out of it."

"He already left."

"Wow, okay, but be ready for the wrath of Noreen O'Callaghan."

She bites her lip as she nods. "But I'm doing the right thing, yeah?"

I hug her tightly and kiss her forehead. "Yes, if ya don't love him, don't marry him."

Unsure, she looks up at me. "But I could maybe, one day."

"Do ya really believe that?"

"No," she says automatically, causing me to grin and hug her tighter.

"Then you're doin' right, love. Don't worry, okay?"

"Okay."

As I hold her in my arms, I can't help but think of all the shite she's been through and how I thought that Micah was the one to bring her back from it. Maybe he was supposed to play a part, but Lena was to do the rest. She will be okay though. She is a strong lass; she'll be just fine.

Especially since that gobshite is going to be in jail for the next fourteen years.

twenty-six

Amberlyn

To say that Mr. and Mrs. O'Callaghan freaked out when Lena told them that she and Micah had decided to part ways would be an understatement.

It was if they went through the five stages of grief.

First was the denial. They didn't believe her; Mrs. O'Callaghan went looking for him, calling him constantly. It was rather insane. Second was anger. They ripped Lena apart, telling her she had made the biggest mistake of her life. Micah came from old money, would be a great husband, blah, blah, blah. Then they decided to hit the third stage, bargaining. Mrs. O'Callaghan thought up every situation that would bring Micah back, while Mr. O'Callaghan tried to talk her into loving him. No matter what, they weren't listening. Mrs. O'Callaghan hit the fourth stage, where she blubbered all over Lena and begged her to take Micah back.

Declan decided he finally had to step in because they were not listening to Lena. Bless her heart, she was crying so much, snot coming down from her nose as she begged them to listen to her. That she didn't love Micah. I held her, my heart breaking for the girl as Declan took the authoritative role and told them this was the way it was going to be. She wasn't going to be with Micah, and that was final.

Which led to the final stage, acceptance. Well, at least Mr. O'Callaghan accepted it. I'm pretty sure Mrs. O'Callaghan is still trying to figure out a way to fix Lena. Crazy. It's been three weeks since it happened, and things are still so tense in the house. Lena doesn't come out of her room much and neither does Mrs. O'Callaghan. Except, of course, to barge in on Declan and me. I'm pretty sure my future mother-in-law is not supposed to walk in on me taking it from behind. It's driving me crazy, but I'm counting down to our wedding. After that, I'm out of this mad house.

Between Mrs. O'Callaghan walking in on us and driving me insane with this wedding, I'm pretty convinced I can't live a decent life with her here trying to dictate it. Like she does with Lena, she's tried it on me. How I dress, how I act, what I do, and even when I'm gonna have kids. Sorry, but I'm not sorry, I'm not dealing with this. Like today, I'm standing here, looking down at the clothes she has picked out for me, and I want to just cry. I am so tired of these ugly, plain tea dresses, the damn shoes that hurt my feet, and just being so proper all the time. I don't even want to go to tea, but I'm trying to make my life easier.

A happy Mrs. O'Callaghan means she doesn't bitch at Declan.

"You don't have to go," Declan calls from bed. He's gloriously naked, only the sheet covering his naughty parts, from where we just caught the bed on fire with our lovemaking. While I was a beginner before, I'm catching on and can make his body sing with my touches. Smiling at him, I shake my head.

"If I don't go, she'll flip her shit," I say, crossing my arms over my stomach, trying to decide which dress I want to torture myself with.

"This is true, but I don't care. You obviously don't want to go."

"I don't."

"Don't, then," he says, sitting up and pulling me down on top of him. Grabbing my butt, he presses himself into me, a grin growing on his face. "Stay in bed with me."

I laugh as I glance at the time while he nibbles on my neck. "For what, ten minutes? You have a meeting this morning."

He groans into my neck, biting softly before pulling back to look at me. "Fine. I'll go to the meeting, and when I come back, I want you in this bed, naked."

I scoff. "So you want me to lie in bed, naked, all day, waiting for you?"

His grin grows. "Now that's a vision to keep me warm all day, yeah?"

He rolls me over, getting on top of me before kissing me hard against my lips. Pulling back, he kisses the side of my mouth before looking down into my eyes. "Ya happy, my love?"

I grin up at him. His eyes are shining, his face flushed, and I can't believe how much I love him. It's all-consuming. Life-altering. Wow, that last thought is truer than I realized. Cupping his face, I know I can't lie to him. "I am when it's me and you."

He leans into my hand, his lashes kissing his cheeks as he rests in my hand. "They still driving you mad?"

"I don't like that while I'm having sex with you, I worry about your mom walking in on us."

"Yeah, I tried talking to her about that, but she doesn't think it's her fault. It's ours for not waiting till we are married. Apparently when we're married, she won't be coming up here."

"I don't believe that," I say quickly and he smiles.

"Didn't think ya would," he says, kissing my palm before looking back down at me. "I really don't want to move out of this house."

"I know," I say, biting my lip. "But I don't think I can stay."

"That's a problem."

"It is."

"So you still want to move out?"

"I do. Buy our own furniture and make a house a home."

He pulls in a deep breath through his nose before rolling out of bed. He reaches for a towel, throwing it over his shoulder. He looks down at me, and I smile as I drink him in. I kinda feel bad for asking this of him, but am I wrong? I'll have to talk to Fiona. We are going to pick out her bridesmaid dress tomorrow. I didn't want her to have a traditional one; I wanted her to have one she could wear later to a ball or something. We've both been busy with registering for school and then starting that, so this is the first day we can do it.

Three weeks before the wedding.

"I gotta get in the shower, but we'll talk more later?"

I go to nod but before I can, a knock comes to the door and then it opens, Mrs. O'Callaghan poking her head in. Covering myself with the blanket, Declan glares as she laughs, saying, "Declan, my goodness, son, put some clothes on."

"Ma! I don't know if ya realize, but this is my room, our room. We're gonna be naked. Knock on that damn door and wait!"

She keeps laughing as she waves him off. A part of me is starting to think she likes catching us. "Ah, you're fine. I've seen ya naked before."

"For fuck's sake," he mutters as he ties the towel around his waist. "What do ya need?"

"Checking to see when Amberlyn will be down for tea," she says, looking at me.

I go to answer, but Declan beats me to it. "She isn't going. She's tired, Ma, working and going to school plus planning the wedding is taking its toll. She's gonna sleep a bit more this morning."

I want to kiss him even more than I usually do.

"Oh, that's disappointing," she says and her lip actually juts out, looking at me as if I am going to do the opposite of what he says.

I'm not.

"Yeah, too bad. Now please leave."

"Declan!" she scolds, but he shakes his head.

"I'm naked, my fiancée is barely dressed. Let us be, Ma. Start knocking."

"Well, lock the door if ya don't want people coming in," she says before shutting the door. To make a point I guess, he goes over and locks the door before turning to look at me.

"When I'm about to take ya to bed, remind me to lock the damn door!"

I laugh as he heads for the bathroom, but before he reaches it, I call out, "Or we could move. At least then we can have sex on every surface and no one can say anything."

"Ah, knowing my ma, she'd come all the way there just to walk in on us."

The door shuts and I roll my eyes. He's probably right, but I'm sure it wouldn't happen that much. When the door opens again, he looks over at me and says, "But I'll think on it, okay?"

I smile. "Thank you."

His mouth pulls up at the side and then the door shuts. As I lie there, I'm a little torn. A part of me wants to leave so that I can be with Declan with no interruptions, but the other part of me wants him to be happy too.

I **DID** sleep some, but when I wake up, I can't just stay in bed naked. I check my online schooling and text Fiona, but she doesn't answer me back. I know I can't bother Declan. He has meetings all day, and I think my uncle is supposed to come to the distillery today too. Declan was really excited for that. After getting dressed, I decide to head to the library, explore the house a little bit. Since I have come to live here, I've seen one room and that's Declan's. Time to check this place out.

Maybe I can find a room no one knows about so that I can have sex with my fiancé in peace.

I'm just kidding.

Kinda.

After spending two hours in the library, I find a whole stack of books that I want to reread. Putting them in a basket that is by the door, I walk out to head upstairs, but before I can go, someone stops me.

"Ms. Reilly, I'll take those to your room."

She reaches for the basket, but I hold on to it. "Oh no, you're fine. I'll do it."

"It's really no trouble," she informs me. "It's part of my job."

Her name is Annabelle and is almost my staff, I guess. She is the one who was assigned to me, and it's really weird to have someone who wants to wait on you hand and foot. She's sweet and I enjoy her company, but I really don't think I need someone to do things for me.

Plus, I truly don't understand why she chose this as a job. Couldn't she do something more? Go to school? Anything other than work for a family that is fully capable of taking care of themselves. But then, who am I to judge her? Declan told me once that the staff here are paid very well with full benefits. So she could be very happy, and I'm over here judging her. How very wrong of me.

Giving the basket to her, my grin grows. "Yes, of course. Thank you."

"You are very welcome. Have a good day, ya hear? Let me know if ya need anything."

"I will, thank you," I say as she turns to head upstairs. I want to say that made me feel good, that I enjoyed that, but I didn't. I hate it. Crossing my arms, I hold myself as I walk through the house, discovering each room and wandering around. The estate is very big, and every room is filled with all kinds of neat things to look at. Be it a book, a gorgeous painting, or beautiful pictures of Declan and his family, I find that I am fully entertained for a few hours.

That is, until I reach the sitting room on Mr. and Mrs. O'Callaghan's floor.

Entering it, it seems just like Mrs. O'Callaghan, a very expensive and floral perfume. I figure this is her room to sit and get away from it all. There are books scattered everywhere, even a little spot for knitting. There is a desk with a computer and mounds of wedding books. This must be where she has been planning my wedding. Going to her desk, I look at each of the books and smile at all the Post-it notes and little notes on her desk about who to call. I wonder why she is doing this herself. Why doesn't she just hire someone to do it all?

Sitting in the chair behind the desk, I reach for one of the books but pause when something catches my eyes.

It's a picture.

A picture of my mom.

Reaching for it, I blink a few times, trying to figure out if I am really seeing what I am seeing. But it is. My mom in all her young glory. She couldn't be over the age of sixteen, so fresh-faced and happy. Her arms are wrapped around a girl I know to be her best friend, Marla. She had died when my mom was twenty-one in a car accident, and I can still remember all the stories of trouble they had gotten into. I had even seen this picture. It was on the table by her chair where she knitted.

Why in the world does Mrs. O'Callaghan have it?

"Amberlyn?"

Looking up, I look across the room at Mrs. O'Callaghan through the tears that have gathered in my eyes.

Turning the picture, I stand and ask, "Why do you have a picture of my mom?"

She looks at the picture and then at me before running her hands down the front of her skirt. In the short time I've known her, I know that it's a nervous tic of hers, but I'm not worried if she is nervous. I want to know why she has a picture of my mom.

Coming toward me, she reaches for the picture, taking it from me before gazing down at it. "You know what the great thing is about pictures, my dear?"

She doesn't look at me or wait for me to answer before she continues, "Everything is standing still. Time hasn't passed. It instantly takes ya back to that moment. This was taken, by me, over thirty years ago. I remember that after I took this, Ciara jumped into the lake and hit her head on a stone. Had to get three stitches, while Marla and I cried and cried." A small smile comes over her face as she gazes at the picture. "We were so worried, ya see. She just passed out on us, and my goodness, her ma was so upset, and so was my ma because we weren't supposed to be swimming in the O'Callaghan lake. We were supposed to be doing laundry, but we got bored and Ciara talked me into it."

She runs her finger along the picture and lets out a sigh. "It's funny 'cause Ciara said that, while she did get hurt, it was meant to be because if she wouldn't have gotten hurt, then Mr. O'Callaghan wouldn't have come up to the hospital with Ivor and we would have never fallen in love.

"We were the three musketeers back then. Everything we did was together, and we promised never to part. But when Ivor fell for me, he decided that I wasn't going to be out of his sight. At first, it didn't bother him that Ciara and Marla were there, but it was hard. When the three of us were together, it was us, no one else, and I tried to include Ivor, but he was so quiet, very stern, but man, did I love him.

"He told me to choose between them and him. I had every intention of picking Ciara and Marla, but my ma, she talked me out of it. We were poor, ya see, very poor, and a rich heir to a very profitable whiskey business wanted me. Ya don't turn that down. So I chose Ivor. I broke their hearts when I told them. Marla hated me, but Ciara, she told me she understood. That I had to follow my heart. She always had such a good soul, one that you instantly loved."

My lip had started to quiver as I sat there listening to her. Tears run down my cheeks because she is right. My mom was a beautiful soul, but I find it so hard to believe that she could be friends with someone like Noreen O'Callaghan.

"I tried to stay in contact with them. Marla, not so much, since she hated me for choosing a man over them, but I sent Ciara letters. But once Ivor and I got engaged, it became very difficult. There is so much that is expected of an O'Callaghan woman."

"You can say that again," I mutter and she finally meets my gaze.

With a small smile, she nods. "We are to be the one who lifts our man up, loves him, even in his darkest hour, have babies, and plan parties. We don't get to go out with our friends, do what we want. It isn't about us; it's about them."

I shake my head, my blood boiling. "That's not how it is with Declan and me."

"Maybe not to that extent, but one day it will be."

"No, it won't," I say back, and it won't. He wouldn't do that to me.

"He idolizes his father. Wants to be him. I used to be like you. Had a plan, but I allowed love to take that from me."

I shake my head, holding her gaze. "I can love him and still be me."

"I thought so too," she says sadly, shaking her head before glancing at me. "Do ya think Declan will want ya to work once you have a baby?" she asks, and I don't answer her. I don't care what she thinks. Declan won't make me do something I don't want to do. "No, he won't. Do you think he is actually okay with you working and going to uni? No, he is not, but he does it because he loves ya, and losing you would not only mean breaking him but also losing his distillery."

"That's not true. He loves me and cares what I feel," I spit back, but she is already shaking her head. How does she know how to hit me where I am weak? Why is she doing this? When I ask her that, she shakes her head, holding her palms up to me.

"I don't mean to do anything to you, my dear. I am trying to warn you. I thought like you do. Ivor was so charming, loved me and cared about what I wanted."

I stand up, the chair falling behind me as I glare at her. "I don't doubt that, but you were submissive to him. You let go of your friends, my mom! So please don't talk to me about how Declan is gonna treat me."

She nods slowly. "I'm sorry," she says softly.

"You should be. How dare you try to pit me against Declan?"

She looks up at me and shakes her head. "That's not what I am doing. I am warning ya, Amberlyn. Once you're married, you won't go anywhere because you love him. Soon it will be one thing after the next that you're willing to let slide because he'll tell ya what's best. It happened to me, and as much as I don't want you to go through what I went through, I also know that my son will not be happy with anyone but you."

"He won't do that to me," I say, and the tears start to roll down my face once more as I hold her gaze.

I don't know if it is the fact that she knew my mom and didn't tell me. Or that she betrayed her friendship, or that she is scaring the living shit out of me, but I am overloaded with emotions. I always thought she was a snob from the start, but if my mom loved her, she must have been a good person at one time. Which means what she is saying is true. Did Mr. O'Callaghan really change her that much?

And as much as I hate to ask it, will Declan do that to me?

Will I lose me and become a hateful snob?

twenty-seven
Declan

Reaching across the table, I take hold of Mr. Maclaster's hand and smile. "Thanks for coming in."

Walking around the table, he comes to my side, cupping my shoulder. "Anything to help out family," he says and I smile.

"Not yet, three more weeks," I say with a wink and he laughs.

"Eh, you've been family since she agreed to marry ya."

That warms my heart for sure, and I know he can see that through the grin I shoot him. "Grand, thank you," I say with a nod. "So you'll come in every Wednesday?"

He slaps his hands together before nodding. "Yup, I'll be here, until the missus complains. When that happens, I'm done."

"Of course," I say in agreement. "I appreciate this."

"I want ya to succeed. Does well for my niece."

I laugh. "I think we both know it isn't about Amberlyn."

He laughs too, a flash of guilt coming over his face. "Eh, I may be getting a bit bored, but don't let that leave this room."

"Wouldn't tell a soul," I promise. He shakes my hand once more, and I watch as he walks away, heading for the stairs to leave. Starting next Wednesday, Mr. Michael Maclaster will be working as my part-time marketing advisor. He says he'll only work that day, but I have a feeling he might come in more than he thought, or maybe work at home. Either way, I couldn't be happier; things are moving. My da doesn't even come to the office anymore. After his retirement party last week, he's slowly been cleaning out his office, and I haven't seen him for the last two days since Cathmor has gone into production.

It's been fuckin' fantastic.

All I need is for Amberlyn to be happy and things will be excellent. Which, I think I got myself a plan for that. Heading out of the boardroom, I start toward my office. My da offered me his office, but I like mine. Probably 'cause it's big enough for Kane and me. Finding my best mate sitting behind his desk, I send him a nod before shutting the door.

"How'd it go?"

"Bloody good, he starts next week and had some great ideas. I'm happy," I say with a grin as I wake my computer up to send some emails.

"Awesome, Fiona said that he was excited and was gonna take the job. Even Sheila was supportive. He must be bored or something."

I laugh. "Yeah, he just said that to me."

"Grand, this will be good for him then."

"And the distillery."

"Oh, for sure. Smart man, he is."

"That's for damn sure," I agree, hitting send on an email to my da before opening another. Even though my da isn't here, I still try to keep him in the loop with this. Just in case I get stuck, he's always up to date and can help me. "Let me run something by ya real quick."

Looking up at me, his brow rises as he nods. "Yeah?"

"Amberlyn's been on me about something, and I'm not sure how I feel about it."

"All right..."

"She doesn't want to live at the house," I explain, and even he is surprised by that.

"Really?"

"Yeah, she hates it. My mom is always walking in on us and shite. She doesn't like people waiting on her hand and foot, as she says, and she just isn't happy."

Kane nods slowly, a worried look on his face.

"What?" I ask.

He shakes his head and shrugs. "Nothing."

"No, tell me. What?"

He lets out a breath and looks down, messing with the pen in his hand. Finally, after a moment, he looks up at me. "You're not gonna dump her, are ya?"

I can't help it. I laugh. Shaking my head, I meet his worried gaze. "Not in a million years."

"Oh," he says, letting out a long breath. "Thank God!"

I'm still laughing when Kane joins in with me as I lean back in my chair, kicking my legs up on the desk. Calming down, I look back over at him.

"All I saw was ya going back to the way you were before her, and I really don't want that guy back. I'm happy, and I want ya to be happy too."

A grin pulls at my lips as I nod. "I know, and I am happy. But I can't be when she isn't. I don't know how to make her happy, short of getting us a place."

"Yeah, but is that what ya want?"

I shake my head. "To be honest, no. But," I say and then pause, thinking for a moment. "I think it was yer da who told me once that marriage is about compromise. Remember that time yer ma painted the cabinet pink, I think, and he lost it. But she said it was what she wanted, and even though it was visibly not something he wanted, he let it be."

Kane laughs as he looks up at the ceiling. "I do remember that. Crazy coots."

I nod in agreement. "Sure, but I figure I won't be happy unless she is happy. Living in my home is what I thought my married life would be, but I'm not marrying someone who wants that life. She just wants me."

"Which is what ya wanted from the beginning," Kane adds, and I couldn't agree more. "Ya always wanted a girl who didn't want this life, and ya found her. So don't expect her to live the life you have."

"No, I know," I say with a nod. "I mean, she doesn't want that part, the house, the service, and parties, but man, Kane, she loves helping people."

He grins at me as he nods. "She's a great lass, Dec. Ya did good."

"I did," I agree, my heart fluttering in my chest like a damn schoolboy. "Did ya see she started a coat drive for those kids?"

"I did and then that yous two is gonna build that library."

"Yeah," I say with a grin. "She wants to work there once it opens."

"She'd be good at that. She's a nerd at heart."

I laugh. "Yeah, when she isn't at school or work, she's either in my bed or reading."

He just grins at me as he nods, and he doesn't have to say anything. I know what I need to do. "So I have to find somewhere, yeah?"

"Yeah," he agrees. "But maybe ya can find somewhere and let it be a compromise, still?"

"Yeah? How?"

"Get a place on the grounds or have something built for ya."

What a great idea! Kicking my legs down, I smack my desk before pointing over at him. "You're a fuckin' genius, Kane."

"Eh, stop. Yer makin' me blush," he teases as he turns to his computer. "Your ma won't like it."

"I don't care," I say. "It isn't about her; it's about Amberlyn."

WHEN I get back to the house, I feel good.

I spent most of the afternoon on the phone with different contractors and have someone who wants to meet with Amberlyn and me to look at designs for a house. He's gonna draw up something nice, he says, and I believe him. I'm pretty sure my family has used him before, but first I have to talk this over with my da.

Walking toward my da's study, I knock on the door and wait for him to tell me to come in. Opening the door, I find my ma is in the room too. Well, I guess I'm gonna tell them both, then.

"Declan, sweetheart," she says as I come in, falling into the chair beside her.

"Hey Ma, Da," I say, sending a nod to him.

"Got your email, good work. Michael will be good for us."

"I agree," I say, resting my ankle against my knee.

"Did you get the email from production?"

I shake my head, pulling out my phone. "No, when?"

"Just a minute ago," he says, a grin on his face. "Cathmor goes to stores and pubs in three months."

Grinning, I nod. "Bloody fantastic," I say, my heart pounding in my chest. Pride is seeping out of my pores, and I can't wait to tell Amberlyn. First though, I have to get this taken care of. "I didn't come to talk about that, though."

"No?"

"What is it? Are you okay?" my ma asks before running her fingers through my hair lovingly. Moving away, sending her a sheepish grin, I nod.

"Yeah, Ma," I say, covering her hand with mine. Looking at my da, I say, "I was on the phone with Mr. Molloy today."

"Molloy? Why?" my da asks.

"Who's that?" My ma wants to know.

"Contractor. What do we need, son?"

"A new house," I say, letting out the breath I am holding as they both stare me down. "There is some land out by the old church and lake. I think I want to build there, if Amberlyn likes it, of course."

"A house? For what?" my ma asks as my da leans back in his chair, crossing his arms.

Clearing my throat, I look over at my ma. "She ain't happy, Ma."

"Who? Amberlyn?"

"Why's that? Is she not being treated right?" my da asks, and I shake my head.

"No, not anything like that. She just doesn't want to live here. She doesn't like being waited on and having my ma walk in on us while we have sex."

My ma blushes as she looks away, and my da booms, "Noreen, I told ya to stop that."

"I don't mean to; it just happens."

"Every week, it seems," I supply and shake my head. "But it's more than that. She wants her own space, and I can respect that."

"Yeah," he agrees, but my ma sure doesn't.

"It just seems a little daft to build a house when this one is perfect for all of us. Take your grandparents' side; they aren't here anymore anyway."

I shake my head. "But they'll be back once they're done traveling. I want her to be happy, and for that to happen, I gotta move her to our own place."

"That just seems a little ridiculous, don't ya think, Ivor?"

Looking over at my da, I see that he is really thinking it through. His chin is resting in his hand as he moves his thumb along it. Looking up at me and then my ma, he shakes his head. I don't realize I've been holding my breath until he goes to speak. What he says matters. Ultimately, he owns everything on this land. If he doesn't want me building on it, I won't be building. Which means I won't even be living on my land because I'm gonna give Amberlyn what she wants.

Shaking his head, he holds my gaze. "I don't, Noreen. It worked for us because my grandparents didn't live here. We really did have everything to ourselves. It's different for them, especially when Lena lives here too."

"Ugh, I don't know. I think it's best they live here. In his home," she says, obviously not agreeing at all.

Sucking in a breath, I want to tell her to be quiet, but when I glance at my da, I feel like he is agreeing with me. I know, even I'm surprised, but his brows are pulled together and he is shaking his head once more. Looking at her, he speaks again, "Yeah, but I get where he is coming from. When you love someone very much, you don't want to share them or be without them even for a second; I understand that. I've felt like that for ya ma my whole life, and I see it in ya eyes when you look at Amberlyn. You love her. Like I love your ma."

I don't know about that, I think my love is stronger, but who am I to disagree. Nodding, I say, "I do. I love her and want to make her happy."

He smiles before leaning back in his chair. "Then it's settled. If that's what ya want, I'm fine with it. With Lena moving to Dublin, it will be nice to just be me and your ma."

While I want to be happy that he agrees with me, I'm a little stunned. "What? Lena is moving to Dublin?"

He nods as my ma says, "Yeah, she needs a change of scenery, from what she is saying." She waves her hand in a dismissive way. "What she needs is to go find Micah and take him back."

I stand, kissing her forehead. "Nah, she won't be happy. Dublin will be good for her. Thanks, guys, gonna go tell my bride the good news."

I turn to head to the door, and as I reach for the handle, my da stops me. As I turn around, we lock eyes and he smiles. "I'm proud of ya, son. She's costing me a lot of money, but ya sure do love her and she adds to your life. Which is what ya needed. Someone that constantly adds. Makes it better."

"Yeah, she does." I scoff as my grin grows, "And she's worth every penny."

Heading out the door, I start to the stairs to go to my room. We have dinner in about an hour, so I can tell her the news and then take her to bed to celebrate.

Good plan, I think.

But when I open our door, she is sitting on the couch with her arms crossed, and I can tell she is seething mad. My brows come together as I shut the door behind me. She is just staring at me, which isn't like her. She usually greets me at the door, kissing me senseless before asking how my day was. Something is wrong. Very, very wrong.

"Amberlyn, love? What's wrong?"

Standing up, she puts her hand on her hips, holding my gaze with her angry one. "Oh, nothing much, just had myself a lovely conversation with your mother!" she says, her sentence dripping with sarcasm.

"Ah fuck," I mutter, falling into the chair. "What happened? I just spoke to her; everything seemed fine."

"What happened?! Oh, let me tell you!" she yells, and I look up surprised. Amberlyn doesn't yell at me. Her eyes are filling with tears, and I stand back up, walking toward her, but she puts her hands up. "Not only did your mom know mine, but she dumped her as a friend for your dad."

My brows are probably in my hairline. "Really?"

"Yes! But that's not the kicker! She stopped being my mom's friend because your dad made her."

Looking at her, I can understand that this is upsetting to her, but I really don't think she should be hostile and taking it out of me. I didn't do anything. "I'm sorry, love, but why are ya so mad about this?"

That only makes her madder. "Because she then proceeds to tell me that he changed everything about her. That being an O'Callaghan wife, you lose yourself!"

I shake my head. "That won't happen to ya. I've told ya that."

"See, that's what I said, but then she made some good points," she snaps, and I don't know why I am being dragged into this.

"Well, please, let me have 'em," I say, crossing my arms over my chest.

"Would you want me to work after I have our first child?"

I feel like I'm walking into a trap, but I answer her. Truthfully. "No, sweetheart, I wouldn't, but only for the fact I don't want anyone caring for our wee baby but you."

"But what if I don't want to raise our wee baby!" she says, mocking my accent. I'm not sure if I should be offended or not, so I go for the latter since there are other things to be offended about.

I eye her as my heart starts to pound in my chest. "I'm sorry, love, but I feel like you're trying to trap me. I don't know the right answer here."

"Just tell me the damn truth!"

Holding her gaze, I shake my head once more. "I'd try to talk ya out of it. At least till the baby is old enough to talk."

She holds my gaze, hers darkening as she shakes her head. "Do you want me to go to school? To work now?"

I feel like I'm digging myself an even deeper hole, but I answer her truthfully. "No, love, I don't. But only because I'm not used to it. I've always been told the wife stays home, the man works."

"We don't live in the fucking 1920s, Declan!"

"Yeah, I know, but that's the way it is around here. I want to provide for ya, make sure you have everything because I gave it to you."

"No! I want to work for what I get!"

"That's fine," I say, holding my palms up. "Calm down, now. No reason to be this upset."

"Yes, there is. You're going to try to change me!"

"I am not!"

"Yes, you are!" she yells, turning to head for the bedroom. "One thing at a time, and I'll let it go 'cause I love you, and soon I'll be unhappy and miserable!"

Following her, I am completely fed up. This is pointless and the stupidest thing in the world to be fighting about. "The hell ya will! I'll make sure you're always happy!"

"Oh, by throwing shiny things in my face or giving me things I ask for, but all while plotting to run my life. Why did you start the library thing? Just so you can shove it in my face when I ask to move? So I wouldn't leave this damn house?"

Completely taken aback by that, I glare. "I mean, fuck Amberlyn, what do ya think of me? Do ya really think I'd do that to ya? Manipulate ya like that?"

She glares back at me. "I don't know. I don't want to think that, but I'm just so mad! Your mom is sitting there, telling me she is just warning me because she doesn't want me to go through what she did."

"So because my ma doesn't know how to keep her mouth shut, I'm being yelled at?"

Whipping her head toward me, her brow furrows more. "So a woman needs to just shut her mouth and do what a man says? Is that what you mean by that?"

Looking up at the ceiling, I let out frustrated yell. When I open my eyes, she's got a bag and is stuffing clothes in it.

"Where do ya think you're going?"

"Why? You going to tell me I can't go?"

I glare, my blood boilin' inside me. I don't know how this escalated so quickly, but it's just ridiculous. Still, I really don't even know what I did wrong.

"Really, Amberlyn?"

"I'm gonna go to Fiona's. We need to have some time apart," she says as a tear rolls down her cheek. "Maybe we rushed into this."

"Really?" I snap.

"Yeah, so you wouldn't lose your precious distillery."

I feel as if she's slapped me. Taking ahold of her arms, I turn her to look at me. "Do ya think I care about that fucking distillery more than you? Is that it?"

"No, but your mom thinks that's the reason you're doing everything to make me happy. So that I don't leave. After that, you'll run my life."

I am going to fucking kill my ma. I've never ever said something like that before, but this is insane. Holding her gaze, I practically plead with my eyes as I say, "I don't care about that distillery more than you, Amberlyn. I'm not doing this to trap ya. I love ya and will give it all up," I say, and she looks down, sucking in a deep breath. "Tell me something. Have I treated you like what you are accusing me of? What is this about? Are ya nervous? Cold feet? What? Tell me. What do I have to do here? I'm not gonna be my da; I'm gonna be me. The man ya love. And I'm gonna make ya happy."

Shaking her head, she looks back at me, her eyes full of tears. Pushing away from me, she goes to the window, crossing her arms over her body. "No, I want to marry you because I love you with every fiber of my body, but I guess I'm scared. I don't want you to change me."

"I'm not going to. Have I yet?"

"No, but all I can think is that my mom was a good judge of character. She loved with all her heart, and if she could love your mom, she had to be a person worth my mom's time. But now, I don't even like being around your mom. And I could be friends with a rock, Declan! It scares me!"

Taking a cautious step toward her, I bend my head to look her in her eyes. "Love, I'm not my da, and yous aren't my ma."

She sucks in a deep breath and shakes her head. "I wonder if your dad said the same thing."

Pulling in a breath through my nose, I stand back and put my hands on my hips. She obviously needs time to think. Nothing I say is gonna change her mind. I could talk until I'm blue in the face and she isn't gonna listen to me. She'll have to do it on her own. Trust that I love her and I would never hurt her. I don't want her to leave, but if that's what she wants, then I'll do it.

"Fine, get ya bag packed. I'll take ya."

She looks up. "What?"

I look at her, confused. "Don't ya want to leave?"

She nods slowly, but I can see in her eyes she doesn't. She's scared. That's all there is to it, and maybe Fiona can help with that. I wish it were me, and I feel it should be me, but apparently not. I hope though that she says no.

But, unfortunately, she doesn't. "Yes."

My heart sinks as I nod. "Fine, then I'll take ya," I say, my own voice breaking. "But don't come back unless you want to marry me and you trust that I won't be my da."

Reaching for the door, I stop at the sound of her voice. "Are you mad?"

I look back at her from the where I'm holding the door handle. "Furious, but that don't mean I don't love ya and can let this go the second you get your head out of your arse. But till then, I'm gonna do as ya ask. Ya want to leave, let's go."

She hesitates and I pray that she'll stay, but then she grabs her bag. Opening the bedroom door, I slam it shut just at the main door to my suite opens and my ma pops her head in. "Declan, I heard yelling."

"Yeah?" I ask, wiping my face free of the tears that burn my cheeks. "Probably the sounds of my fiancée deciding to leave to go to her cousin's because you chose to warn her about how I'm gonna change her."

She pauses, her eyes glassing over as I hold them with heated ones. "Why would ya do that to me, Ma? To her? Scare her like this? Do ya really think that of me?"

"I don't want her to end up like me," she answers.

Confused, I shake my head. "If yer unhappy, change it. Don't bring everyone down with ya because you decided to be unhappy."

"I didn't decide this; it was chosen for me."

"Again, not my fault or Amberlyn's. Yours and da's. I'm not him. I won't hurt her. I actually love her. Just like I think he loves you."

"And I love him, but now everyone is leaving me. I'm lonely."

I can't believe what I am hearing. Shaking my head, I yell at her as my skin burns with anger. "So you're trying to ruin my marriage? To keep me here?"

"No, Declan, no. I love you and I want you to be happy," she pleads, reaching for me, but I brush her to the side. "But I loved her ma, and I don't ever want her to live like I have."

Glaring, I go toe-to-toe with her, glaring at her. "She fuckin' won't because I'm gonna make her happy and love her for her. I'm not your husband. I'm you. The you from before what now stands in front of me."

Tears stream down her face as we hold each other gazes. It's like I'm not looking at the woman that has loved me unconditionally my whole life. The person who I believed loved her life. No, I don't even know this person, nor do I have the need to. She might have pushed Amberlyn away from me.

"Declan, I'm sorry."

Shaking my head in complete disgust, I hear my bedroom door open and then Amberlyn behind me. "It's too late for sorry now, Ma. Yer words have spread like wildfire, and now I have to figure out how to put them out."

Looking back at Amberlyn, I see that she is looking down, her bag on her shoulder, tears falling down her cheeks. I want to wrap her up in my arms, kiss her, tell her it all will be fine, but I know she won't let me. My ma has poisoned her vision of me. Glaring back at my ma, I fight back the tears. I'm supposed to love her unconditionally, but how can I when she may have taken my life away? Clearing my throat of the sobs that threaten to break free, I basically growl, "Now, if you'll excuse me, I'm gonna take Amberlyn to her cousin's because she doesn't want to be here."

Not waiting for either of them to say anything, I head for the door, stomping to the front of the house. My heart breaks a bit, but I believe in Amberlyn and me. I do, and maybe by the time I get to Fiona's, she'll remember she does too.

Or maybe my ma has ruined everything.

twenty-eight
Amberlyn

I don't know if I am doing the right thing.

I remember when my mom and dad got into a big fight once, they fought for hours, screaming and yelling at each other. My mom was crying and shaking, my dad shouting, his face red with anger. I remember hating that they fought and wanting them to stop. My mom packed a bag, told me to grab a few things, and that's when my dad stopped screaming and started begging. I started to cry because I didn't understand. I couldn't have been over six, but I can still hear my dad's voice.

Don't leave. Stay. Talk this out. Don't give up on me.

She didn't leave. She told me to go to my room and I did, putting my head under a pillow as I cried. I didn't know what was going on, and it scared me. I feel asleep, and when I woke up, they were fine. She was sitting in his lap, and they were looking at the checkbook as if nothing had happened.

Before she died, I asked her what had happened. She smiled and shook her head as she looked me deep in the eyes. My dad had a gambling problem and lost the college fund they had started for me. She was furious with him and said he needed a wake-up call. I thought for so long they were crazy, but really, she was trying to help him and did. Losing my mom and me would have been his downfall.

Looking over at Declan, I know I would be his.

I can see the whites of his knuckles; his jaw is taut and he just looks miserable.

I started this, but I know I have just cause for it. His mother has scared me shitless. I want to live a happy life, but can I do that being an O'Callaghan? I know that, being with him, I have all these expectations of me, and they mean I'll have to change. He keeps promising me that he won't do that to me, but all I keep hearing is his mom's warning.

My mom wouldn't want me to do anything until I was completely sure. While I am completely sure I love him more than anything in this world, I don't know if I can go into marriage with him believing that I'll still be me in the end. I mean, I love who I am with him, but when his parents, and even his sister, get involved, all of a sudden I'm a tea dress-wearing snob. I just don't know. I'm so scared, but then I don't want to be without him. I just don't know what I want.

When we pull into the lot of Fiona and Kane's apartment, Declan turns the car off and taps his thumb along the steering wheel. I know this is where I'm supposed to get out, but I'm scared to. My heart is pounding, my hands feel clammy, and even my eye is twitching. I don't know what to do; I'm just so fucking scared of everything, which is very unlike me. I'm usually a jump-in kind of girl, but his mom really fucked me up. My biggest fear is to lose the woman my parents raised. They wouldn't want me to be what Noreen O'Callaghan is.

Over the last couple months, I've seen firsthand that she only cares about appearances. I couldn't care less what I look like or who I'm supposed to impress. I just want to be comfortable. She wants to have parties, impress people all the time, yeah, again, I don't care. I also don't want to be in a loveless marriage. If she loved her husband, she'd spend more time in bed with him rather than walking in on me in bed with her son. Again, gross. She's lost herself, and I don't want to ever lose me. I love me.

But I love Declan.

Ugh, I'm so confused.

Reaching for the door handle, I pull it and push the door open. Letting one leg out, I look back at him. Should I kiss him bye? Or is he too mad at me? I mean, I've caused one hell of a mess with my explosive freak-out.

Before I can ask though, he says, "I'll be waiting for you."

My brows furrow as I look at his beautiful profile. "Waiting for me?"

"Yeah," he says with a curt nod. "Go on inside, sleep on it. When yer ready to tell me one way or another, I'll be here."

"I can call you," I supply, but he shakes his head.

"No, I want to be here."

"But I'm going dress shopping with Fiona in the morning."

He nods and then finally looks over at me. His eyes are so dark, even hard, like a gorgeous marble, but I can see the pain. I've really fucked up here, and even with all that, he doesn't want to leave. He wants to be here. He wants to wait for me to get my "head out of my arse" as he said. Clearing his throat, he says, "And I'll be waiting for ya, then."

My lip starts to wobble as I nod slowly. "I'm sorry."

He looks at me. "For what?"

"For being scared, for not believing in you the way I did before your mom messed it up."

"It's a part of life, Amberlyn, to be scared. The other thing, I know it's in there, the trust, the believing. Ya just have to find it again. It's lost in the shitstorm my ma has caused. I can't help ya find it; ya won't let me. So go on, I'll be waiting."

Tears stream down my face as I shake my head. I don't want to be in a shitstorm without him. I want us to face it together, but why don't I say that? What is wrong with me? Why am I so fucking scared?

Clearing my throat, I close my eyes before glancing back at him, sucking in a deep breath. "Do I kiss you goodbye?"

His eyes soften then. "Do you still want to?"

"Declan, I still love you. More than anything. I'm just so fucking scared."

"There isn't anything to be scared of, though. I'm not gonna to hurt ya, change ya, or anything else ya can come up with. I want only to love ya back."

A tear runs down my cheek, splashing against my hand. "I'm just scared."

Holding my gaze, he nods. "Fine, go on in there, then. Maybe Fiona can help ya with your fear since I can't do shite, apparently."

"It isn't that; it—"

"Go on, Amberlyn," he says, interrupting me. "I'll be waiting."

"So you don't even want to talk about it?"

Looking back at me, he glares. "Amberlyn, do ya want to talk? 'Cause I've tried, and you want to leave. I bring ya here, and now ya want to talk? I don't know what to do here, lass, and you aren't helping me at all. Tell me what I have to do to make you feel better, to make this fear go away. I want you to be confident in us."

"I am."

"Then what do you want me to say?"

"I don't know," I answer honestly because I don't. I don't know how to make this fear go away.

"Sure. Then, go on with ya," he says, shaking his head.

I watch him for a moment, tears still streaming down my face as I try to figure out what to do. Do I leave? Do I stay? I have no clue. I'm so inexperienced when it comes to men, but I'm not stupid. I'm scared, and there has to be a reason for that.

Biting my lip, I wipe my face before asking, "So do you want to kiss me goodbye?"

Looking over at me, he just looks so sad. "Yer killing me, love."

"I know," I answer with a slow nod.

"But, I do. C'mere," he says, his brogue thicker with all the emotion in his voice. Reaching for me, he holds my face for a second, his eyes searching mine. "This isn't goodbye, though. You'll go in there. Talk a bit with yer cousin and hopefully decide to believe me when I say I'm not gonna change ya." Before I can say anything, his lips press against mine, my eyes drifting shut as we slowly kiss. I want to get lost in his kiss; I want to forget his mom altogether, but what if I'm right for feeling like this? What if I go upstairs and Fiona begs me to leave him?

Will I?

Could I?

Pulling my mouth from his, I know it won't be easy, but I need someone's input. I need to talk to someone.

But what I really need is my mom.

Getting out of the car, I go to shut the door as Declan says, "I love you, Amberlyn."

Unable to look at him because I know if I do, I'll lose it even more, I say, "I love you too."

I then shut the door and head to the front door. After I knock on it, Fiona opens the door and a huge grin comes over her sweet face. I must have pulled her from bed; she's wearing sweats and a tee with her hair pulled up on her head. She looks a little pale and I worry she's sick, but before I can ask, she looks at my bag and then back at me, her brows furrowed.

"Oh no, what happened?"

"Can I come in?"

"Yeah, of course," she says ushering me in, holding me close to her. "Yous didn't break up, did ya?"

I shake my head, my tears coming faster down my cheeks. Sitting on the couch, she takes my bag, throwing it on the floor before gathering me into her arms.

"Now tell me what's wrong?"

I explain it all. How I feel like I don't fit in, how his mom is always trying to make me into this person I'm not, how I found my mom's picture in her study, and all about their past. Then about Declan and my fight.

"He's out there, waiting. Like a fucking gentleman, and it kills me, Fiona. But what if I'm making a mistake?"

She nods, her head leaning on mine as she sucks in a deep breath. "But what if leaving him would be the biggest mistake of your life?"

Hiccupping on a sob, I close my eyes. "I don't want to leave him. I want to be with him, but I don't want to be what they want me to be."

"Then don't."

"It's hard though. *'Being an O'Callaghan, you have expectations,'* you're the one who told me that from the beginning."

Pulling back, she looks at me, a grin forming on her lips. "And you've not become one of them. You are still the same girl you were when you came here, just more in love than anything." Moving a piece of my hair out of eyes, she holds my gaze as she goes on, "What is a name, Amberlyn? Just 'cause that name is one thing doesn't mean it's you. He isn't going to do that to you. He loves you too much."

"I'm just scared."

Holding me tightly, she whispers, "My dad once told me that fear is a liar. That it makes you believe something that isn't true. Or something that will never even happen. Do you really, in your heart, believe that Declan would have you be anyone but who you want to be? Hasn't he been the one changing? I mean, the Declan now versus the one before, whoa! And you? It's easy to see you're loved. You're glowing. He wouldn't dim that for nothing. He feeds off yer light. I mean ya ask him to move out of his house and he's considering it; that's huge since he wants to live there till his dying day, yeah?"

"Considered it. He's probably waiting for the moment to tell me he doesn't want to go, and then it starts. I'm stuck in that damn house 'cause I'm not going to leave him. I love him. That's probably why he wanted me to wait till after we were married. I'm not going anywhere, then!"

Looking deep into my eyes, Fiona shakes her head. "Do ya really think that? I mean, everything I've seen, he's bent over backwards to make sure you had, or he went against everything his parents said. He's been doing that from the beginning. Is it really this, or is it because she did your ma dirty and you still don't like her?"

"It isn't that I don—"

"Ya don't like the woman, and that's fine. Who really likes their mother-in-law? Well, minus Kane's ma; she's a true sweetie."

I shrug as tears flood my eyes. "I don't know. It just bothers me that she felt she needed to warn me of how Mr. O'Callaghan changed her."

"Did ya think maybe she isn't happy and sees how happy you and Dec are? That she is losing her son to ya? Misery loves company, Amberlyn."

"I know," I say with a nod. "But I don't want to think of her as being deceptive like that."

"Well, don't. But don't hold Declan to it."

"No?" I ask. "What if it's a sign to run?"

"Would ya run?"

I look at her with wide eyes. "I came to your house."

"'Cause ya knew I would tell ya to go back," she says just as the door opens and Kane comes stomping in.

"I smell like hell. Don't come near me 'cause I'm going right back out."

"Didn't plan on it," she calls back at him. "Where ya off to?"

"Well, since yer best friend and my best friend are fighting, I'm gonna go sit with mine and get smashed while yous two cry in ya ice cream or whatever ya lassies do," he says as he rustles through the fridge.

With a grin, she says, "Love ya, honey."

"Love ya too. Get yer head out yer arse there, Amberlyn," he calls before going back out the door, slamming it behind him.

Fiona grins over at me and says, "Ya know, I love that man."

I roll my eyes. "'Cause he's a good guy. You two complete each other."

"Yer right. Do ya think he'd love Declan the way he does if Declan weren't a stand-up guy?"

Looking down, I shake my head. "I don't think he isn't. I'm just scared to lose myself."

"Ya won't. Yer too strong, Amberlyn."

I know this. I do, and I know that I am being a little ridiculous, but something is holding me back from getting up and going back home with Declan.

"Amberlyn, what do you want?"

Looking down, I bite my lip. Tears gather in pools in my eyes, making my vision blurry. I know what I want. "I want my mom."

"Aw, sweetie, come here."

As she gathers me in her arms, I don't know why I said that. Yes, I want my mom—I would do anything to have her back—but maybe it's because I need her here. I need to hear from her that I am being dumb and that I won't change. That I'll be me no matter what. I want her to meet Declan and love him the way I do. I want my dad to walk me down the aisle and tell me how gorgeous I am as he gives me away. Is this really what my problem is?

"Didn't ya tell me that she loved Declan in your dream?"

Squeezing my eyes shut, I nod. "She did."

"Okay, don't ya think that means something?"

"Yeah," I say, nodding my head. "I just miss her."

A sob escapes my lips as I fall into her lap, closing my eyes tightly as I cry. She doesn't say anything as she runs her hands through my hair, slowly massaging my head as we sit in complete silence. Gathering me tighter to her, she kisses my forehead.

"What if ya went back to the States?"

Opening my eyes, I look up at her. "Huh? What for?"

"To go see her. Yer da too. Maybe it will make you feel better, and maybe it will also help with knowing that you'll never change because they raised ya."

"Maybe."

"Maybe it's the fact that everything is changing so fast, ya know? You need that reassurance. Go back to your roots and get that. I think it might help."

Holding her gaze, I think that through. It's a good idea. Maybe it will help. But then I shake my head. "The wedding is in three weeks."

"Yeah, so? Go this weekend. We can go dress shopping when you get back.

I look good in anything."

I scoff as I nod, but then my grin falls. "I really don't want to leave Declan behind though. He might think I'm leaving him or something."

She laughs. "Well, tell him of course, but also, how ya gonna say you don't want to leave him, but you come over here unsure if ya should marry him?"

I shake my head as I laugh. "I love him and maybe I'm blinded by that. That's why I would change."

With a deadpan look, she asks, "That's dumb. Ya haven't changed yet, why ya going to later?"

She does have a point.

Standing up, I grab my bag and lean to her, kissing her forehead. "Thank you."

She smacks my ass playfully. "Anytime. Call me when ya get back so we can go shopping."

"I will," I say, opening the door. Declan and Kane look up from where they are drinking beers against his car.

"Hey there, ya get yer head out yer arse?" Kane calls to me, and Declan smacks his chest.

"Shut up, Kane," I say as I walk toward them.

"Well, here's to hoping, yeah?" Kane says, smacking his shoulder, but then he pauses, whispering something before he turns to head toward the apartment. When he reaches me though, he leans into me, giving me a side hug and then whispering, "He's really hurting over this, Amberlyn. Don't go over there saying *Fiona* helped you to realize yer outta ya Godforsaken mind thinking he would change ya 'cause he'd never do no such thing. His ma is off her rocker too. Don't listen to a word from her. He loves ya, okay? Let him help you realize this. All he wants is for ya to be happy. Okay, lass?"

Looking up into his dark eyes, I smile. He loves his friend so much, and maybe I was completely out of my mind for thinking Declan would do anything but love me completely. Hoping to convey that to him, I nod my head before saying, "You smell like death, Kane."

Giving me a lopsided grin, he nods. "I know, see ya."

"See ya," I say, and then my gaze meets Declan's. Leaning against the car in all his sexy glory, he holds his beer by the neck of the bottle, his eyes trained on me. Sucking in a breath, I head toward him and his eyes don't leave mine as I stop before him. Neither of us says anything for a moment, both of us searching each other's eyes as we stand in the last light of the day.

Clearing my throat, I say, "Hey."

"Howya," he says, taking a pull of his beer. "That didn't take long. Only two beers."

I nod as I look down, kicking the dirt. I hate feeling like this. I just want to go back to us. Before all this. I've messed everything up, and I feel that the root of the problem is my grief. I'm so scared to lose the person my parents molded me into that I'll believe anything that could threaten that.

"So?"

I look up, biting my lip. "I want to go back home for a visit. I miss my mom and dad a lot."

He nods his head. "Before or after the wedding?"

"Before."

He looks down, swinging the bottle at his side. "When?"

"This weekend."

Looking up at me, he holds my gaze. "I'll make it happen."

"Oh, you don't have to. I just wanted to let you know where I was going."

"I want too. I'll have our jet take ya."

Surprised, I ask, "You have a jet?"

"Yeah," he says with a nod.

"That's cool, I guess."

"Eh, being O'Callaghan has its perks. Today though, no perks. Just a shitestorm."

I smile as I look back down, wringing my hands together. He then asks, "Are ya coming home?"

I meet his gaze and shrug. "If you want me to."

"Of course I do," he says, reaching for me and wrapping his arms tightly around me. Nuzzling my neck, he kisses it as his fingers dance along my ribs. I can smell the beer on his breath and it reminds me of the pub. Of the first few days here when I was a crying heap of sadness. He helped me out of that, but yet, I'm trying to push him away.

Why? What is wrong with me?

"I want to go with ya and meet yer parents, Amberlyn."

Cuddling my nose in the crook of his neck, I feel how hot his skin is underneath my lips as my tears splash against his face. I want that more than anything, I do, but I really don't understand how he still wants to be around me after all the hell I've caused. Whispering still, he says, "I also don't want to be away from ya a second longer."

Kissing his neck, I nod my head. "I don't want that either."

"So we'll go together?"

Pulling back, I met his gaze as my eyes drip with tears. "I would like that."

twenty-nine
Amberlyn

I can barely see the two tombstones that sit before me.

My eyes are full of tears and my lip starts to wobble as my heart pounds in my chest. There are flowers all over both their graves, and I wonder if my uncle had something to do with this. I spent most of the morning at my old family home, packing and going through my parents' things and also the things I left behind. It was hard, but I was happy with what I kept.

Which was almost everything.

Declan has been very sweet, saying that we'd "find a place for it" whenever I asked if I could have it shipped back home. He has been a saint since we left Fiona's. I assumed we would leave that Friday, but he had us on the jet this morning with arrangements for us at a hotel with the promise that we could stay as long as I wanted. When I told him that I wanted to have stuff shipped, he had a moving company at the house within an hour. I'm not sure how my uncle feels about it all, but then, he is getting my house at a steal of a price, so he will be okay.

My only complaint so far is that we haven't talked much. It's been very simple yes-and-no questions. It's weird and I don't like it, but then I think that maybe he is giving me space to think. I never did tell him that we were good, but then he never asked. All he's really been doing is talking on his phone or checking emails. Even when I was going through everything, he was on his phone. I don't know if it's his way of letting me be or what. I know he still cares and loves me—he's done nothing but show that since we left—I just wish he'd get off his phone. But then I feel like an asshole because he's missing work to be here with me. We are not there to do last-minute planning for the wedding because I wanted to come home. He won't even answer his mom's calls. He's shutting down on me, on everyone, and it's all my fault.

He brought me here to see my mom and dad. Here I am, and I have no clue what to do or even how to move.

Seeing their names on the tombstones is so very real. I am used to seeing my dad's name. There wasn't one Wednesday or Sunday a month that we didn't come to clean off his grave and set new flowers out. The flowers that lie on their graves now are gorgeous, and I'm surprised that someone took the time to put them there. Especially if it was my uncle since he hated my dad. My mom always said that he thought my dad was bad news, but he was completely wrong.

My dad was a great man.

Looking at his grave, I swallow my sob as I read the words that will be etched in my brain for the rest of my existence.

Tomas Albert Reilly
7-2-1970 to 9-23-2007
His soul to Amberlyn.
His heart to Ciara.

"Wow, that is beautiful," Declan says from beside me, and I look back at him, wiping away my tears with the back of my hand.

Glancing back at the stone, I close my eyes, wanting to hear him say it to me. But I don't hear anything. Nothing, except my sobs. Whispering, I say, "He always said that to us. That my mom had his heart and I had his soul. I was the one who told her to put it on his tombstone."

Lacing his fingers with mine, he brings my hand up to his lips, kissing it softly as he cocks his head to my mom's. "I think that's my favorite though."

Glancing at my mom's stone, I fully expect to lose my mind crying, but I don't.

I smile.

Ciara Lynn Reilly
5-16-1970 to 5-25-2014
The heart of Tomas.
The best mom in the whole entire world to Amberlyn.

Reading the words on the tombstone, my tears start to fall faster, but my grin remains. I'm drawing strength from Declan as he moves my hand into his other, while his hand moves up and down my back. Kissing my temple, he whispers, "That is the most amazing thing I have ever seen. When I die, do something like that for me, yes?"

I shake my head, closing my eyes as I lean into him. "Please don't leave me first. I couldn't do it."

"Neither could I," he says. "So let's wait till we're old and gray, yeah, and die together."

"Sounds like a plan," I say, even though I know that is the silliest thing we could ever plan for. Life is the most uncertain thing in the world. One day things are great, next day they aren't. One day you're alive, the next you're dead. There is no promise for the next breath. It can be taken from you in a blink of an eye. There is no guarantee.

But in this moment, maybe I can hope that Declan and I will go together. Content and ready.

Kissing me again, he says, "Ya gonna say hi to them? Wanna put the flowers down?"

I nod silently as I walk closer, dropping to my knees as I crawl onto their graves. I know that it's silly, but I feel closer doing this. I used to lie on my dad, so did my mom. We'd lie for hours the first year of his death; it's morbid and silly, but it was comforting to us. And it is now.

To my surprise though, Declan drops to his knees beside me and we go to work, brushing off the little bits of leaves and other debris that has gotten on their graves. Since the flowers are fresh, we leave them but add in mine, making the front of their graves so bright and vibrant.

The day is dreary. It's about to get supercold here, but that didn't stop me from getting bright pink and blue flowers for my mom and orange ones for my dad. When I was younger, they were the ones we brought my dad. My mom used to say that it would make him laugh to know we girlied up his grave. It always made me happy then, and it doesn't fail to do it again.

"Hi Mom, Dad," I say as I wipe away some bird poop on my mom's grave with the rag I brought just for that. "Came to visit. Sorry, I didn't come sooner. As you both know, I've moved to Ireland like you wanted, Mom." My voice breaks a bit, and I swallow my sob as I go to clean my dad's. As I scrub, I blink back my tears as Declan's hand rests on the middle of my back. "Things are great. I'm going to school, I work for Shelia, and I met someone. His name is Declan. He's here too." I swallow around the lump in my throat as I continue to scrub. "I love him so damn much and things are moving fast, but we are getting married in two weeks," I say as his hand comes up into my hair, cupping my neck. "I'm happy, he makes me happy, but I do miss you guys. So much."

I don't know what I am expecting. For them to come out of their graves and wrap their arms around me? I don't know, but soon I am crying as I wait for some kind of response. A butterfly, a rainbow, shit, anything. When nothing happens, I stand up quickly, leaving Declan at my feet.

"I forgot something in the car. Be right back," I say, turning quickly and heading to the car. I need to be alone. I need to pull it together.

But Declan being Declan, he says, "Do ya want me to come, love?"

I shake my head. "I'll be one minute," I call back as I rush to the car.

Getting there, I collapse against the car and just cry. I cry so hard my body is shaking and my heart feels as if it is coming out of my chest. This was supposed to help. This was supposed to make me feel better, but all I feel is agony. Wiping my face, I reach in the car for my purse. I wasn't lying when I said I had to get something. I figured I'd get it later, but here I am, pulling out the picture of Declan and me at the engagement party and then a picture of Shelia, Michael, and Fiona with a message from my aunt to my dad on the back.

Wiping my face once more, I look back at where Declan sits on my parents' graves, his hand on my mom's tombstone. He's talking to it. My brows come up as my eyes fill with tears once more. What is he doing?

Heading for him, I wonder what he is saying, but before I can get there, the clouds part and the sun starts to shine down on me. I'm hot within seconds, and when I look up, two cardinals are sitting in the tree. My mom always said that cardinals were good luck. Is this my sign? Gooseflesh explodes over my body as I fight for breath. Am I really seeing this? Looking back at Declan, I go to call him, but he moves to my dad's grave, putting his hand on his tombstone as he starts to speak.

"I'm not worthy of her, not in the least, but I'll love her. With everything inside me. I'll care for her, make sure she's never unhappy. When she wants to see yous two, I'll bring her. I don't know how I got lucky enough to meet her and then to fall in love with her, but I have and don't plan on ever letting her go. I'll do anything and everything to protect, provide, and love her for the rest of my life." I cover my mouth with my hand as the two birds fly overhead, leaving me alone as I close my eyes, my tears rushing down my face. "I brought ya an O'Callaghan pin too. Everyone who joins our family gets one. Yous may not be here physically, but yer here in her heart, in my heart, and I promise to always keep yer memory alive, along with Amberlyn. Our wee little ones will know their grandda and grandma. And the wee ones after that. Yous will worry for her, I understand that, but ya have my word, as a man, I'm gonna love her and make her proud to be my wife."

"I'm already proud," I finally say, and he turns to look at me, a grin on his face.

"C'mere, love. Let's sit a bit, yeah?"

Coming to him, I drop down into his lap as he wraps his arms around my waist, kissing my jaw. Leaning forward, I set the picture of him and me on my mom's stone and then the one of my aunt's family on my dad's. Leaning my head against his shoulder, a calm falls over me like the sun, warming Declan and me as we sit in contented silence.

"I saw you talking to my mom. What did you say?"

He smiles in my hair as he kisses my temple. "It's a secret."

I smile moving my nose along his jaw. "Tell me."

"Ah, can't say no to ya, can I?"

I flash him a grin and he holds my face. "I asked her to help ya. To give ya a sense of peace, if she could. I know her not being here hurts ya, my love. Since I can't fix it, maybe up there, she can figure out a way to help, ya know?"

My lip wobbles as my throat burns with a sob and I nod. As much as I would love that, I also don't want it to happen. I like the pain; it reminds me of what I've lost and to always cherish the life I have. To live it to the fullest and the greatest I can. To do that, I know I need Declan in my life. I have to let go of this fear that has me thinking he is going to change me.

No one can change me but me.

And Declan wouldn't do that anyway.

He loves me.

He just told my mom and dad that.

WE LEAVE the following day with everything that I wanted to bring home on its way. I also left with a pretty check for my family home. It was hard when my uncle handed it to me, but seeing him with his arm around his new wife and their child growing in her belly, I felt that my home was going to be filled with love the way it had been before. That my parents' memory would still live on. At least I hope so.

As much as I didn't want to leave, Declan promised we'd come back soon, and that made me feel a little better. I knew that he had to get back to work and I needed to get Fiona a dress since the wedding is going to be here before we know it. There is so much to do, and I also have to deal with the fact that I don't want to live with his family.

I wish I could talk him into moving to the States, but being back did nothing for me. We were only gone a day and I missed Mayo so damn much. I missed the green of the country, the friendliness of the people, and the air. It's just so crisp in Ireland. I missed it and it surprises me, but somehow, Mayo has become my home.

Maybe I was always meant to be here, that it was always my home, but the States was my detour. I don't know, but the moment we stepped off the plane, I was glad to be home. The trip was good, the weight I had on my chest was gone, and I was ready for our future. Just some things had to change. Quickly, before I lose my ever loving mind.

Riding in the car, Declan takes my hand and squeezes it. Looking over at him from where I am texting Fiona, I smile. "Thank you."

"For?"

"For taking me," I answer. "For being there for me."

"I always will be." He sends me a grin then and says, "I need to show ya something."

"What's that?"

"We are almost there."

I nod before looking down at where I am texting Fiona.

>Me: *It was a great trip. I feel a billion times better. You're a genius.*
>
>Fiona: *Like ya doubted me. Grand. I'm happy.*
>
>Fiona: *Yous two good?*
>
>Me: *Yeah, I think. We need to address some things. Like the fact I need out of his mom's house tomorrow.*
>
>Fiona: *Yeah sure, do that but remember that's his home. The one he grew up in.*
>
>Me: *I know.*
>
>Fiona: *Grand. Have fun and make sure things are good between yous two before I see ya tomorrow.*
>
>Me: *I will.*

When the car stops, I look up to see that we are parked by a field as Declan gets out of the car. Looking around, I see the lake and know where we are, but I don't understand why.

"Come on," he says, opening the door and letting me out. I take his hand and we walk around the car to where a large spot has been marked off. Raising an eyebrow, I look up at him and he is grinning at me, pointing to the space.

"It's the most gorgeous blank spot in the world?" I say and he laughs.

Shaking his head, he gathers me in his arms and takes in a deep breath. "The other day when I came home and I walked in and ya ripped my head off, ran off to Fiona's, and then we flew to the States?"

"Not still upset about that, are ya?" I ask with a teasing tone, but he doesn't laugh, he sets me a look and I press my lips together. "Sorry, no filter, remember? Anyway, as you were saying."

A grin pulls at his lips as he shakes his head. "Yeah, that night, I came home excited to tell ya about this."

"The blank spot?"

"Yeah," he says with a nod. "This where our house is gonna be."

Scrunching my face, I look up at him from the blank spot. "Huh?"

"We are gonna build a house here. I want to be on my land; I understand that you don't want to live with my family, and that is fine, but I want to be on my land. It takes seven minutes for anyone to get here. By then, surely we will be done, or at least we will remember to lock the door," he says with a suggestive wag of his brows. But I'm too stunned to really comprehend what he just said.

Looking back at the spot that is marked off with bright orange tape, I sort of can't believe him. "Are you for real right now?"

"Yeah, ya wanted out of the house. I'm giving you that."

"Why?"

"Because I love you."

It was that simple. Turning to look at him, my lip starts to wobble as our eyes meet. As my eyes search his, my heart jackhammers in my chest, Fiona's words playing over and over again in my head. She was right. Fear is a liar and the truth is right in front of me. Declan wouldn't change me; he only wants to love me. Wrapping my arms around him, I squeeze him tightly as I press my lips to his. Holding me in his arms, he kisses me thoroughly as all the love we have for each other floods our senses.

Parting, he kisses my nose as I look up at him. "I'm sorry I'm a pain in your ass."

He gives me a lopsided grin as he shakes his head. "Ah, maybe, but I wouldn't want any other pain in my arse but ya. And I knew we'd be okay. Ya just had to realize it."

"I wouldn't have without you. I knew when I saw you at my parents' graves that I couldn't even think you'd change me. You just want to help me grow."

"That's fuckin' right, *mo stór*. I want only that because yous have helped me grow. I couldn't be who I am without ya. I love you."

"I love you too," I promise.

"Grand, now come on, let's go home."

He kisses me again before we get back in the car, and I am on cloud nine. Basically bouncing in my seat as we start to drive again.

"Do we get to design it ourselves?"

He nods. "Yup."

"Eek! I'm so excited! When can we start? Are we gonna live with your parents until then? I'd rather we didn't, but if you want to, and you think it won't take long to build us a new house, then I can bear with it a bit. Wait, where are we going?"

Declan grins over at me as we head up a hill. He doesn't answer me, even when I ask again. When a small little cottage comes into view, I look over at him as he stops in front of it. Shutting the car off, he looks over at me and lets out a breath.

"Welcome home, Ms. Reilly." My jaw drops as he gets out and opens the door for me. "It's not much, but it's got the basics. I have had it furnished a bit, not a lot, but it will get us by till the big house is done."

"Oh my God," I mutter as he pushes open the door and we go in. It's adorable. Only a living room and a small kitchen with a bathroom attached to the bedroom. It's the size of his room on the estate.

"It's got a kitchen, food in the fridge, so you'll be cookin' my dinner, ya know," he says with a wink and I giggle. "But it will do us good, I think."

Looking back at me, he pulls me into the crook of his arms as I agree, "I think so too."

"Grand. So ya happy, love?"

My eyes glaze over as I wrap my arms around his waist, looking around our small little home before looking back up at him. "More than you'll ever know."

thirty
Amberlyn

"It's so damn cute! I love it so much!"

Fiona looks over her shoulder and grins at me. "I am so excited for ya. Invite me and Kane for dinner. I did for yous two."

"You did, and maybe I won't burn the food."

"Ah, fuck off. It was a little crisp is all."

"If you call charcoal-black crisp, then yeah, it was only a little crisp," I tease, and she sticks her tongue out at me.

"I've gotten better."

"Good!" I cheer for her since she could burn water. "Hey, maybe you guys can come over the night the contractor drops off the plans. We'll eat and look everything over."

"Sure, let me know," she says before lifting the top of the dress up her arms and snapping the back before turning to show me the dress. "Has he talked to his ma?"

"A little. She's apologetic of course, but he isn't listening. He's still so mad."

"Can't blame him."

"No, but I know it hurts him to be mad at her."

"He'll get over it. Yer still marrying him," she says, still messing with the snap.

"This is true," I say with a nod.

When she gets it, her honey brown hair falls down her shoulders as she models the dress she wears for me. The dress is cream, plain, and hugs her in every single place. I wanted something very simple, a showstopper since Fiona is so gorgeous, but nothing that would take away from my dress. I know, I'm confusing and I make no sense, but I'll know it when I see it.

This one is good, I guess. It's stunning, but I don't like it. For one reason and one I think she sees too. Putting her hands on her gut, she looks in the mirror and then at me.

"So I guess you aren't burning everything you cook?" I ask with a forgiving grin.

She laughs as she shakes her head. "No, that's not it. I forgot to tell ya."

"What?" I ask, drawing my brows in. She holds my gaze, gnawing on her lip as she starts to blush. "What?" I ask again.

"I'm pregnant," she whispers with a grin.

"Shut up!" I exclaim, hopping up and rushing toward her. "Really?!"

"Yup, only eight weeks, but yeah, got us a wee baby growing."

I hug her tightly, kissing her cheek as we part. "Oh my God! Why didn't you tell me?"

She smiles as she holds me by the back of my arms. "Ya see, at first I didn't believe it. Threw the test away and waved it off as a fluke. But then I got supersick, and I was like, shite, I think I am. So I took another test. Positive. Told Kane. We go to the doctor, positive again," she says with a laugh, and I can't stop grinning. "And so we sat on it for a minute, to digest really 'cause this was very unplanned. I was on the pill."

"Oh, I didn't know that."

"Yeah, well, obviously his sperm didn't either," she jokes and I smile. "But yeah, it's a big surprise and not something we were ready for. But he's gonna ask for my hand after the wedding, and then we will get married quick before telling my parents."

Grinning even bigger, I wrap her up in my arms, hugging her tightly. "You're gonna be a great mom."

"Ah, I don't know, but we'll see. I'm excited."

"Eek! I can't wait!" I exclaim, kissing her again on her cheek. "I'm gonna be an auntie!"

"Ya are," she says with a nod. "But enough about that. Let's get us a dress, yes?"

"Yeah," I say, letting her go, but then I hug her again. "If it's a girl, Amberlyn is a great name."

She laughs as she pushes me away, heading to the dressing room for another dress. She sends me a look over her shoulder, and I love how happy she is. I don't know how I didn't see before that she was glowing. It's like our lives are at full speed. She's pregnant and gonna get married real quick. I'm getting married, and then it will be time for me to be a mommy. Not anytime soon, but it will happen, and I honestly can't wait.

WHEN I get home later that afternoon, I can't wipe the grin off my face. Between being so damn happy for Fiona and then adding in the fact that I'm alone in my own home, marrying the man of my dreams, it's easy to say that I'm one of the happiest girls on earth. Only thing missing is my parents, but I feel them with me. A lot lately, which is comforting.

After picking up a bit since apparently, my husband-to-be is very messy—must have not noticed that since someone was always picking up after him on the estate—I do some schoolwork and then check my emails. I have emails from the movers, who send me an email with every stop they make. My stuff won't be here for another two weeks, and we've already decided to put it in storage until the big house is ready.

That's what we've dubbed it. The big house. It won't be anywhere near the estate's size, but it will be a good size for us and whatever children we decide to have. When I come to an email from his mom, I groan. I haven't spoken to her or seen her since I walked out of her office the day Declan and I got into that horrid fight that I still feel I need to apologize for.

Sucking in a deep breath, I open the email and start to read it.

Amberlyn my dear,

I wanted to let you know you have a dress fitting Monday at three. Shelia and Fiona are welcome to join us. Lena and I will be there too. Everything with the wedding is sound and ready to go. Should have no hiccups. I even got you a bit of a surprise to bring ya in. I think you and Declan will appreciate it.

While I have you, I want to apologize for upsetting you the other day. I've been thinking a lot about Ciara, and I wish I had told ya sooner about her. I miss her. I was even at her funeral. I saw ya that day and thought how gorgeous you were, so much like her. When word of Declan dating an American came to us, I didn't even think of you until I saw your picture. I cried for hours, pulled Ciara's and even Marla's pictures out to have a look for a bit. I didn't tell anyone about this. That I knew you or even who you were. I let it be, but now I wish I hadn't.

I would have defended you to Ivor. I would have pushed Declan to you sooner, because any daughter of Ciara's is bound to be a beautiful and strong soul, and I'm not wrong about that. That's why I worried. I had already done her wrong once, and I couldn't let ya go into this marriage without the warning. As much as I know it hurt you both, I had to tell you. You will be a fine wife for my boy, and I hope that one day we can have a relationship too. I do think very highly of you and do worry for ya, like I knew your ma would. I'm sorry if I hurt you, scared you, or ever upset you. I wish nothing but the best for you.

Let me know if you need anything.

I hope you love the cottage. It was my ma's. I grew up there. I made sure to hang the picture of your ma and da in your living room for ya. I thought you'd appreciate that.

With lots of love,
Noreen

Wiping away the tear that ran down my face, I look across the room at the picture she hung for me. It's a beautiful picture, one of them at their wedding under the big tree by the lake. Soon, I'll have a matching picture just like that. Wiping another tear free of my face, I hit reply and write a quick message.

Mrs. O'Callaghan,

Thank you for all you are doing for our wedding. I can't wait for the day to finally be here so I can join your family. Thank you also for my picture of my parents. It made me happy to see that when Declan brought me home last night. I also want to thank you for sharing this side of you with me. I look forward to getting to know you and soon loving you. Maybe we can have some tea tomorrow afternoon when I get off work? I can guarantee you, though, I won't be wearing a tea dress.

Love,
Amberlyn.

I hit send and then check some more emails before my email dings with another one. Seeing that it's from Mrs. O'Callaghan, I hit open and smile at her response.

I wouldn't expect you any other way. See ya tomorrow around three. I look forward to it.

Love, Noreen

With a grin on my face, I shut my computer and lean back in my chair. I feel good about this. I don't know if I'll be comfortable with Mrs. O'Callaghan soon, but maybe one day I will. Like Fiona said, not everyone gets along with their mother-in-law, but I need Declan to fix it with his mom. He loves her, and while it was rough there, we made it through.

Standing up, I go to the kitchen to start dinner. I'm gonna make my Aunt Shelia's shepherd's pie, one of Declan's favorites. He wasn't joking when he said he had the fridge stocked. We'll eat the food in there for at least two weeks, and it makes me giddy to know I'll be cooking him meals. My husband in less than two weeks!

With a grin on my face for the unexpectedly great day, I dance around the kitchen, mixing and cooking as I wait for Declan to come home. He usually gets home around five, and today he isn't a minute late. Just as I'm taking the pie out of the oven, I see his car coming up the hill. Placing it on the stove, I grin as I wipe my hands on the apron my mom used to use when she cooked before going to the door to greet him.

As soon as he gets out of the car, he sends me a grin. "Is this the way I'll be greeted every day?"

I giggle as he gathers me in his arms, kissing me deeply. He smells like death, but I've missed him and I really don't care. Pressing my lips to his chin, I grin up at him as I say, "Maybe."

"Then getting through the day is gonna be even harder than it already is," he says, kissing me again. "I missed ya."

"I missed you. Come on, dinner is ready."

"Grand, let me get a shower. I worked in the malting room for a bit with Kane. I stink."

I smile as he squeezes my shoulders, walking past me. "Just a bit."

"Wee bit, yeah?" he says with a grin before disappearing into the bedroom. My heart explodes in my chest as I start to cut the pie, plating him some before putting it on the table and getting us both something to drink. Sitting down, I cross my legs just as he comes out of the bedroom in only a pair of shorts. Looking at me, he moves his hand up and down his body. "Can I come to dinner this way?"

I laugh as I nod. "In our home, you can."

"Smart woman talking me into this, ya know?" he says, coming around to kiss the top of my head before dropping into the seat beside me. "Mm, looks damn good, love. C'mere, one more kiss."

I come willingly, and he kisses me hard on the lips before we part to dig in. Cutting into my pie, I let out a contented sigh as I take a bite, looking around the house, loving our little home. "We could stay here forever, you know," I say, and he looks at me with a brow up.

"Ya love it, do ya?"

I nod. "I do. It's so adorable."

"For now. But soon it will be cramped, and it's a bit drafty in here in the winter from what my ma says," he adds, pointing his fork at me.

"Yeah, I didn't know it was her old home."

"Yeah, when my grandma found my other grandma with the baby, they gave her this house and didn't take rent from her. My grandma loved my ma's ma. Good worker, they didn't want to lose her."

"That's sweet."

"Yeah," he says with a nod.

"Have you talked to her?"

He nods. "She came to the office today."

I wait, and when he doesn't go on, I say, "And?"

Swallowing the bite he just took, he shrugs. "I forgave her."

"Good."

"In some twisted way, it's sweet that she tried to warn ya for your ma's sake, but it still makes me mad that she didn't think higher of me. That she just assumed I'd be my da."

I nod. "Yeah."

"But it is what it is. We are done with it," he says, squeezing my hand. "What I am not done with is this. It really is good."

I give him a pleased smile. "Thank you."

Digging in, he cleans his plate before getting more. Looking over at me, he points his fork at me, and asks, "How did ya know this was my ma's old home?"

"She wrote me an email."

"Did she?" he asks, surprised. "What did she say?"

"She apologized and talked a bit about my mom."

"Hm. Ya okay?"

I nod earnestly. "More than okay."

"Grand," he says, cupping my knee under the table before digging in.

"She asked me to tea tomorrow. Want to come?"

He shrugs. "Yeah, I'll meet ya there."

Smiling, we go back to eating as we talk about our days, and I love how private this is. No one is serving us; we aren't talking about what his family wanted to talk about. It's just us. It's perfect. It's what I've always wanted. To feel completely complete with the man I love.

"Did I tell ya Lena is moving to Dublin?"

Shocked, I say, "Really? When?"

"After the wedding, apparently. She came to talk to me a bit today too. I think it's best for her."

"Me too, new change."

"Yeah, I think so."

"Has Micah contacted her?"

He shakes his head. "Guess he must not be hurting much. She hasn't heard from him."

"Maybe it was for the best, then," I suggest and he agrees.

"Yeah, I think so too," he says, sitting back and placing his hand on his stomach. He's so lean and sexy, the tattoo on his shoulder begging me to lick it. I could gobble him up like I am this pie for sure. Leaning on my hand, I say, "You full?"

"No, just preparing for round three," he says, causing me to laugh. "How'd the dress shopping go for Fiona?"

I scoop up some of the gravy with my finger and put it in my mouth before looking over at him. I can't believe how freeing it is to do that since for the last couple months, I couldn't even have my elbows on the table. Remembering my day with Fiona, I grin really big as I nod. She told me not to tell anyone, but I'm not sure if that means Declan too. Surely not. But just in case, I take my phone out of my pocket to text her real quick as I tell him about the dress.

"Did yous two talk?"

I look up from my phone, my brow coming up. "About?"

He shrugs. "Stuff?"

"What kind of stuff?" I ask, searching his eyes as he does the same to me. Finally we both say, "You know!"

"I do! A baby! I can't wait!" I gush, and he laughs as he leans on his hands.

"Yeah, Kane is very excited—but nervous, of course."

"So is Fiona. I can't wait," I say with a bright grin on my face. "We were trying on dresses, and she has a little gut now! I'm like, um, Fiona, the dress doesn't fit you, and she's like, oh yeah, I'm pregnant."

He laughs as he shakes his head. "The reason I was in the malting room was because Kane didn't know how to tell me. I was so confused as to why he was nervous to tell me. Did he think I wouldn't be happy? Still blows my mind a bit."

"For sure! Weird. But yay! A baby. I love babies," I say, leaning on my hand. He does the same, his nose against mine as he grins at me.

"Do ya, love?"

"I do," I say, holding his gorgeous gaze with mine.

"Wanna make one of our own?"

I giggle as I shake my head. "Not yet."

"Grand 'cause I don't want to either," he says with a wink. "But nothing says we can't practice."

Standing up, he pushes everything off the table in a crashing heap.

"Declan!"

He looks over at me. "What? I haven't been able to make a mess like that and make love to a woman on my kitchen table a day in my life."

Taking ahold of me, he lifts me before setting me down on the table. "I sure as hell hope not," I mutter against his lips as he pulls my panties and shorts down my legs.

He chuckles against my lips before saying, "Now that I have my own home, my own table, and my own soon-to-be wife, yer gonna get it against the table."

"Many times, right?" I ask with desire filling my eyes.

"Oh yeah," he promises. "And not just tonight—for the rest of yer life."

"Mm, can't wait," I say as he slides his fingers inside of me, but then I stop him, mock panic on my face. "Did you lock the door?"

Needless to say, there was more laughter happening than actual lovemaking, but I don't think we'd have it any other way.

thirty-one

Amberlyn

"Beautiful."

I look over my shoulder as Fiona enters the room, and I smile at her. She looks stunning in the light pink dress that gathers under her breasts before flowing down her body. Her hair is in a braid that comes down her shoulder, big white blossoms in it, complementing the dress perfectly. Her makeup is done softly and beautifully, and as she stands beside me, I think we look magnificent. The perfect balance of color.

"Do you think so?" I ask as I take myself in. The dress fits me perfectly, flowing down, and the blue looks amazing on my skin. I love the dress more now than I did when I first picked it out. My hair is up in a loose bun, tendrils falling down in my face around the ribbon that is wrapped around my head. A huge blue blossom is at the side of my head with my birdcage veil covering my face. "Do you think Declan will love it?"

"He'll be knocked on his arse for sure," she tells me, and I wrap my arms around her waist, pressing my forehead to her temple.

Closing my eyes, I swallow back my tears for how much I love this woman I hold. Unable to keep it in, I say, "I honestly don't know how I would have made it this far without you, Fiona."

She starts to laugh, and when I open my eyes, she is waving her hand in front of my face. "Don't do that to me, Amberlyn. I'm an emotional mess! I want to make it down the damn aisle with my makeup on!"

I smile as I wrap my arms around her, kissing her cheek. Looking deeply into my eyes, she goes, "But I will say, yer ma and da are looking down on us right now, and they are both saying that you are gorgeous, Amberlyn. Stunning. Really."

Tears gather in my eyes as I nod, and then I'm the one waving my hand in front of my face, hoping to keep my tears in. "Talk about making someone cry!"

Laughing like little girls, we lean against each other as we stare at ourselves in the mirror.

"So much is changing," she whispers and I nod. "It changed when ya came—I got a sister—but now, we are starting our lives. With two men who would give us the world."

"It's going to be good. We will be happy," I whisper back. "It won't be easy."

"When is love ever easy?" she asks and I smile. "But we'll have each other?"

"Always," I answer as I hug her tightly. Then the door opens and my aunt Shelia comes in, fussing and blubbering all over me and Fiona. When Mrs. O'Callaghan comes in, I smile at her as her mouth falls open.

"Perfection, yes?"

Shelia nods her head quickly as she wipes her face. "That's what I said. Just truly gorgeous."

Coming toward me, Mrs. O'Callaghan kisses my forehead, holding my gaze. "Ya look every bit like yer ma. To a tee, I think."

"Yeah, she does," my aunt says, wiping her face again. "They would be so proud."

"They are," Mrs. O'Callaghan says, moving a tendril behind my ear. "We all are."

"Thank you."

She waves me off. "Declan looks dashing."

I smile. "Is there any other way that man looks?" I ask and she laughs.

"I don't seem to think so. It's time. Are ya ready?"

Sucking in a deep breath, I smile as I let it out. "I've been ready since the moment he asked."

And those words could not ring any truer in my soul. As we head out of the living room of what was my home for a bit, I can't believe this day is finally here. For the last week and a half, Declan and I have fallen into a routine we'll have for the rest of our lives. We are apart throughout the day, but when he is home, we are together, and it's honestly magical. We are so happy and my soul is joyful.

Don't get me wrong, I miss my mom and dad so much. But after going back to the States with Declan, listening to him promise them that he will love me until our dying day, it really helped me. It was like tons of bricks fell off my chest, and I knew I was starting a life with the man who was made for me. Our love story isn't perfect. We've had people try to kill us, break us apart, and even had fear rear its ugly head, but we made it through.

We didn't give up. We fought.

Because we love each other too much to be apart.

And now I'm about to make him my husband.

It's a little bit of a walk to the spot where everyone is gathered to watch Declan and me get married, and I'm bouncing on my heels, ready to do this. This morning when I woke up, Declan had a package waiting for me with a two hundred and ten roses, one for each day he's loved me. It was a beautiful thing to see, but when I opened the gift with two Mickey Mouse-ear hats and two shirts, one that said Mr. and the other saying Mrs., I about lost my shit. I was screaming so loudly as I read the note that told me he was taking me to Disney World for our honeymoon. And then when I saw that we'd stop to see my mom and dad, I cried for good little bit.

It was insanely sweet, and I've been waiting hours to see him.

To thank him for constantly surprising me.

Coming out the door, Mrs. O'Callaghan stops me. "Ready for your surprise?"

I look around, confused. "Now?"

She nods as Mr. O'Callaghan comes up, leading Cathmor with him. "Surprise! You're gonna ride in on the horse."

My grin grows as I hug her tightly. "Declan will love it."

"He will."

Soon they are helping me up on Cathmor. They tried to make me sit like a lady, but that wasn't happening. I was scared I was gonna fall, and finally, they gave up, letting me be. I know I look insane with my legs open and my dress falling like a cape on the gorgeous horse, but oh well, it's me.

"Good luck, sweetheart, and congratulations," Mrs. O'Callaghan says, patting my legs.

"Yes, we are very lucky to have ya in our family," Mr. O'Callaghan says with a boasting grin. "Declan is going to hit the ground at the sight of ya. Yer gorgeous, ya are."

"Thank you," I say before they wave and then they are gone.

I'm supposed to wait for the signal to go, and as I sit here, I'm surprised that I'm not the least bit nervous. I'm excited. Ready to start my life with the man I love. I can't wait to see what our future holds, and while I do miss my family, I have people here who love me and a man who would give up everything just to have me. The man who was made by the hands of God just for me.

Slowly I close my eyes, my fingers tangling in Cathmor's mane as I send a little prayer up to my mom and dad. For some reason, I can feel them around me. I know they are watching, probably crying in heaven from being so happy for me. I'm living the life they wanted for me. One where I plan on taking more risks than I already have. Where I plan to do something drastic just to drive

Declan mad and to make me happy. And one where I will continue to fall in love with the love of my life every single day of my existence. What more could they want?

When Tom, one of the stable hands, whistles, I open my eyes to see that he is waving me on. I kick lightly into Cathmor, and he starts a slow trot as I head toward the field where the person with whom I'm going to start the rest of my life is waiting. The ride isn't long, and soon all I see are rows and rows of people. They have put up a huge, gauzy-type tent that will shield us some from the sun, but it also just gives a certain elegance to the spot. I know that my mom is probably grinning from the mere perfection of it all. There are fields of white blossoms, so big they look like clouds all over the place. They even are hanging from the gauzy curtains on the tent. It's gorgeous.

Fiona starts walking down the aisle, looking like a beautiful pink flower floating along the way, but that isn't who I see first.

No. It's my groom.

Standing all dashing and commanding the attention of everyone around him is my forever. Clad in a very chic and tailored black suit, I almost bust a gut when I see a black beanie on his head. When he sees me, his face lights up, and there is no way I'm going to make it down the aisle with my makeup in place. His eyes are locked with mine, and I'm not looking anywhere else as our whole love story plays on rewind in my head. I can still remember the first time I saw him, how I hated that damn beanie. But now, I love it and can't wait to pull it off so I can run my fingers through his spectacular curls. I can still feel his lips against mine the first time we kissed. I remember the first time he touched me and recall the burn of the bullet when I was ready to give up my own life for him. I can still feel him as he laid me down in the field and every time after that. Every stolen glance, every sweet touch, everything, and it was all just so damn perfect.

But now, I'm starting the rest of my life, and it's bound to be even better.

When Cathmor comes to where I am supposed to get down, gracefully, mind you, I see that he is coming toward me and I'm confused.

"I was supposed to walk down by myself," I call to him as he reaches up to get me.

He shakes his head as he helps me down. Coming down on my feet, I look up at him, scowling since he was supposed to wait for me. But soon he is cupping my face, grinning at me, and, of course, his grin gets me every time. Clearing his throat, he says, "No, yer never gonna be alone again, *mo stór*, not while I'm breathing."

My God! Really? Swallowing back my tears, I shake my head as I reach up, pulling the beanie off and throwing it over my shoulder.

"Declan, you're a dream," I breathe, and he flashes me a saucy grin.

"Not even close. You're the dream, my love, simply gorgeous. Ya got me choking up," he says before kissing my forehead softly. Pulling back, he looks deep into my eyes, and I can see the tears gathering in his own eyes. It hits me straight in the gut, and I honestly don't know how I am not crying right now.

Probably because I am unbelievably happy.

"Plus, I want to walk with ya into our forever. It's more for me than you," he says with a wink as I take his arm, looking up into his beautiful face. As the music starts with something soft and sweet, we head down the long aisle with all eyes on us, but we aren't looking anywhere but into each other's eyes.

When a grin pulls at his lips, I squeeze his arm. "What?"

Shaking his head, he says, "Ya came on a horse?"

I smile back. "I did."

He laughs. "Of course ya would, yer my princess."

"I am," I agree, leaning into him. "Because didn't you hear?"

"Hear what?"

"I'm becoming the Whiskey Princess today."

"No, the queen, my love, and don't ya forget it," he says with a wink.

And as we hold each other's gaze, love pouring out of us in waves, I don't even know how I could forget that I'm going to be tethered to him for the rest of my life. Because the Whiskey Prince is no longer just a person, no, he is the one and only love of my life.

And what a love I picked.

A note from Toni Aleo

You know, I really don't like acknowledgments. My people know I love them. My family, they know. Friends, they are aware, as are the people who work to make me a success. Everyone knows. So I'm gonna skip that and take a moment to thank you. I really do appreciate everything you do for me. Buying my books, getting lost in my worlds, and loving my characters as much as I do. It's great, and you truly mean the world to me.

I love this book. I love how it ended, I love Declan, I love Amberlyn. I am so proud of it and a little sad it's over. In my heart, I don't think this is the last you'll see of Declan and Amberlyn, but I don't know. We will see what happens.

Thank you again.

Love,
Toni

Upcoming from Toni Aleo!

Clipped by Love (Bellevue 2) Spring 2015
Overtime (Assassins 7) Spring 2015

And a brand new series is coming in Summer 2015 from Toni Aleo

The Spring Grove Novels
Bring on the cowboys!

Make sure to check out these titles and more on Toni's website:
www.tonialeo.com

Or connect with Toni on Facebook, Twitter, Instagram and more!
Also make sure to join the mailing list for up to date news from the desk of
Toni Aleo:
http://eepurl.com/u28FL

More books by
TONI ALEO

The Assassins Series
Taking Shots
Trying to Score
Empty Net
Falling for the Backup
Blue Lines
Breaking Away
Laces and Lace
A Very Merry Hockey Holiday
Overtime (Spring 2015)

The Bellevue Bullies Series
Boarded by Love
Clipped by Love (early 2015)
Hooked by Love (late 2015)

Standalone
Let it be Me

Taking Risks Series
The Whiskey Prince
Becoming the Whiskey Princess

Made in the USA
Lexington, KY
16 March 2015